U0099032

# 戰勝GEPT全民英檢

## 中級 Intermediate 的16堂課

用心智圖搞懂
英文作文與句型

# 目錄

# 學習計劃表

| 堂次 | 內容 | 頁數 | 學習日期 | | 複習日期 | |
|---|---|---|---|---|---|---|
| 第一堂 | 前言 — 統一<br>（一段一概念） | vii~015 | 月 | 日 | 月 | 日 |
| 第二堂 | 主動語氣勝被動語氣<br>— 強而有力的動詞 | 016~032 | 月 | 日 | 月 | 日 |
| 第三堂 | Variety 句型 101 Part 1<br>（Ⅰ） | 033~062 | 月 | 日 | 月 | 日 |
| 第四堂 | Variety 句型 101 Part 1<br>（Ⅱ） | 063~090 | 月 | 日 | 月 | 日 |
| 第五堂 | Variety 句型 101 Part 2<br>（Ⅰ） | 091~118 | 月 | 日 | 月 | 日 |
| 第六堂 | Variety 句型 101 Part 2<br>（Ⅱ） | 119~148 | 月 | 日 | 月 | 日 |
| 第七堂 | 主題句、段落發展及支<br>持的論點、連貫及緊密 | 149~160 | 月 | 日 | 月 | 日 |
| 第八堂 | 轉承詞與連接詞、結論 | 161~176 | 月 | 日 | 月 | 日 |
| 第九堂 | 書信文 | 177~182 | 月 | 日 | 月 | 日 |
| 第十堂 | 說明文 | 183~190 | 月 | 日 | 月 | 日 |
| 第十一堂 | 議論文 | 191~198 | 月 | 日 | 月 | 日 |
| 第十二堂 | 記敘文 | 199~207 | 月 | 日 | 月 | 日 |
| 第十三堂 | 描寫文 | 208~219 | 月 | 日 | 月 | 日 |
| 第十四堂 | 比較性文章 | 220~228 | 月 | 日 | 月 | 日 |
| 第十五堂 | 看圖寫作、自傳、履歷<br>表 | 229~254 | 月 | 日 | 月 | 日 |
| 第十六堂 | 標點符號、文法、淺談<br>中譯英 | 255~281 | 月 | 日 | 月 | 日 |

前言

## 閱讀為墊腳石

多閱讀是個提升寫作能力的好途徑。從閱讀中，可以學到字彙、片語、句型、文法、文章結構、正反論點的辯證，最重要的是：由閱讀所得到知識，將可作為往後寫作的資源。

閱讀的來源基本上越廣越好，各文類的英文多接觸，對於寫作必大有助益。英文報紙是個很好的閱讀材料，不但讓自己和世界及周遭發生的時事連結，報紙中的社論更裨益於論說、議論方面的寫作。多看多背別人的佳句、論點的切入，實為寫好英文作文的一大利器。 其他如英語雜誌、讀者文摘、英文小說……等等。另外，等寫作有一段時間後，亦可以拿閱讀的文章來分析、訓練大意寫作，或改寫，如此，亦可增進自我對文字、文章結構的熟悉度。

## 充實單字庫

講話怕詞窮，寫作更是如此。你曾經有過要表達一個英文字，想破頭也想不出來，只好寫出"平易近人"的單字嗎？考試的時候又不能按按電子字典找中翻英，怎麼辦？其實這只凸顯一個問題：單字背太少、又不夠熟。比較一下，現在有兩篇文章，兩篇都是在表達同一件事和論述相同觀點，在各方面都一樣之下，只差別於一篇用字難易度在國中 1200 字，另一篇為 5000 字的難易度，孰優孰劣，不用多說。我想強調的是，平常多閱讀多背單字及片語，其實就是增進你英文實力的不二法門，更不用說寫作時可以避免詞窮的窘境。

# 英檢作文考題及評分標準

## 英檢中級作文到底考什麼？

以往作文考題出題方向不離：論說文（含說明文或議論文）、書信（email）為兩大寫作文體，但也不是說其他文體完全不會考，所以讀者應就本書內的各文體寫作方法多加練習。全民英檢中級作文網站公告的題目如下：

### 例題 I

說明：請依下面所提供的文字提示寫一篇英文作文，長度約 120 字（8 至 12 個句子）。作文可以是一個完整的段落，也可以分段。（評分重點包括內容、組織、文法、用字遣詞、標點符號、大小寫。）

提示：一般說來，孩子表現良好時，父母常會給孩子獎勵。請寫一篇文章說明

(1) 你表現好的時候，你的父母通常會用哪些方法獎勵你？你覺得這些方法有效、適當嗎？

(2) 如果有一天你為人父母，你會用相同的獎勵方式嗎？

### 例題 II

請依以下提示寫一封英文 email，長度約 120 字（8 至 12 個句子）。作文可以是一個完整的段落，也可以分段。（評分重點包括內容、組織、文法、用字遣詞、標點符號、大小寫。）

提示：你住在美國的筆友 Ted 最近剛轉學，正在煩惱新學校的交友問題。請寫一封英文 email 給他，信的內容必須包括以下兩點：

(1) 分享你適應新環境的經驗。

(2) 建議他幾個交新朋友的方法。

## 英檢英文作文評分標準？

不外乎內容、組織、文法、用字、標點符號等 5 大面向，以下茲以全民英檢中級寫作評改標準，提供讀者參考：

| 級分 | 分數 | 說明 |
|---|---|---|
| 5 | 60 | **寫作能力佳**<br>內容適切表達題目要求,清楚有條理;組織甚佳;能靈活運用字彙及句型;文法、拼字或標點符號偶有錯誤。 |
| 4 | 48 | **寫作能力可**<br>內容符合題目要求,大致清楚;組織大致完整;能正確運用字彙及句型;文法、拼字或標點符號雖有錯誤,但不影響理解。 |
| 3 | 36 | **寫作能力有限**<br>內容大致符合題目要求,但未完全達意;組織尚可;字彙及句型掌握不佳;文法、拼字、標點符號錯誤偏多,影響理解。 |
| 2 | 24 | **稍具寫作能力**<br>內容局部符合題目要求,大多難以理解;組織不良;能運用的字彙及句型有限;文法、拼字、標點符號有許多錯誤。 |
| 1 | 12 | **無寫作能力**<br>內容未能符合題目要求,無法理解;缺乏組織;能運用的字彙及句型非常有限;文法、拼字、標點符號有過多錯誤。 |
| 0 | 0 | **未答 / 等同未答** |

官方網站上有範例文章可以參考,讀者可至以下網站去感受一下,什麼文章可以拿高分,什麼文章級分低:

https://www.lttc.ntu.edu.tw/geptscoreremark/icomposition.pdf

# 如何使用本書

除了足夠單字量、基本文法讀者必須先具備,閱讀本書時,應遵循 4 大步驟,如此才能精練英文作文:(1) 可以先就前言、寫作原則章節部分,先了解一篇文章基本的架構與寫作應注意的原則、細節,(2) 接下來,翻閱 Variety 章節,即英文句型,將每一個常用句型充分練習以達熟練,如此才能於下筆寫作時,輕易變換句子,而非一成不變的直述句:主詞 + 動詞,Variety 章節中,筆者透過實際教學現場所發明的記憶口訣,搭配淺顯易懂的例子,相信讀者應該可以很輕鬆駕馭這些句型。當基本寫作原則與句型都已掌握,(3) 其次應細讀各文體寫作細節及技巧,並實際反覆練習,當然,(4) 如果有專業人士(如英文老師),可以幫忙批改是最佳,但並非人人都還在求學階段,為此,提供幾個線上資源:

**國外資源：**

1. 劍橋語言測驗中心建置之線上批改（需註冊）（免費）

   http://www.cambridgeenglish.org/learning-english/find-free-resources/write-and-improve/

2. 國外 essayforum（免費）

   http://www.essayforum.com/

3. English test net（免費）

   http://www.english-test.net/forum/forum16.html

4. lang 8（免費）

   http://lang-8.com/

**國內資源：**

5. 加入臉書粉絲團（免費）

   https://www.facebook.com/learnthenlove

6. Xuite 隨意窩上，有老師免費批改（免費）

   http://blog.xuite.net/playenglish/cc/42816952

7. 國內 iCorrect（須付費）

   http://www.correctwriting.com.tw/

8. 筆者粉絲團：

   FB 搜尋 "Ronnie's English Cafe"

**文法檢查：**（以下皆免費）

1. Grammarly（可安裝到 Word, 瀏覽器）

   https://www.grammarly.com/?AT2250＝4

2. Online Text Correction

   http://www.textcorrection.com/

3. After the deadline（除了標出錯誤，還會建議用字）

   http://www.polishmywriting.com/

# Chapter 1

## Writing Principles
## 寫作原則

### The framework of a good composition（文章架構）

> 審題→主題句→鋪陳→結論

I. 審題：依據題目判斷應該書寫的體裁，可分為：論説文、記敘文、描寫文、議論文、比較對比文、甚至是應用文（書信類）。

II. 主題句：主題句為該段的大意，通常出現在段落的第一句，下筆時，可對題目提出概括的意見，或是前言（論説文、比較對比文章）；亦可善用 5W1H 將事件的人、事、時、地、物、發生原因等大概敘寫（描寫文或記敘文）。

III. 鋪陳：

A. 列點：文章短的時候，可以在一段內就把各點列出並加以闡述，提供支持論點的句子（supporting ideas），甚至可舉例、引經據典；至於如果要長篇大論，則必須一段一主題句，再加以闡述（論説文或議論文）。

B. 開始依據事件發生的時間順序（time order）加以敘寫（記敘文）；或客觀描寫該事物、該人物，使用空間順序的概念（space order），由內到外或由外到內、由遠至近或由近至遠來書寫（描寫文）。

IV. 結論：

    A. 用換句話說的方法把結論前的各段加以綜合、歸納、總結（論說文或議論文）。

    B. 與自身感受做連結，如：感想、對個人影響、帶來的教訓；或隨事情發生的節奏自然結束（描寫文或記敘文）。

       切記：英文作文很重邏輯。千萬不要在結論段引入新的議題或主題！

下圖為作文基本架構：

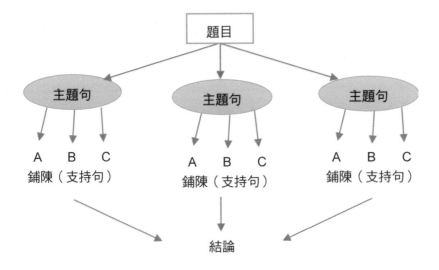

# The "cement" of a good composition（好文章的成分）

> **I. 字彙、II. 文法、III. 多采多姿的句子、IV. 思路清楚**

I.  字彙：有"深度"的字彙 vs. "簡單"的字彙。英文初學者剛接觸寫作，用字可能只能侷限於 1000-2000 字（國中畢業門檻），但隨著不斷學習，應該將單字量提升到至少 3000-4000 字（高職畢業門檻），6000-7000 字（高中畢業門檻），更好的是，用字可以隨著學習不斷往上提升，如此文章才有「可看之處」。但也要注意一點：整篇作文的用字難易度要一致，不可通篇都是 2000 字難度書寫，但中間插入一些 6000 字難度以上的字，這種感覺會像中文裡，白話文中突然出現一些古字或文言文的落差感。

II.  文法：如果文法錯誤百出，就算字彙再深、句型再多變，亦是枉然。大文法包含各時態的使用（現在簡單式、過去式、未來式、完成式等等，請見附錄）、語態（被動句、主動句），語氣（假設語氣、祈使句、直述句）。小文法包括單字和片語的使用：動詞（protect…from…）、形容詞（be allergic to）、名詞（an obstacle to）與介系詞（in the middle of）等的搭配使用。

III.  多采多姿的句子：句型要多變化，不呆板。除了本書介紹常用的各種句型外，也應熟練將同一個意思用不同角度表達或不同主詞轉換改寫。

IV.  思路清楚：

    A.  論點要能切中題意，且強而有力、不互相矛盾、浮誇不實，目的只有一個 ⇨ 說服讀者（論說文或議論文）。

    B.  時間優先順序：時間由先到後或由後到先；地點優先順序：由小地點到大地點或由大地點到小地點（描寫文或記敘文）。

## **1** Concise｜簡潔有力

> **說明**
>
> 英文作文著重句子簡潔有力，不拖泥帶水，所以不應該為了拖字數，而增加一些累贅的字眼（redundancy），如此只會模糊讀者的閱讀重點，也會失去文章的流暢度，以下列出幾個常見的累贅寫法。

**1** 避免不必要的強調與太過普通的用詞。

**(1)** We just need very extraordinarily talented workers for our company.

**解析** just 是個口語用字，且太過普通的字，應刪除，句子才會直接了當；very 及 extraordinarily（格外地、非凡地），兩字則是過度強調，且語意重疊。

**建議例句**

We need talented workers for our company.

我們公司需要有天分的員工。

**(2)** Yesterday I walked in the park and met one of my friends.

**解析** 這句文法與語意都沒問題，但用字太普通且累贅，我們可以巧用 bump into, run into, come across 來表達 "巧遇" 而不是只有 "遇見"，如此，句子變精簡而且語意更明確。

**建議例句**

Yesterday I bumped into one of my friends in the park.

昨天，我在公園巧遇朋友。

**2** 更換或刪除不夠明確的詞語（特別是上一句沒有提到的名詞，不要在下一句突然出現一個代名詞，如此會讓讀者摸不著頭緒）。

**(1)** People had better take measures to do something for trash reduction now.

**解析** do something 中文是 "做某事"，如此用字不夠明確、過於模糊，應該選用更準確的字詞。因為後面接垃圾減量，所以應思考與其搭配的動詞，如：回收（recycle）、再利用（reuse），或分類（sort）等等。

People had better <u>recycle and sort</u> trash for trash reduction now.

人們最好現在為垃圾減量開始回收和做好分類工作。

(2) <u>It</u> can help us learn the importance of give-and-take.

**解析** 所有的代名詞都是用來代替前面已經提過的名詞或整件事情，如果前面都沒提過，突然用代名詞，放主詞、所有格或受詞位置，只會困惑讀者。假設本例句於文章中，都沒有提過 it 所指稱的事物，修改方式，就是替換成明確的事件即可。

建議例句

⇨ <u>Joining clubs at school</u> can help us learn the importance of give-and-take.

參加學校社團幫助我學習到施捨的重要性。

(3) The purpose of our charity aims to provide education funds for <u>children</u>.

**解析** 此句中的小孩（children）意思亦不夠明確，建議在小孩前面加一些精確的形容詞來限制這慈善機構所要幫助的小孩。換句話說，我們也可利用形容詞的修飾來讓原本不清不楚的名詞，使其明確化。

建議例句

⇨ The purpose of our charity aims to provide education funds for <u>poor or abused children</u>.

我們慈善會的目的是要提供貧困或受虐小孩教育基金。

(4) This medical breakthrough extends many <u>patients</u>' lives.

**解析** 此句中的病人（patient），並沒有指明是哪一類的病人，總不可能全部適用，所以建議改法可仿造上一例句，在病人前加一個形容詞，或者，可以在病人後加一個介系詞片語來修飾與限定。

建議例句

⇨ This medical breakthrough extends the lives of many <u>patients with terminal lung cancer</u>.

這醫學突破延長了肺癌末期病患的生命。

**3** 避免不必要的重複。

(1) Dogs are human's <u>loyal and faithful</u> **friends.**

**解析** 此例句中的 loyal 與 faithful 意思皆是 "忠實的、效忠的"，意思重複，顯得累贅，建議只留其中一個即可。換句話説，在寫作時，意思如果可以用一個字表達時，不要硬加另一個同義字或相似字來表達強調，這其實都很不必要；相反地，我們應該用其他詞性來強調，如：加一個副詞來修飾形容詞等等。

**建議例句**

⇨ Dogs are human's <u>most</u> <u>loyal</u> friends.

狗狗是人類最忠實的朋友。

(2) Listening to music is a <u>joy</u> for me and makes me <u>feel happy</u>.

**解析** 此句中的 joy 與 feel happy 要表達的意思相同，形成累贅多餘。修改方式，同樣地，留其中一個即可。另外，建議例句中，另加 such，來強調 joy。

**建議例句**

⇨ Listening to music is such <u>a joy</u> for me.

聽音樂對我而言是如此的快樂。

(3) Only by <u>cooperating together</u> can we turn the tables this time.

**解析** 例句中的 cooperate（合作）本來就有 together（一起）的含意，所以 together 在此例句中是多餘的。換句話説，當我們在使用副詞要修飾動詞時，也須留意是否該副詞已有動詞的內在涵義。

**建議例句**

⇨ Only by <u>cooperating</u> can we turn the tables this time.

只有藉著合作我們才能扭轉這次的局勢。

(4) <u>In my opinion, I think</u> we should develop mutual respect for each other.

**解析** In my opinion（依我之見）與 I think 意思重疊，應只保留其中一個，畢竟作文是正式文體，建議還是用 in one's opinion（=in one's view, in one's point of view, as far as one is concerned, etc）比較合適；I think（I feel, I guess）比較常用於口語之中。

⇨ In my opinion, we should develop mutual respect.

或

I think we should develop mutual respect.

我認為我們應該培養相互尊重。

(5) Never postpone something urgent until later.

**解析** postpone（耽擱）與時間片語 until later（直到之後），意思也部分重疊，因為耽擱本來就是會拖到之後。建議改法：將 until later 刪去。

**建議例句**

Never postpone something urgent.

絕對不要耽擱緊急的事。

(6) The reason Rita dressed up as a vampire was because she was invited to a costume party.

**解析** the reason 與 because 一起連用也是常見的正式寫作中常見錯誤，建議改法：可用 that 代替 because；或者將原本一長句，利用連接詞 because 來連接兩句，但須刪去 the reason。

**建議例句**

The reason Rita dressed up as a vampire was that she was invited to a costume party.

或

Rita dressed up as a vampire because she was invited to a costume party.

Rita 裝扮成吸血鬼的原因是她受邀去參加化裝舞會。

(7) The plane suddenly descended down dramatically, terrifying all of the passengers.

**解析** up 與 down 亦是常見用錯頻率很高的副詞。例句中的 descend（下降）本來就含有 down 的意思，故應刪去 down。因此，如果動詞本身已含有上或下方向的概念，就不宜再加 up 或 down。

The plane suddenly <u>descended</u> dramatically, terrifying all of the passengers.

飛機突然急速下降，嚇壞所有乘客。

另外類似錯誤如下：（畫線的字是多餘的，因為意思重複）

| | |
|---|---|
| <u>am</u> in the morning 早上<br>（am 或 in the morning 留一個就好） | <u>pm</u> in the afternoon/evening 下午 |
| manually <u>by hand</u> 手動地 | <u>past</u> history 歷史 |
| pursue <u>after</u> 追求 | <u>free</u> gift 禮物 |
| <u>current</u> incumbent 現任的 | repeat <u>again</u> 重複 |
| <u>sudden</u> impulse 衝動 | face <u>mask</u> 口罩 |
| few <u>in number</u> 稀少 | <u>completely</u> eliminate 剔除 |
| follow <u>after</u> 跟從 | invisible <u>to the eye</u> 看不見的 |
| blend <u>together</u> 混合 | <u>new</u> innovation 創新 |
| cancel <u>out</u> 取消 | blue <u>in color</u> 藍色 |
| assemble <u>together</u> 組裝 | rise <u>up</u> 上升 |
| drop <u>down</u> 掉落 | <u>end</u> result 結果 |

**4** 刪除無意義的字眼。

(1) The accident <u>which occurred</u> last year messed up John's plan for studying abroad.

**解析** 此句中的 which occurred 顯得無意義，因為車禍一定是發生了，不然怎麼會影響後續 John 所做的事。類似的尚有 happened 與 in the past 連用，都應避免。

**建議例句**

<u>The accident last year</u>/<u>Last year's accident</u> messed up John's plan for studying abroad.

去年車禍搞亂了 John 去國外求學的計畫。

(2) The runner dashed through the finish line <u>in the end</u> and earned enthusiastic cheers.

**解析** 此句中的 in the end 也是累贅，因為跑者當然 "最後" 會衝過衝點線。換句話說，寫作時，邏輯也是很重要的。

**建議例句**

The runner dashed through the finish line and earned enthusiastic cheers.

這跑者衝過終點線並贏得熱烈歡呼聲。

(3) <u>It goes without saying that</u> honesty is the best policy.

**解析** 此句中畫線部分意思是 "不言可喻"，這個老套的句型，只會讓文章變得囉嗦，應該換成簡單的副詞或根本不用寫出，直接將所要說的話說出才直接了當。

**建議例句**

(<u>Undoubtedly,</u>) Honesty is the best policy.

（無疑地）誠實為上策。

(4) It is thought that all the artist's works are <u>very unique</u>.

**解析** unique 本身已經是 "獨一無二"，不可再加 very 來修飾。換句話說，如果形容詞已經有 "極端" 的涵義時，就不能再加 very。類似的有：gorgeous（很棒的）、fantastic＝excellent（極好的）、terrible（極糟的）、exhaustic（筋疲力竭的）、furious（盛怒的）、freezing＝chilly（極冷的）、obese（肥胖的）、tiny（很小的）等等。當不確定是否可加 very 修飾，則必須翻翻英英字典看看該字的英文定義。至於要修飾這些極端形容詞，建議使用：completely, absolutely, totally 等等。

**建議例句**

It is thought that all the artist's works are <u>unique</u>.

一般認為這位藝術家所有的作品都是獨一無二的。

**5** 用字簡潔：用一個單字勝過於用一個軟弱的片語，不該因為拖字數而捨棄簡潔的動詞、名詞、或形容詞。

(1) My little unhealthy sister has a tendency to catch a cold.

**解析** 句中的 has a tendency to 意思是 "有…的傾向"，使用上當然沒有錯，但是，有更好的選擇，我們可以用動詞 tend 來書寫。

**建議例句**

My little unhealthy sister tends to catch a cold.
我那身體欠佳的小妹常感冒。

(2) Our new advertisement is to recruit people who are experienced in fashion design.

**解析** 例句中使用形容詞子句來寫，句子顯得冗長，倒不如換成一個簡單的形容詞 experienced。因此，當書寫完後發現有類似冗長情況，可以試著換個角度或是用另一個說法來陳述相同的事實或概念。

**建議例句**

Our new advertisement is to recruit experienced fashion designers.
我們新廣告目的是為了招募有經驗的時尚設計師。

(3) The first stop of our trip is Hong Kong, which is known as a shopping paradise.

**解析** 本例句文法和語意都沒問題，但總不如建議例句中的簡潔，可以直接省略關代，用過去分詞來書寫。

**建議例句**

The first stop of our trip is Hong Kong, known as a shopping paradise.
我們旅程的第一站是香港—知名的購物天堂。

另外類似累贅例子如下：

| | |
|---|---|
| due to the fact that ⇨ because | because of the fact that ⇨ because |
| given the fact that ⇨ because | by means of ⇨ by |
| during the time that ⇨ when | tall in height ⇨ tall |
| in today's world ⇨ today | small in size ⇨ small |
| in spite of the fact that ⇨ although/though | in a hasty manner ⇨ hastily |
| have the ability to ⇨ can | in an efficient way ⇨ efficiently |

6 有時盡量避免使用 there is, there are。因為語氣顯得比較弱，可直接用動詞代替。

(1) There was a burglar breaking into the tycoon's villa.

解析 there was 除了語氣較弱以外，因為例句裡面又有另一個動詞，所以，整句變得相當不自然，直接用一般動詞寫，比較強而有力。

建議例句

A burglar broke into the tycoon's villa.

有個竊賊闖入這企業大亨的別墅。

(2) There were four earthquakes happening in a row in ten minutes.

解析 此句與上一句改法相似；若硬要留 there were，則應該將 happening 省略。

建議例句

Four earthquakes happened in a row in ten minutes.

或

There were four earthquakes in a row in ten minutes.

十分鐘內一連發生 4 次地震。

**7** 避免書寫委婉語（euphemism）。除了因為字數不精簡外，讀者不容易從字面上看出意思，導致語意不清不楚，所以應該清楚表達才是正確。

(1) Several bank robbers were put into the correctional facility.

**解析** correctional facility 意思是 "矯正設施"，其實就是 "監獄"。

**建議例句**

Several bank robbers were put into jail.

數個銀行搶匪入監服刑。

(2) Anna was introduced to a wealthy but vertically-challenged man.

**解析** vertically-challenged 字面上意思是 "垂直高度上受挑戰"，白話點就是 "矮"。

**建議例句**

Anna was introduced to a wealthy but short man.

Anna 被介紹給一位富有但個子矮的男人。

(3) The careless driver crashed into a road tree and bought the farm last night.

**解析** buy the farm 是 "死亡" 的委婉語。

**建議例句**

⇨ The careless driver crashed into a road tree and died last night.

這粗心的駕駛昨晚撞路樹並身亡。

**牛刀小試** 請找出不適當的字詞，並改正。

1. The bomb completely destroyed the village at the foot of the mountain.

→ _____

2. It is reported that the tragic plane crash happened at around 4 pm in the afternoon.

→ _____

3. They are to blame for polluting the Love River.

→ _____

4. There are many ants circling and savoring a cookie on my desk.

→ _____

5. Jefferson said he needed to answer the call of nature.

→ _____

## Answer

1. The bomb destroyed the village at the foot of the mountain.

   解析 destroy 本身即有 "完全破壞的意思"，內含有 completely 的意思。屬於上述 3 避免不必要的重複。

2. It is reported that the tragic plane crash happened at around 4 pm.

   或

   It is reported that the tragic plane crash happened at around 4 in the afternoon.

   解析 pm 與 in the afternoon 表達的意思相同，應留一個即可。屬於上述 3 避免不必要的重複。

3. The factories which discharged wastewater into the Love River are to blame for the pollution.

   解析 They 指稱不明，應換成具體主詞。屬於上述 2 更換或刪除不夠明確的詞語。

4. Many ants are circling and savoring a cookie on my desk.

   解析 There are 語氣較弱。屬於上述 6 有時盡量避免使用 there is, there are。因為語氣顯得比較弱，可直接用動詞代替。

5. Jefferson said he needed to go to the toilet.

   解析 answer the call of nature 為 go to the toilet 的委婉語。屬於上述 7 避免書寫委婉語（euphemism）。

## ② Unity: One paragraph one idea 統一

**說明**

在中式作文中，可能採迂迴環繞的過程行文，有時候要看到文章最後才知道作者要表達的目的與中心思想，就像開山路一路蜿蜒才到山頂。相較之下，英文作文則比較"直來直往"。所謂的直來直往就是英文作文思考的模式比較直線式，不會拐彎抹角。而 unity（一段一個中心思想），便為這些直線，想像一下金字塔，除了頂點外（就像文章的題目），這些直線不會有交叉點。

舉個例子來說：

今天題目為 My Favorite Night Market Snacks

第一段寫 tempura（天婦羅），第二段寫 pig blood cake（豬血糕），第三段寫 oyster omelet（蚵仔煎），最後一段結論。在發展第一段 tempura 的時候，就不會把 pig blood cake 的相關內容寫進去，同理，在第二段時，就不應該把 oyster omelet 的敘述寫入，而最後一段，則需綜合全部內容，提出感想或建議，但不宜增加新的概念，如下圖所示：

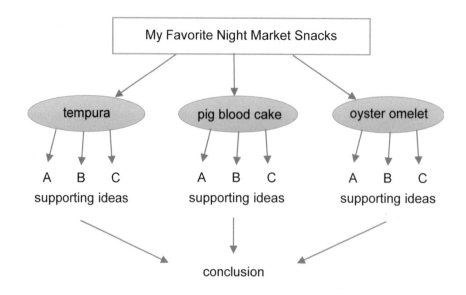

 牛刀小試 依據題目，請寫出三個段落可能發展的主題關鍵字 / 詞。

Topic: The Importance of Sense of Humor

Paragraph 1: _____

Paragraph 2: _____

Paragraph 3: _____

Answer （僅供參考）

Paragraph 1: relieving stress

Paragraph 2: positive attitude toward life

Paragraph 3: better relationship with people

## ❸ Active voice is better than passive voice
### 主動語氣勝被動語氣

> **說明**
>
> 相信大家在求學過程中一定作過很多主動及被動句型的轉換練習。在英文寫作中，句子以被動句來寫是很不好的，不但語氣弱而且字數會因此而拖長，跟上章節的簡潔 Concise 原則有所違背。換句話說，盡量還是用主動寫語氣來書寫，以達句子簡潔。

例句：

1. Elsa has learned French since she was ten.

   Elsa 從她 10 歲開始就在學法語。

   ⇨ French has been learned by Elsa since she was ten.（不自然）

2. People in Taiwan eat rice as their staple food.

   台灣人以米為主食。

   ⇨ Rice is eaten by people in Taiwan as their staple food.（不自然）

然而，在平常的閱讀中最常見被動句的地方不外乎教科書、科學科技相關報導、報紙、口語英文。

以下情況為作文中為常見的被動句：

A. 所要強調的是動詞及受詞而非行為執行者

   **例句**

   Residents in this village lack a sense of public moral. Bags of trash were thrown on the roadside.

   這村子的居民缺乏公德心。成包的垃圾被棄置在路邊。

B. 句中的行為者不明

**例句**

The textile factory was burned down.

紡織工廠遭大火燒光。

⇨ Someone/They set fire on the textile factory.

C. 行為者顯而易見

**例句**

New laws against drunk driving were passed (by the lawmakers).

酒駕新法過關了。

D. 特殊句型

It is reported/said/thought/announced/believed/expected that S+V.

**例句**

It is said that there are some traces of water on the Jupiter.

據說木星有水的痕跡。

進階學習

1. 有些動詞本身已有被動意思，所以常以主動代替被動，例如：sell, print, open, increase（增加）, decrease（減少）, happen/take place/occur（發生）, look, smell, taste, sound, feel, cost, etc.

**例句**

Horrace's new books <u>sold</u> like a hot cake.

Horrace 的新書大賣。

2. 大多數靜態或有關情感的動詞亦無被動式寫法，例如：have, own, want, belong to（屬於）, remain（仍然）, take after（長得像…）, resemble, last（持續）, exist（存在）, etc.

**例句**

This castle belongs to an old man in my hometown.

這城堡屬於我家鄉一位老人的。

**牛刀小試** 改為主動句或被動句。

1. Someone hacked the computers in our office.

→ _____

2. The defending champion was finally defeated by the challenger.

→ _____

**Answer**

1. The computers in our office were hacked.

2. The challenger finally defeated the defending champion.

## ④ Third person dominates the article

### 多使用第三人稱

**說明**

以第三人稱觀點寫文章比起以第一人稱或第二人稱還要來的公正客觀、不武斷。建議讀者可多用 people, they, those who, almost everyone, anyone, one, no one, etc。甚至，亦可使用虛主詞 it、動名詞、不定詞片語、名詞子句等等來串寫。更多句型請見本書後面章節。

例句：

1. <u>People</u> who often dine out are likely to eat something with problematic cooking oil.

   常外食的人很容易吃到有問題食用油的食物。

2. <u>It</u> is hard to believe that the miser donated half of his wealth to the charity.

   令人難以相信的是：這個小氣鬼竟然把一半的財產捐給慈善機構。

3. <u>Playing</u> with smartphones for too long can cause damage to people's eyes.

   手機玩太久會對人們的眼睛造成傷害。

另外，盡量避免用 you 來貫串全文。因為若全篇以 you 來行文，會讓讀者閱讀文章有壓力，有種指著鼻子說教的感覺，而且這種文章比較不正式。

例句：

（劣）If <u>you</u> hit and run, <u>you</u> will face a harsher punishment.

如果你肇事逃逸，你會面臨更嚴厲的懲罰。

**建議例句**

If <u>people</u> hit and run, <u>they</u> will face a harsher punishment.

如果人們肇事逃逸，他們會面臨更嚴厲的懲罰。

**解析** 原例句中，讀者會有種我是肇事者的感覺，如此，讀你的文章便不輕鬆，好像被指責或指控的感覺。

當然也並非所有寫作文章都不用 you 來書寫。在「描寫文」中，在寫結論段時，可以用 you 當主詞一句以來做為結束，建議讀者可至景點一遊，反而達到效果。

例句：

> If you happen to pass by Lukang, be sure to visit the century-old temples and try delicioius local snacks.
>
> 如果你恰好路過鹿港，務必要拜訪歷史悠久的寺廟和品嚐當地可口小吃。

除此之外，在「論說文」中，前言部分為了吸引讀者而穿插一句，詢問讀者是否有論說議題相關的經驗時，再繼續發展文章。好比如以下的例句，就可放在作文題目是 On Insomnia（失眠）的開頭段裡。

例句：

> Do you have trouble falling asleep? If you do, then you might suffer too much pressure from life.
>
> 你有睡眠問題嗎？如果有，你可能生活壓力太大了。

其次，也不要通篇全部用 I 來開始每一個句子，有時會讓讀者認為你過於主觀或沒自信，而且使用第一人稱（I, we, me, us）會變的不正式，口語才會講 I think 或 we think；另外也會讓讀者覺得這些字太累贅，文章不用刻意強調 I think that, I believe that, I feel that, etc. 此種寫作缺點最常出現在以下這些題目：自傳、我最難忘的旅遊（打工、考試、恐怖）等等個人經驗。當然，也不是說都不能用第一人稱來開始句子，而是要交錯其他種不同主詞，才能避免單調，畢竟作文句子的句型要力求多變。解決辦法就是：換句話說的方式或以另一種觀點來表達相同的概念，請見例句。

例句：

1. （結論句）Next time, if I have to ride in a heavy rain, I will slow down and wear a bright yellow raincoat.

   下一次，如果我在大雨中騎車，我會減慢速度並穿亮黃色的雨衣。

   **解析** 在記敘文，而且是書寫有關自己的經驗或發生的事情，而得到一些反省或反思，用 I 來開頭是非常合理的。

2. （段落中）

（劣）I have undergone many unhappy experiences in my first year in America and I am in serious depression now.

⇨ Having undergone many unhappy experiences in my first year in America leads to my great depression now.

在美國第一年經歷這麼多不愉快的經驗導致我憂鬱症。

**解析** 原句用 I 開頭，修改過後的句子使用動名詞，就可避免太多的I。另外，將原句 I am in serious depression. 用換句話說方式改成：…leads to my great depression. 也是另一種變換句型的呈現。

除了記敘文外，在論說文的結尾，除非要是以訴諸道德口號或是提供建議時，才會用到第一人稱 we，如此可以達到加強語氣的目的。

例句：

1. Only when we cut down on carbon dioxide emission can global warming slow down.

只有當我們減少二氧化碳的排放，全球暖化才會減緩。

2. We should pay more attention to the problem of the wealth gap.

我們應該多注意貧富差距的問題。

## ⑤ Diction 遣詞用字

**說明**

Diction 的意思是「用字遣詞」。很多英文初學者因為受到中文的影響，所以在寫英文作文時，用中文的思考模式，用字往往是以中文翻英文的方式，更糟糕的是使用手機的字典 app，將中文直接翻成英文單字，再由單字湊成句子，這樣的寫作方式十之八九會有用字遣詞上的問題。因為直接中翻英的字會因為字本身的用法（usage）及上下文邏輯（logic）問題而間接產生令人啼笑皆非的句子。而改善這個問題的方法不外乎多看報章雜誌上的文章，看看別人是怎麼用的。另外，身邊最好準備一本字典（英漢或英英），遇到生字應先查清楚字的用法之後再使用，在此介紹幾本較具權威的英英字典：Longman Dictionary of Contemporary English、Oxford Learner's Dictionary、Macmillan Dictionary、Merriam-Webster Learner's Dictionary、Cambridge Dictionary 等等，以上亦有線上版；而平常在背單字的時候不要光背意思，重點是要背這個字的用法及這個字或片語的搭配詞（collocation）。以下例句所列舉的就是用字及搭配詞的錯誤。

例句：

1. Mr. Chang attended to the board meeting last Friday.

   ⇨ Mr. Chang attended the board meeting last Friday.

   張先生上禮拜五參加了董事會議。

   **解析** attend 為及物動詞時，意思是 "參加"，但當不及物動詞時，常跟 to 連用，意思則變成 "（服務生於餐廳）服務客人"。

2. Customers had better take a room reservation as early as possible.

   ⇨ Customers had better make a room reservation as early as possible.

   顧客最好盡早訂房。

   **解析** reservation 意思為 "預定（房間、餐廳等）"，搭配動詞為 make；reserve 則是動詞。

3. Every item in our shop is on sale in half price.

   ⇨ Every item in our shop is on sale at half price.

   我們商店內每項商品都打 5 折。

   **解析** price 搭配的介系詞為 at，而不是 in。

4. Mandy tried hard to get to her parents' high expectations.

   ⇨ Mandy tried hard to live up to her parents' high expectations.

   Mandy 努力地要達要她父母的高期待。

   **解析** expectation 意思是 "期待 / 期盼"，而 "實現" 期待的動詞，可以搭配 meet, fulfill, match, satisfy, realize, etc.

5. The company rolled out a new environmentally-kind detergent product.

   ⇨ The company rolled out a new environmentally-friendly detergent product.

   這家公司推出一款對環境友善的清潔商品。

   **解析** environmentally-friendly 意思為 "對環境友善的"，也就是環保，屬慣用語。

6. I would die for something than live for nothing.

   ⇨ I would rather die for something than live for nothing.

   我寧願有意義地死去，也不願白活。

   **解析** would rather... than... 意思是 "寧願…也不願…"。

以上例句説明了：不管是動詞、名詞、形容詞、甚至是介系詞都有其搭配固定用法，絕非憑感覺任意書寫。另外，有些容易混淆的單字或片語，在使用上也需仔細小心，如：hope vs. wish，因為 wish 所帶出的 that 子句通常需使用假設語氣，倘若在 hope 的情境下，卻使用 wish，則會貽笑大方，因此字詞用法的重要性，不言可喻，對此，可參考筆者另一著作《英語易混淆字速查辭典》，其中收錄 1,300 則字義、字形容易混淆的單字及片語，協助讀者更聰明地選詞用字。

我們除了可以從文章的上下文得知該字用法、字典搭配用法外，「語料庫」亦是相當好的搭配詞查詢來源，所謂的語料庫，是指由電腦收集相當大的英文語料（至少都上千萬字），簡單説就是英文文章，進行對比、分析、檢索。使用方法很簡單，只要在查詢框裡鍵入要查詢的單字或片語，網站會顯示該字或片語在句中的使用情形。

在此筆者提供幾個語料庫及搭配詞網站供讀者查詢：

## 語料庫

- BNC（British National Corpus）：http://www.natcorp.ox.ac.uk/
- COCA（The Corpus of Contemporary American English）：http://corpus.byu.edu/coca/
- Macmillan Dictionary Corpus：http://www.macmillandictionary.com/corpus.html
- Tango 語料庫：http://candle.cs.nthu.edu.tw/collocation/
- Voicetube：https://tw.voicetube.com/?mtc=t3_blog_3595（亦可看影片學習）
- Google：www.google.com

以下茲以 Tango 語料庫為例，它是由國內清華大學所開發：

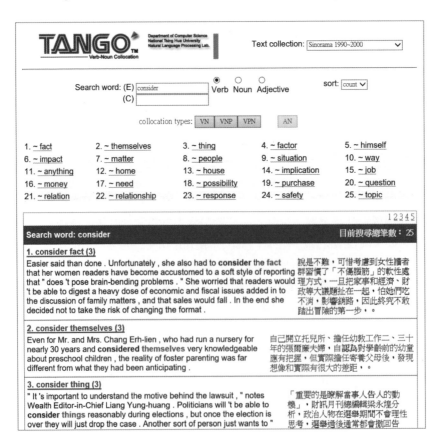

步驟：

❶ 進入網頁後，選擇該查詢字的詞性，並鍵入關鍵字，例如：consider

❷ 查詢中間頁面會有 consider 常搭配的字。

❸ 再往下，則會看到 consider 在文中的位置，右邊亦有中文翻譯。

## 搭配詞

- Netspeak：http://www.netspeak.org/#
- Online OXFORD Collocation Dictionary of English：
  http://oxforddictionary.so8848.com/
- Corpus Concordance English：http://lextutor.ca/conc/eng/
- iwill 搭配詞：http://collocation.stringnet.org/
- Just the Word：http://www.just-the-word.com/
- Ozdic：http://www.ozdic.com/

搭配詞查詢，以 Online OXFORD Collocation Dictionary of English 為例：

**Online OXFORD Collocation Dictionary**

**possibility** *noun*

ADJ. **exciting, interesting | endless, many** *The resort offers endless possibilities for entertainment.* | **further, other | different, various | future | distinct, great, real, serious, strong** *There's a strong possibility that it will rain today.* | **reasonable | faint, remote** *There is a faint possibility that he might have got the wrong day.* | **practical | theoretical | obvious**
VERB + POSSIBILITY **allow sb, offer sb, open up, raise | see | consider, discuss, examine, explore, study** *Have you explored the possibilities of setting up your own business?* | **accept, acknowledge, admit, concede, countenance, entertain, recognize | ignore, overlook | deny, discount, dismiss, eliminate, exclude, preclude, rule out** *We cannot rule out the possibility of mistaken identity.* | **face** *The club is facing the real possibility of relegation.* | **risk** *We don't want to risk the possibility of losing all our money.* | **allow for, cover** *Some reserves were named to cover the possibility of withdrawals.* | **avert | lessen, reduce**
PREP. **~ for** *She was quick to see the possibilities for making money that her new skills gave her.* | **~ of** *Careful checks will reduce the possibility of unpleasant surprises.*
PHRASES **beyond/within the bounds of possibility** *It's not beyond the bounds of possibility that a similar situation could arise again.* | **a number/range of possibilities** *The course offers a wide range of possibilities for personal development.*

步驟：

❶ 鍵入 possibility。

❷ 從查詢結果得知：possibility 可與很多形容詞搭配使用，如：exciting, further, reasonable, etc.

❸ 另外，possibility 也可與一些的動詞連用，例如：consider, accept, etc.

除了以上所列專屬的查詢網頁，其實 Google 也是一個龐大的語料庫與搭配詞查詢工具：

步驟：

❶ 當你不確定寫出的句子是否正確時，你可以用引號，框住要查詢的字或詞，例如：“relieve my pressure”。

❷ 首先你可以看到這種寫法共有幾筆，此例有 12,800 筆。

❸ 如何確認用法是否正確？你該選擇搜尋出來是圖書的網頁；或具公信力、權威的網站，例如：CNN，英美國家的政府機構、教育單位；論文研究；科學、醫學報告等等。

除了以上的單字查詢、語料庫查詢、搭配詞查詢等工具網站，在平常練習作文時，對於一篇文章會一再使用的單字或片語，應該多翻翻同義字字典，使用其同義字或相似字來取代，如此一來，才不會單調，但特別注意：選定一個同義字或相似字後，請務必在英英字典中確認是否英文解釋及用法可互通，在查詢過程中，相信讀者一定可以收穫滿滿！

在此推薦幾個好用的同義字線上字典：

* Collins Thesaurus：http://www.collinsdictionary.com/english-thesaurus

* Merriam Webster：http://www.merriam-webster.com/

* Cambridge：http://dictionary.cambridge.org/dictionary/british/

* Oxford：http://www.oxforddictionaries.com/thesaurus/

* Macmillan：http://www.macmillandictionary.com/

* Thesaurus.com：http://www.thesaurus.com/

* Wordreference：http://www.wordreference.com/thesaurus/

## 6 Muscular Verbs｜強而有力的動詞

**說明**

英文詞性分為：主詞、動詞、形容詞、副詞、介系詞等等。其中動詞是最多采多姿，也是句子的靈魂，句子可以沒有主詞（如：祈使句 Be quiet.），更可以沒有形容詞、副詞、介系詞（如：Time flies.），不過就是不能沒有動詞，這也代表著動詞是英文裡用法最多也最複雜的詞性，因為它會搭配主詞（有些動詞只能用於人或物），最麻煩的是它還會搭配介系詞使用（如：consist in 存在於 vs. consist with 與……一致）。而動詞也有分強弱，在好文章中是很少看的到語氣弱的動詞（be, seem, appear…），以下就來介紹哪些情況會用到弱動詞及如何去修改。

A. 避免使用語意弱的 be 動詞。我們可以把句中的補語轉換為不同的修飾語。

(1) **Weak and lengthy**: The man's leg <u>was crippled</u>. He <u>was dressed</u> in rags and <u>hungry</u> for money and food.

這男子的腳殘了。他穿破衣並渴望金錢與食物。

**Strong and concise**: The <u>crippled</u> man <u>in rags</u> <u>desired for</u> food and money.

這穿著破爛的殘廢男子渴望食物與金錢。

**解析** 修改後的句子，只有短短一句就可呈現全部資訊，將 crippled 當形容詞；in rags 置於名詞後面來修飾；was hungry for 則是直接用動詞 desired for，語氣較強。

(2) **Weak and lengthy**: It <u>was over</u> between my girlfriend and me. My heart <u>was broken</u> and my body <u>was weak</u> now.

我和我女朋友之間到此為止。我的心碎了而且現在的我很虛弱。

**Strong and concise**: <u>Breaking up</u> with my girlfriend <u>broke</u> my heart and <u>weakened</u> my body.

和我女朋友分手深深傷了我的心而且耗弱我的身體。

**解析** 原本三句，簡潔用一句表達，使用動名詞（breaking up）帶出分手這件事，並把原本例句中的形容詞皆改為動詞（was broken ⇨ broke; was weak ⇨ weaken）。

B. 將作 be 動詞後用的形容詞或名詞變為動詞。

(1) **Weak**: John is a <u>hard-working</u> man.

John 是個努力工作的人。

**Strong**: John <u>works hard</u>.

John 工作努力。

【解析】hard-working 詞性為形容詞，意思是 "努力工作的"，我們可以將其改為動詞 work hard。

(2) **Weak**: Mark's failure <u>is the result of</u> his laziness and dishonesty.

Mark 的失敗是懶惰和不誠實的結果。

**Strong**: Mark's failure <u>resulted from</u> his laziness and dishonesty.

Mark 的失敗起因於他的懶惰和不誠實。

【解析】名詞的 result 意思是 "結果"，它也可以當動詞，result from 意思是 "起因於…"；result in 則是 "…導致…"。

C. 在以「here」或「there」開頭的句子中，去除「be」，並改成語氣強的動詞。

(1) **Weak**: Here <u>is</u> your chance.

你的機會來了。

**Strong**: Your chance <u>comes</u>.

你的機會來了。

【解析】雖然兩句翻譯都一樣，但語氣強度上明顯分出高下。

(2) **Weak**: <u>There</u> <u>is</u> a <u>possibility</u> that Hannah will deliver a speech tomorrow.

明天 Hannah 可能會有一場演講。

**Strong**: Hannah will <u>possibly</u> <u>deliver</u> a speech tomorrow.

明天 Hannah 可能會有一場演講。

【解析】there is a possibility 其實就等於副詞的 possibly，用副詞來寫可以避免主要動詞是 be 動詞，如此句子既精簡又有強度。

D. 用字要精準，避免籠統字眼，如：go, eat, drink, walk, cook, etc.

(1) **Vague**: James drank two cans of soda and burped loudly.

James 喝下兩罐汽水並大聲打嗝。

**Clear**: James guzzled down two cans of soda and burped loudly.

James 狂飲下兩罐汽水並大聲打嗝。

**解析** guzzled down 可以翻譯為 "狂飲"，比起 drink，來的明確精準，更能凸顯後面的大聲打嗝。

(2) **Vague**: Lillard went around the campus, showing off his gold medal.

Lillard 在校園到處走動，炫耀他的金牌。

**Clear**: Lillard strutted around the campus, showing off his gold medal.

Lillard 在校園到處趾高氣揚地走，炫耀他的金牌。

**解析** strut（趾高氣揚地走），比較能搭配後面的 "炫耀他的金牌"。

溫馨提醒：關於各種動作的明確用字，請參考本書中的描寫文單元，會有更詳細補充。

E. 多用主動。只要多使用主動語氣，自然就不會出現被動語氣中的：be+p.p.。

(1) **Weak**: I was encouraged by my mentor to pursue an active life.

我受我的心靈導師鼓勵去追求更積極的人生。

**Strong**: My mentor encouraged me to pursue an active life.

我的心靈導師鼓勵我去追求更積極的人生。

(2) **Weak**: The safety of nuclear power plants has been emphasized by the government.

核能發電廠的安全受政府所重視。

**Strong**: The government has emphasized the safety of nuclear power plants.

政府重視核能發電廠的安全。

**解析** 以上這兩句主動句的寫法不但精簡，且語氣也更強。

1. **Weak**: Ronnie was attentive to the teacher's lectures.

   **Strong**: _____

2. **Weak**: The bank was robbed. Five million dollars was gone and the police are searching for him.

   **Strong**: _____

3. **Weak**: There is a tendency for people in Taiwan to get married after 30 years old.

   **Strong**: _____

4. **Weak**: The chef is cooking a fish which this restaurant is famous for.

   **Strong**: _____

5. **Weak**: Our new smartphone will be demonstrated by the CEO herself at today's exhibition.

   **Strong**: _____

1. Ronnie paid attention to the teacher's lectures.

   **解析** was attentive to 意思是 "專注於…"，可以換成動詞片語 pay attention to。

2. The police are searching for the criminal who robbed the bank of five million dollars.

   **解析** 將第一句的 The bank was robbed. 用主動句表達，並將所損失的五百萬，巧妙用 rob 這個動詞來搭配寫出。

3. People in Taiwan tend to get married after 30 years old.

   **解析** tend to（傾向於做…）會比 there is a tendency 語氣來的強烈。

4. The chef is steaming a milkfish which this restaurant is famous for.

   **解析** steam 意思是 "清蒸"，烹煮的意思較 cook 來的明確許多。

5. The CEO herself will demonstrate our new smartphone at today's exhibition.

   **解析** 主動句比被動句來的精簡有力。

# Chapter 2

## Variety
## 句型 101

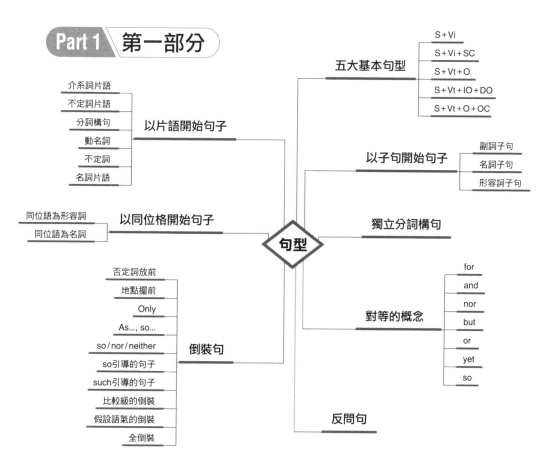

## 一、S+V

口訣：主動付點錢

一般句子，皆必須有主詞、動詞，後面修飾的副詞、地點、時間可有可無，另外，副詞有時可置於動詞前面。

Curry practices basketball hard in the gym almost every day.

Curry 幾乎每天都在體育館認真地練籃球。

| 主 | 主詞 | Curry |
|---|---|---|
| 動 | 動詞 | practices basketball |
| 付（副） | 副詞 | hard |
| 點 | 地點 | in the gym |
| 錢（間） | 時間 | almost every day |

## Imperative sentence（祈使句）

此一句型是省略主詞 you，並以動詞開始一個句子；否定句時，可加否定詞 never 或 don't 於句首，來形成否定。祈使句目的是希望 / 要求對方可以照著自己的意思來做或不要去做。在實際寫作上，適用於開頭段引起讀者注意或於結論段給予讀者建議。

例句：

1　Consider the job offer and reply to me next week.

考慮一下這工作機會，下禮拜再回覆我。

2 <u>Never</u> transfer money at the ATM simply because of a phone call from a stranger.

絕對不可因為一通陌生人電話，就乖乖到 ATM 轉帳匯錢。

### 🖊 牛刀小試

1. 把辣椒加到菜裡，再炒一下就好了。

   _____ chilli to the dish and stir-fry it for a few seconds.

2. 手濕濕時，不要碰觸插座。

   Do not _____ the socket when your hand is wet.

3. 你開太快了。慢一點。

   _____

4. 千萬不要考試作弊。

   _____

### ✓ Answer

1. Add

2. touch

3. You drive too fast. Slow down a little bit.

4. Never cheat on the exam.

# 五大基本句型

## (1) S+Vi（Nothing matters.）

口訣：主動

> **說明**
>
> 此句型中的動詞為不及物動詞（Vi），句子可以簡單到只有兩個字，即：主詞與動詞，不用另外加補語或受詞；如果動詞後想加受詞，則需先加入適當的「介系詞」（Vi＋介＋受詞），因此在背不及物動詞時，要連同搭配的介系詞一併學習。此外，可加副詞來修飾。

例句：

1. The wind *blew* hard.

   風吹很大。（加副詞）

2. My dog always *barks* in the middle of the night.

   我的狗總在半夜汪汪叫。（加副詞片語）

3. Everyone is *laughing at* my new haircut.

   每個人都在笑我的新髮型。（Vi ＋ 介 ＋ 受詞）

## 牛刀小試

1. 他總是在喝酒後，講話大聲。

   He always ＿＿＿＿＿＿＿＿ ＿＿＿＿＿＿＿＿ after drinking too much alcohol.

2. 這個 5 歲小孩跑得比成人還快。

   The five-year-old kid ＿＿＿＿＿＿＿＿ faster than an adult.

3. 一台噴射機消失在雲裡。（vanish 消失）

   ＿＿＿＿＿＿＿＿＿＿＿＿＿＿＿＿＿＿＿＿＿＿＿＿＿

4. 這老人獨自住在一間房子。

   ＿＿＿＿＿＿＿＿＿＿＿＿＿＿＿＿＿＿＿＿＿＿＿＿＿

**Answer**

1. talks loudly

2. runs

3. A jet vanished in the clouds.

4. This old man lived in a house alone.

## (2) S+Vi+SC（It sounds awful.）

**說明**

此句型之動詞亦為不及物動詞，此類動詞又稱為「連綴動詞」，後面須接主詞補語，否則句子將不合乎文法。用法上，動詞後常接「形容詞」。

常見的動詞如下：

| Be 動詞 | be |
|---------|-----|
| 5 感覺 | look, sound, taste, smell, feel |
| 似乎 | appear, seem |
| 變得 | get, grow, go, fall, turn, become |
| 保持 | keep, stay, remain |

**補充說明**：5 感覺（smell, look, taste, sound, feel），若要後接名詞作為主詞補語，則可利用 like：She looks like a super model. 此外，become/remain 後面也可直接加名詞：She became a successful doctor. We still remain friends.

例句：

1. Alice stayed calm when there was a fire, and was finally saved by firefighters.
   Alice 當火災時仍保持冷靜，最後順利被消防員救出。

2. You will know it is difficult to walk upstairs when you <u>grow</u> <u>old</u>.
當你老了，就會知道爬樓梯是件很困難的事。

### 牛刀小試

1. 明年，我就要 20 歲了。

   Next year I'll _____ 20.

2. 在山裡迷路時，你還是得保持冷靜。

   When lost in the mountain, you still have to _____ calm.

3. 這運動員比賽前似乎太自信了。（運動員 athlete）

   _____

4. 這西瓜嚐起來一點都不甜也不多汁。

   _____

### Answer

1. turn

2. keep

3. The athlete appeared too confident before the game.

4. This watermelon doesn't taste sweet and juicy at all.

### (3) S+Vt+O（It hurts me.）

> **說明**
>
> 此類動詞為及物動詞，換句話說，動詞後須接受詞，可為「名詞」或「動名詞」或「不定詞」。一般的及物動詞，在背單字時只需留意即可，以下介紹一些特殊動詞，其後必須加「動名詞」或「不定詞」來作為受詞。

| 常見口語用字<br>（後必須加動名詞 Ving） | enjoy, finish, miss, practice, keep, mind, mean, quit, spend |
|---|---|
| 進階版<br>（後必須加動名詞 Ving） | appreciate（感謝）, admit（承認）, avoid（避免）<br>consider（考慮）<br>delay（延誤）, dislike（不喜歡）, deny（否認）,<br>detest（討厭）<br>imagine（想像）, include（包括）<br>postpone（延遲）<br>risk（冒險）, resist（抵抗）, resume（再從事……）,<br>recommend（建議）suggest（建議） |
| 有些動詞後可加「動名詞」當受詞，亦可加「不定詞」為受詞，且意思幾乎毫無差別。 | 忍受：bear, endure<br>繼續：continue<br>停止：cease<br>討厭：hate<br>喜歡：love, like, prefer<br>開始：start, begin |
| 不同於上述兩類動詞，有些動詞後加動名詞與不定詞，意思則相異。簡易辨別方式為：to 可翻譯為「去……」。 | 停止：stop<br>記得：remember<br>試著：try<br>忘記：forget<br>繼續：go on |

試比較以下例句：

1. Mobby stopped making a noise.

   Mike 停止製造噪音。

2. Mobby stopped to make a noise.

   Mike 停下原本在做的事，去製造噪音。

3. I forgot renewing my passport.

   我忘記已經換新我的護照了。

4.  I forgot <u>to</u> renew my passport.

    我忘記去換新我的護照了。

---

補充學習：

| 常見片語（後必須加動名詞 Ving） | burst out（突然）, end up（結果成為）, feel like（想要）, give up（放棄）, put off（延遲） |
| --- | --- |

---

### 牛刀小試

1.  老闆所說的話困惑著每一個人。

    What my boss said really ＿＿＿＿＿＿＿ each of us.

2.  妳有曾想像過躺在沙灘上，曬個古銅色皮膚嗎？

    Have you ever imagined ＿＿＿＿＿＿＿ on the beach, getting a suntan?

3.  很多人都討厭住在工廠旁邊。

    _____

4.  Leo 說他記得去關瓦斯，但事實上他並沒有。

    _____

### Answer

1.  confused

2.  lying

3.  Many people hate to live/living right next to a factory.

4.  Leo said he remembered to turn off the gas, but in fact he didn't.

## (4) S+Vt+IO+DO（He made me a cake.）

**說明**

句型中的動詞為授與動詞，後面需加「兩個受詞」即：IO 為間接受詞（通常為人）、DO 為直接受詞（通常為事物）。若要將 IO 與 DO 互換，則需加適合的「介系詞」，即主詞＋動詞＋物＋介＋人。

茲以介系詞做以下分類：

| 需接 of | ask |
|---|---|
| 需接 from | borrow |
| 需接 for | buy, make, choose, get, bring, cook, leave |
| 需接 to | give, offer, show, teach, sell, write, lend, send, bring |

試比較以下例句：

1. Thank you for lending me your car for my first date with Eve.

   ＝Thank you for lending your car *to* me for my first date with Eve.

   謝謝你借我車讓我可以去跟 Eve 第一次約會。

2. Remember to buy me a bottle of soy sauce on your way home.

   ＝ Remember to buy a bottle of soy sauce *for* me on your way home.

   記得回家路上幫我買一瓶醬油。

### 牛刀小試

1. Anthony 送老婆一台平板電腦當作生日禮物。

   Anthony ＿＿＿＿＿＿ his wife a tablet computer as her birthday gift.

2. 我跟我鄰居借了一把螺絲起子。

   I ＿＿＿＿＿＿ a screwdriver from my neighbor.

3. The old man asked me a favor = The old man asked a favor _____ me.
這老人要求我幫忙。

4. A con man sold me a fake watch. = A con man sold a fake watch _____ me.
一個金光黨賣我一支假錶。

## Answer

1. gave

2. borrowed

3. of

4. to

## (5) S+Vt+O+OC（I watched her dancing.）

**說明**

此類動詞亦為及物動詞，但是在加完受詞後，必須再加一個「受詞補語」，如此，語意才完整。

| 使役動詞 | make, have, let（語氣由強到弱） |
|---|---|
| 感官動詞 | 3 看（see, watch, look at）、2 聽（listen to, hear）、feel、observe（觀察）、notice（注意） |
| 狀態動詞 | 受詞後可接形容詞、地點、甚至是動詞，若接動詞，則視受詞與動詞的關係：主動 Ving、被動 p.p.。<br>leave 讓……處於……狀態<br>find 發現……處於……狀態<br>keep 使……處於……狀態 |
| 其他 | 常以名詞為補語的動詞：<br>name（命名）；elect（選為…）；appoint（任命為…）；call（稱…為…）等等 |

例句：

- **使役動詞**

  (1) She let/had/made me submit my report by tomorrow.

   她要我明天前繳交報告。（受詞與後面動詞，若為主動關係，用原形動詞）

  (2) Benny had/made the reservation date changed to July 6th.

   Benny 將訂位日期改為 7 月 6 日。（過去分詞 p.p.）

  (3) I let the door be closed in case the cat should sneak out.

   我讓門關著以免貓偷溜出去。（have, make, let 的受詞與後面動詞，若為被動關係，用過去分詞 p.p.，但 let 後須另加 be 動詞）

  ---

  補充說明 make 其他用法：

  (1) After the two-year training, the coach made Ford a better tennis player.

   經過兩年的訓練，教練讓 Ford 成為一個更好的網球選手。（可用名詞為補語）

  (2) Jason can always make his grandmother happy by saying something sweet.

   Jason 總是可以藉著說一些甜蜜的話讓奶奶開心。（可用形容詞為補語）

  ---

- **感官動詞**

  (1) I never heard Pete mention/mentioing his family.

   我從來沒聽過 Pete 提過他的家人。（受詞與後面動詞，若為主動關係，用原形動詞或現在分詞 Ving）

  (2) It is sad to see the historic building destroyed in an earthquake.

   看到這在歷史上有意義的建築物毀於地震真令人難過。（受詞與後面動詞，若為被動關係，用過去分詞 p.p.）

- **讓 / 發現 / 使……處於……狀態**

  (1) I left my alarm clock ringing without stopping it.

   我讓我的鬧鐘響而不按掉它。（主動 Ving）

(2) I found the *baby* bitten by mosquitoes.

我發現這小嬰兒被蚊子咬。（被動 p.p.）

(3) I always keep my *windows* open for better air ventilation.

我保持窗戶開啟以利空氣流通。（加形容詞）

(4) Mr. Wang found Sam in the classroom alone.

王老師發現 Sam 獨自在教室裡。（亦可加地點）

- **其他**

She was named the most popular actress this year.

她被選為今年最受歡迎女演員。（以名詞為補語）

### 牛刀小試

1. 警察要我交出我的駕照。

The police officer had me _____ in my driving license.

2. 我們從沒看過病人像這樣被糟糕地對待。

We never saw a patient _____ so badly like this.

3. 這女士注意到有人尾隨她回家。

The lady noticed someone _____ her all the way home.

4. 這位醫生當選台北市市長。

The doctor was _____ mayor of Taipei.

5. 沒人發現我們迷路於山中。

_____

6. 我讓我的車子一個月修理三次。

_____

## Answer

1. hand
2. treated
3. follow/following
4. elected
5. No one found us lost in the mountains.
6. I had my car repaired three times a month.

## 二、Starting a sentence with an appositive
### 以同位格開始句子

> **說明**
> 我們可利用名詞與形容詞，來和其後的主詞形成同位語，功能上，是用來補充說明主詞，並免去將名詞與形容詞放入直述句中的單調感。

例句：

**a** 同位語為形容詞

(1) Stupid and fat, the dog was bullied by a kitten.
又笨又胖，這隻狗竟被一隻小貓欺負。

(2) Cold and hungry, the traveler lost his consciousness.
又冷又餓，這旅人失去了知覺。

**b** 同位語為名詞

(1) A successful businessman, Mr. Wang donated a fortune to help those in need.
身為一位成功的企業家，王先生捐鉅款來幫助那些需要幫助的人。

(2) Rose finally found Jack—the man that she would spend the rest of her life with.

Rose 終於找到 Jack—是她能夠託付一生的男人。

**補充說明** 使用破折號帶出同位格，另以關係代名詞補充說明該同位格，會讓句子看起來更漂亮。

(3) As he is a child, he takes care of his bedridden mother all by himself.

⇨ Child as he is, he takes care of his bedridden mother all by himself.

即使他只是個小孩，他獨自照顧久病臥床的媽媽。

(4) Though they are robots, they are capable of many difficult tasks.

⇨ Robots though they are, they are capable of many difficult tasks.

雖然它們只是機器人，它們可以執行很多困難的任務。

**補充說明** as 與 though 可互換，但不可用 although，若為單數名詞，則不須加冠詞 a/an。

## 牛刀小試

1. Lovesick and _____, Nash guzzled down liquors to drown his sorrows.

   為愛所困及思鄉心切，Nash 只能借酒澆愁。

2. After retiring, Jack moved to Hualien—a city _____ is famous for its spectacular scenery.

   退休後，Jack 搬去花蓮 — 一個以絕美風景聞名的城市。

3. Though she is an office lady, she turns out to be a rock singer at a club at night.

   → _____ though she is, she turns out to be a rock singer at a club at night.

4. Miranda is a slim girl.

   She can move a freezer upstairs.（以同位格合併）

   → _____

 **Answer**

1. homesick

2. that/which

3. Office lady

4. A slim girl, Miranda can move a freezer upstairs.

## 三、Starting a sentence with a phrase 以片語開始句子

### (1) 介系詞片語

 **說明**

我們可利用介系詞片語來開始一個句子，此介系詞片語可來修飾主詞或整句。目的是除了讓句子多變化之外，也可強調該介系詞片語。

例句：

1. <u>With a lollipop in hand</u>, the child was as happy as a lark.
   棒棒糖在手，那個小孩快樂的不得了。

2. <u>In front of the excited fans</u>, the singer went down the stage to shake hands with them.
   在興奮歌迷前，這位歌手跑下舞台和他們握手。

3. <u>With a view to perfecting roller-skate riding skills</u>, Kevin practices in the gym three hours every day.
   為了要使溜冰技巧完美，Kevin 每天都在體育館練習 3 小時。（with a view to 意思是「為了」，其中 to 是介系詞）

4. <u>On hearing Mr. Huang's steps</u>, students went back to their seats in no time and pretended to study hard.
   一聽到黃老師的腳步聲，學生們迅速地坐好並假裝認真念書。（On+Ving, S+V 可表「一…就…」）

 **牛刀小試**

1. _____ _____ _____ the musical chart, Jay's album sold like a hot cake.
   高居排行榜第一名，周杰倫的唱片大熱賣。

2. _____ the _____ of the road, the poor dog didn't know what to do.
   在馬路正中央，這隻可憐的狗狗不知該怎麼辦。

3. 在這棟房子的後面，我發現一條很乾淨且充滿魚的河流。

   _____

4. 一喝到這麼美味的湯，Tim 不停稱讚廚師。（praise 稱讚）

   _____

**Answer**

1. On top of

2. In；middle

3. In the back of the house, I found a very clean river full of fish.

4. On eating such delicious soup, Tim couldn't stop praising the cook.

## (2) 不定詞片語

> **說明**
> 此一句型中，我們可以用不定詞（to V 或 in order to V）來開頭，可表示後面句子主詞的目的。

例句：

1. <u>To increase work efficiency</u>, the boss offered a bonus to any hard-working employees.
   為了增加工作效率，老闆提供紅利獎金給認真工作者。

2. <u>In order to attract female birds</u>, the male bird never feels tired of showing off its beautiful feathers.

為了要吸引母鳥，這隻公鳥對於展示它漂亮羽毛都不厭倦。

溫馨提醒：with a view to, with an eye to, with the intention of 皆有「為了……」的意思，但差別於 to 為介系詞，後面需接動名詞。

例句：

<u>With a view to</u> winning more votes, the candidate promised to seek free lunch for students.

為了吸引更多選票，這候選人承諾為學生爭取免費營養午餐。

### 牛刀小試

1. _____ _____ _____ slow down the global warming, scientists urged people to use alternative energy.

   為了要減緩溫室效應，科學家們力勸人們使用替代性能源。

2. _____ _____ the heavy traffic, Mr. Chen usually takes shortcuts to his office.

   為了避開壅塞交通，陳先生通常抄捷徑去辦公室。

3. _____

   為了照顧小北鼻，Helen 辭掉工作。

4. _____

   為了要激勵學生，張老師告訴他們一個感人的故事。（inspire 激勵）

### Answer

1. On top of

2. To avoid

3. With an eye to taking care of her baby, Helen quit her job.

4. With the intention of inspiring his students, Mr. Chang told them a touching story.

## (3) 分詞構句

**說明**

使用分詞構句的目的在於讓句子更精簡，步驟如下：(1) 確認前後兩句的主詞相同；(2) 省略連接詞（and, or, but 等等）；(3) 並將其中一句，或有副詞連接詞那一句的主詞省略；(4) 省略主詞的那句，動詞做變化，口訣為：主動 Ving 被動 p.p.。而副詞連接詞可留可不留。另外，可在分詞前面加 not，來形成否定。

例句：

1.  If you download this bus app, you will know when the bus will come and leave.

    ⇨ If downloading (Downloading) this bus app, you will know when the bus will come and leave.

    如果你下載這公車 app，你會知道公車何時來何時離開。

2.  Because the little girl was frightened by a fake snake, she cried for her mother.

    ⇨ Frightened by a fake snake, the little girl cried for her mother.

    被一隻假蛇嚇到，這小女孩哭著找媽媽。

3.  Although he didn't succeed in the job interview, Clark didn't feel discouraged.

    ⇨ Although not succeeding/(Not succeeding) in the job interview, Clark didn't feel discouraged.

    雖然工作面試失敗，Clark 仍不氣餒。

### 牛刀小試

1.  _____ on a shopping spree, Monica splurged all her salary of this month.

    Monica 瘋狂大血拚，花光了她這個月的薪水。

2.  After _____ by you twice, I won't believe whatever you say anymore.

    被你騙了兩次，我以後再也不相信你講的話了。

3. _____

為新法所禁止，這種藥不能再給病人服用。

4. _____

雖然無法實現夢想，Tina 仍然不放棄並且繼續嘗試。

## ✅ Answer

1. Going

2. cheated

3. Banned by the new law, this kind of medicine can't be given to patients.

4. Although failing to realize her dreams, Tina didn't give up and kept trying.

## (4) 動名詞

**說明**

動詞變成動名詞後，具備名詞功能，因此可以當作句子的主詞、受詞或主詞補語。如果做為主詞功能時，需視其為單數，因為是指整件事情；另外，not 加於動名詞之前，可以形成否定。

例句：

1. Reflecting what she did in the diary has become a daily routine for Connie.（當主詞）

   反省日記中所做的事已成為 Connie 每天必做的事。

2. The prime minister admitted making a serious mistake and stepped down afterwards.

   總理承認犯下大錯，隨後並下台。（當受詞）

3. Not following the traffic rules results in many road accidents every year.

   沒有確實遵守交通規則每年都導致許多道路意外事件。

1. _____ to this torch song reminded me of those unhappy days.

   聽到這首感傷的情歌讓我想起以前不愉快的日子。

2. _____ _____ a mantis behind, this butterfly was soon eaten up.

   沒注意到有隻螳螂在後面，這隻蝴蝶很快就被吃了。

3. _____

   老實說，我還蠻享受去當義工在週末去淨灘。

4. _____

   對智慧型手機上癮會對人們的眼睛造成傷害。

## Answer

1. Listening

2. Not noticing

3. To be honest, I quite enjoy volunteering to clean up the beach on the weekend.

4. Being addicted to smartphones does damage to people's eyes.

## (5) 不定詞

**說明**

動詞作為名詞功能，除了動名詞外，亦改成不定詞（to V）。不定詞可當作句子的主詞、主詞補語、受詞。同樣的，如果放於主詞位置時，需視其為單數；另外，not 加在不定詞之前，可形成否定。

例句：

1. <u>To give</u> green light to the fruit import had a great impact on farmers in Taiwan.

   開放水果進口對台灣農民有重大影響。（當主詞）

2. The opposition party threatened to block any bills proposed by the ruling party.
在野黨威脅要阻擋執政黨所提的任何法案。（當受詞）

3. The purpose of this study is to find out if drinking red wine before bed helps?
本研究的目的是找出睡前喝紅酒是否有助睡眠？（當主詞補語）

4. Not to reserve a table beforehand can leave people waiting outside a restaurant for a long time.
沒有事先訂位可讓人們在餐廳外等待很久的時間。（加 not，來形成否定）

## 牛刀小試

1. _____ _____ the latest news in the battlefield is quite risky.
在戰地報導新聞還蠻有風險的。

2. 沒有在路上浪費太多時間將使我們可以及時搭上飛機。
_____ _____ _____ too much time on the road will enable us to get on the plane in time.

3. 帶著較少行李旅行總是讓我有好心情。（go on a journey 旅行）
_____

4. 英文要說的流利需要足夠的練習和自信。
_____

## Answer

1. To report

2. Not to waste

3. To go on a journey with less baggage always puts me in a good mood.

4. To speak English fluently needs enough practice and confidence.

## (6) 名詞片語

說明

名詞片語是由名詞子句變化而來，只是長相是「片語」，功能亦為「名詞」，用法上，可當整個句子的主詞、主詞補語、及受詞。相同地，如果放在主詞位置，則要視為單數主詞，適用單數動詞。公式：5W1H+to+V。

例句：

1. <u>Who to be starters for the next basketball game</u> will be decided by the coach later on.

   （當主詞）下一場籃球賽先發球員等等會由教練決定。

2. What worries the government now is <u>how to put our economy back on track</u>.

   （當主詞補語）現在政府所擔心的是如何將經濟步入正軌。

3. The instructor will cue all the musicians <u>when to start playing</u>.

   （當受詞）指揮者會暗示所有樂手何時開始演奏。

### 牛刀小試

1. Sam 完全處於困惑當中，因為沒人告訴他該怎麼做。

   Sam was completely at a loss since no one told him _____ to do it.

2. _____ to start building this tunnel will be decided by the city government.

   何時開始建造這隧道將是由市政府所決定。

3. _____

   所有的士兵需要將軍選擇該在何處紮營。（tent 帳篷）

4. _____

   我們下一個問題是誰要代表我們公司去這場會議。（represent 代表）

## Answer

1. how

2. When

3. All the soldiers needed the general to select where to put up their tents.

4. Our next question is who to represent our company to the meeting.

## 四、Starting a sentence with a clause 以子句開始句子

### (1) 副詞子句

**說明**

副詞子句定義上，是以副詞連接詞引導出的句子，常見的副詞連接詞包括：while, when, before, after, if, even if, though, although , even though, since, unless（除非）, until, till（直到…）, as, as long as（只要…）, as soon as, once（一旦…）, by the time (=before), etc.

溫馨提醒：副詞子句不可單獨存在，必須連接另一主要子句；但可擺主要子句前或後。特別注意：有些連接詞本身有兩個意思，請注意例句後面的說明。

例句：

1. Before I go to work, I usually check what the weather report says.

   在我上班前，我都會看看氣象報導怎麼說。

2. Cathy has been depressed since she was diagnosed with liver cancer.

   自從 Cathy 被診斷出肝癌，她就一直很沮喪。（since 當句需接過去式句子）

   Cathy has been depressed since September 2.（since 後亦可加時間點）

   vs. Since you made a promise to me, you will have to keep it.

   既然你都對我承諾了，你就應該要遵守。（since 可當「既然 / 因為」）

（註：since 當自從時，當句用過去式，主要子句用完成式；since 當既然 / 因為時，左右兩句的時態沒有特別限制。）

3. While I was dozing off in class, my teacher suddenly loudly called my name.

當我在打瞌睡時，我的老師突然很大聲喊我名字。（while 當句常用進行式）

vs. Some people are vegetarians while others can't eat without meat.

有些人是素食者，但有些人不能沒有肉。（while 此處有 although/but 的意思）

4. My grandmother still haggled over the price through body language even though she couldn't speak Japanese.

我奶奶仍然透過肢體語言在殺價即使她根本不會講日語。

5. Although (Though) Rose loves you so much, it doesn't mean you can cheat on her again and again.

雖然 Rose 如此愛你，但不意味著你可以一再的出軌。（although 與 though 可互換）

6. As animals were drinking water near the pond, a crocodile jumped out of water to attack them.

當動物們在池塘邊喝水，一隻鱷魚從水中衝出進行攻擊。

Vs. As it's getting dark, bats fly out, hunting for dinner.

隨著夜色低垂，蝙蝠飛出，進行晚餐獵食。

Vs. As you are short of ideas for writing, why don't you watch a movie for inspiration?

既然 / 因為你寫作已經沒想法了，為何不去看場電影來獲得靈感？

7. By the time the police *came*, all the gangsters *had scattered* in all directions.

在警方到達之前，所有的幫派份子就鳥獸四散。（By the time 當句用過去式，主要子句用過去完成式）

Vs. By the time the rescue team *arrives*, the missing mountain climber *will have died* of hunger.

在搜救隊抵達前，這失蹤的登山客將早已餓死。（By the time 當句用現在式，主要子句用未來完成式）

**牛刀小試**

1. _____ I took a little rest, I got my second wind to make it to the top of the mountain.

    (A) Before  (B) By the time  (C) Although  (D) After

2. _____ your flight is delayed for 12 hours, why don't you stay for one more day in Paris?

    (A) While  (B) Since  (C) Though  (D) By the time

3. Some of my friends keep pets, _____ others think it troublesome to have one.

    (A) after  (B) since  (C) while  (D) so

4. By the time the alarm clock went off, Mark _____ for another new day.

    (A) wakes up  (B) has woken up  (C) will wake up  (D) had woken up

5. The writer won't sign his name on the contract _____ he sees a satisfying one.

    (A) until  (B) though  (C) while  (D) since

6. _____ all the animals noticed a lion nearby, they escaped right away.

    (A) Since  (B) Until  (C) Although  (D) As soon as

 Answer

1. (D)    2. (B)    3. (C)    4. (D)    5. (A)    6. (D)

## (2) 名詞子句

例句：

1. How the hacker stole the data of our bank is still being investigated.（當主詞）
   駭客如何偷走我們銀行的資料仍在調查。

2. An enough supply of tap water is what we need most now.（當主詞補語）
   足夠的自來水供應是我們現在最需要的。

3. The housewife didn't understand why cockroaches sometimes came out of the sink.（當受詞）
   這家庭主婦不了解為何蟑螂有時從洗手台冒出來。

4. What caused our ceiling to leak troubled my father.（what 可當主詞，若子句內主詞不明時）
   到底甚麼導致天花板漏水困擾著我爸爸。

5. Would you tell me who won the Best Actor of the Golden Horse last night?（who 可當主詞，若子句內主詞不明時）
   你能告訴我昨晚誰贏得金馬獎最佳男主角嗎？

6. That the earth is not round has been proved.（當主詞）
   地球不是圓這件事已經被證實。

7. No one is so sure to say <u>whether a big earthquake will occur in the next ten years or not</u>.

沒人可以很確定的說未來十年是否會發生大地震。（=whether or not a big earthquake will occur in the next ten years.）

### 牛刀小試

1. _____ the ship was robbed by pirates was unclear.

   尚不明船隻在何處被海盜搶劫。

2. It was said that Kim knew _____ the price of gold would rise.

   據說 Kim 知道金價何時上揚。

3. _____

   創造這好用 app 的人一定是個聰明人。

4. _____

   火車是否會誤點取決於有多少旅客上下車。

### Answer

1. Where

2. when

3. Who created this useful app must be a clever person.

4. Whether the train is delayed or not depends on how many passengers get on and off it.

## (3) 形容詞子句

| 功能 ＼ 先行詞 | 人 | 物 |
|---|---|---|
| 主格 | who | which |
| 受格 | whom | which |
| 所有格 | whose | whose |

**說明**

以上表格為所有關係代名詞（關代）的列表，由關代引導出來的子句為形容詞子句，是用來修飾／說明先行詞，相同地，因為形容詞子句亦為子句的一種，所以寫作時，不可單獨存在，詳情請見底下例句寫法。另外，特別注意以下幾點：

1. 用法上：口訣：主格關代 +V；受格關代 +S+V；所有格關代 +N+V 或所有格關代 +N+S+V

   溫馨提醒：*所有格關代後面必須先加名詞，其後所加的東西，綜合了主格關代及受格關代。*

2. 受格關代可省略，省略後句子仍是正確；

3. which 可以代替前面整個句子，不過 which 前面要使用逗點；

4. 主格關代及受格關代皆可用 that 代替，但若關代前有介系詞或標點符號，則不可用 that 代替；

5. 先行詞若為人和非人的名詞、the very、the only、序數、最高級、any、all 等等，關代常用 that；

6. 主格關代原則上不可省略，若要省略，則必須將其後的動詞改成 Ving（主動）或 p.p.（被動）；

7. 若先行詞為獨一無二、地名、人名、或專有名詞，則關代前須逗點，稱為非限定用法；反之，先行詞若無上述特點，則不需逗點。

例句：

1. In this store, most electronic products <u>which</u> are on sale were all made in China.

   在這家店裡，大部分特價的電器都是大陸製的。（主格）

2. An apology is the only thing <u>that</u> you owe me.

   一個道歉是你唯一欠我的東西。（受格）

3. Viewers complained about this TV station <u>whose</u> <u>weather</u> <u>forecast</u> <u>is</u> often incorrect.

   觀眾抱怨這家電視台的氣象預報常失準。（whose＋N＋V）

   Vs. Viewers don't like this TV station <u>whose</u> <u>weather</u> <u>forecast</u> <u>no</u> <u>one</u> <u>trusts</u>.

   觀眾不喜歡這家電視台，它的氣象預報沒人信任。（whose＋N＋S＋V）

4. The Love River, <u>which</u> looks more romantic at night, becomes a popular spot for dates.

   愛河在晚上看起來更浪漫變成約會的熱門地點。（the Love River 為專有名詞）

5. Patients <u>receiving</u> chemotherapy usually feel extremely weak and tired.（＝who receive…）

   接受化療的病人通常會感覺特別虛弱和疲倦感。

6. Our new game app <u>targeted</u> at young people earned us a lot of money.（＝which is targeted…）

   我們新的遊戲 app 以年輕朋友為目標為我們賺進不少錢。

7. Smartphones nowadays feature many functions, <u>which</u> indeed makes our lives more convenient。

   現在的手機都具備許多功能，這讓我們的生活更便利。（which 代替前面整個句子）

牛刀小試

1. I know a professor _____ has been doing research on liver cancer for 30 years.

   (A) which  (B) who  (C) whose  (D) , that

2. A brick _____ fell down from the building hit a man passing by.

   (A) whose  (B) who  (C) ,which  (D) which

3. May I introduce the man _____ I work with to you?

   (A) whom  (B) ,that  (C) which  (D) whose

4. This is a popular TV channel _____ programs I watch every night.

   (A) who  (B) that  (C) whose  (D) which

5. Some people in China still eat dog meat _____ really terrifies me.

   (A) whose  (B) , which  (C) which  (D) that

6. Cruise is the most hard-working actor _____ I've ever seen.

   (A) that  (B) , which  (C) who  (D) whose

7. Have you heard the famous TV host _____ travel books?

   (A) published  (B) publishes  (C) to publish  (D) publishing

8. Hardy is a great soldier _____ in a battle last year.

   (A) injured  (B) injuring  (C) to injure  (D) injures

9. 你沒什麼可以爭辯的。你完全錯了。（argue 爭辯）

   _____

10. Jeff 傷了 Annie 的心，但被另一個女人背叛。（betray 背叛）

    _____

**Answer**

1. (B)   2. (D)   3. (A)   4. (C)   5. (B)   6. (A)   7. (D)   8. (A)

9. There is nothing that you can argue about. You are all wet.

10. Jeff, who broke Annie's heart, was betrayed by another woman.

## 五、A question sentence（rhetorical question）反問句

**說明**

有一種問句叫做反問句，並非要對方回答，而是有反諷、帶點聽天由命、或要對方反思的意思，後者（反思）在論說文的寫作中，可以使用，而這種問句並不需要去回答。

例句：

1. Who do you think you are?
   你以為你是誰？

2. Who knows you won't meet a better man?
   天曉得你不會遇到更好的人？

3. How can we expect a corrupt government like this to provide us with any welfare?
   我們要如何期待如此貪腐的政府提供我們福利？

4. Shouldn't we stop and smell the flowers, instead of getting snowed under with heavy workload?
   我們不該停下腳步，欣賞沿途風景，而不是被沉重工作量壓的喘不過氣？

**牛刀小試**

1. _____

    我們不該多多關心我們的地球並試著和其他生物和平共處嗎？

2. _____

    我們為何要浪費這麼多時間做像這種無意義的事呢？

**Answer**

1. Shouldn't we care more about our earth and try to live peacefully with other creatures?

2. Why do we waste so much time doing something meaningless like this?

## 六、Absolute participle 獨立分詞構句

> **說明**
>
> 簡單的說，獨立分詞構句就是因兩邊主詞不同而無法省略，故需將兩邊主詞皆保留下來，一樣不留連接詞，動詞改分詞的處理上，口訣亦為：主動 Ving 被動 p.p.。

例句：

1. After the couple had a quarrel, the man carried his comforter and pillow to the sofa for the night.

    ⇨ The couple having a quarrel, the man carried his comforter and pillow to the sofa for the night.

    這對夫妻吵架，男子拿著棉被和枕頭去睡沙發。（將 after 刪除，因兩邊主詞不同，皆保留，並因為夫妻 "主動" 爭執，所以動詞改為 Ving）

2. <u>The criminal was caught</u> in his sleep, so the police didn't use any bullets or get hurt.

⇨ <u>The criminal caught</u> in his sleep, the police didn't use any bullets or get hurt.

罪犯在睡夢中被抓，所以警方並沒用到任何子彈或受傷。（先將 so 刪除，因兩邊主詞不同，皆保留，又因為罪犯與動詞 "逮捕" 的關係為被動，所以動詞改為 p.p.）

## 牛刀小試

1. The weather ＿＿＿＿＿ unstable, we had better bring umbrellas with us.
   天氣不太穩定，我們最好帶傘。

2. The cricket's hole ＿＿＿＿＿ with water, it couldn't help but dash out.
   蟋蟀的洞大淹水，它只好趕快從洞口衝出。

3. ＿＿＿＿＿＿＿＿＿＿＿＿＿＿＿＿, most the villagers decided to move out.
   這村莊一個月淹水五次，大部分居民們都打算搬出去。

4. ＿＿＿＿＿＿＿＿＿＿＿＿＿＿＿＿, the city government hardly cares about it.
   流浪狗問題越來越嚴重，但市政府卻鮮少關心。

## Answer

1. being

2. filled

3. The village flooded five times a month

4. The problem of stray dogs getting worse and worse

補充學習：

有些片語雖為獨立分詞構句的寫法，但已成為固定片語

Considering N, S+V（就 ...... 而論）

Regarding/Concerning N, S+V（關於 ......）

Generally speaking, S+V（一般說來）

Strictly speaking, S+V（嚴格說來）

Theoretically speaking, S+V（理論上來說）

Provided that S+V, S+V（假使）

Providing that S+V, S+V（假使）

Supposing that S+V, S+V（假使）

Given that S+V, S+V（假使）

Judging from N, S+V（由……判斷）

Weather permitting, S+V（天氣許可的話）

例句：

1. Considering your young age, it was amazing that you could make such first-rate cakes.

   就你年紀輕輕而言，你可以做出頂級蛋糕實在驚人。

2. Generally speaking, most newborn babies spend plenty of time sleeping.

   一般而言，大部分的小嬰兒大部分時間都是在睡覺。

3. Providing that you have no lighters or matches with you in the wild, how do you make a fire?

   假使你在野外沒有打火機或火柴，你要如何生火？

4. Judging from her facial expressions, we can easily tell that she was deeply depressed.

   從她的臉部表情判斷，我們可以很輕易地分辨出她很憂鬱。

## 七、Inversion 倒裝句

> **說明**
>
> 所謂的倒裝句，是將原本主詞 + 動詞的順序，顛倒為動詞 + 主詞，倘若動詞為 Be 動詞，可直接倒裝；但如果為一般動詞，則需使用符合該時態的助動詞，而原本的一般動詞要變為原形動詞或因為完成式而變成過去分詞（p.p.）。

特別注意，並非任何一句都可任意倒裝，以下介紹常見的倒裝句：

### (1) 否定詞放前

never, rarely, scarcely, hardly, seldom, none, nobody, nothing, nowhere, no sooner, not until, not at all, on no account, in no way, by no means, under no circumstances, not only…but also, little, no longer

例句：

1.  Tim is never hostile to anyone he meets, even strangers.
    ⇨ Never *is Tim* hostile to anyone he meets, even strangers.
    Tim 從來未對他見面的人帶有惡意，即便是陌生人。

2.  We seldom see Emy irritated by what people say about her fat figure.
    ⇨ Seldom *do we see* Emy irritated by what people say about her fat figure.
    我們很少看到 Emy 因為別人説她胖胖的身材而憤怒。

3.  On no account *should you give* up treatment.
    妳絕對不可放棄治療。

4.  Not until the sun is about to set *does the farmer finish* farm work and go home.
    非得要太陽快下山，這農夫才會結束農場工作並回家。

5.  Not only *did the monkeys damage* farmers' crops, but they also broke into people's houses for food.
    這些猴子不但會破壞農夫的作物，牠們還會破門而入尋找食物。

6. No sooner *had my dog seen* the mailman than it began to chase him and bark.

我的狗一看到郵差就衝去追及狂吠。(一 ...... 就 ..... )

7. Hardly *had the drivers yielded* the road when they noticed an ambulance behind.

= Scarcely *had the drivers yielded* the road before they noticed an ambulance behind.

駕駛們一注意到一台救護車在後面就馬上讓路。(一 ...... 就 ..... )

### 牛刀小試

1. Hardly _____ any conclusions if we keep turning a deaf ear to what is said.

   (A) we reached  (B) did we reach  (C) we reach  (D) can we reach

2. Not only _____ the game, but he also lost the spirit of being an athlete.

   (A) did Dick lose  (B) Dick lost  (C) does Dick lose  (D) lost Dick

3. In no way can human beings _____ living if all bees die out.

   (A) have kept  (B) keep  (C) keeps  (D) kept

4. Not until the plane landed _____ Mr. Lin feel relaxed and no longer nervous.

   (A) has  (B) will  (C) did  (D) does

### Answer

1. (D)   2. (A)   3. (B)   4. (C)

## (2) 地點擺前

介系詞帶出的地方片語（如：at the restaurant）或地方副詞（如：there），一般都擺動詞後，但若為了強調，可擺句首，但此時要注意：當主詞為代名詞時，不用倒裝，即：代名詞 + 動詞；但若為一般名詞，則需倒裝，即：動詞 + 主詞，值得注意一點是：這些動詞皆為不及物動詞；另外，試與比較前一單元的否定詞擺句首的倒裝，本倒裝句型，是不用借用助動詞喔。試比較以下例句：

例句：

1. They come here.
   ⇨ Here they come.（代名詞 + 動詞）
   他們來了。

2. A small cottage stands on the top of the hill.
   ⇨ On the top of the hill stands a small cottage.（倒裝）
   丘陵上坐落著一間小茅屋。

3. A pride of lions lay under the big tree.
   ⇨ Under the big tree lay a pride of lions.（倒裝）
   大樹下躺著一群獅群。

### 牛刀小試

1. On the beach _____ a crowd of tourists who are enjoying sunshine and sea breeze.

   (A)was (B) are (C) were (D) is

2. Next to a church _____ who collected garbage for recycling.

   (A) lived an old couple (B) an old couple lived (C) an old couple live
   (D) an old couple lives

3. On the top of the mountain _____ waving our national flags.

   (A)were they   (B) they will   (C) they were   (D) they could

4. In the middle of the road _____.

   在路正中央躺著一個酒醉男子和一個空酒瓶。

## Answer

1. (B)    2. (A)    3. (C)

4. lay a drunk man with an empty wine bottle

## (3) Only

說明

> only 所引導出來的介系詞片語（only in, only by, only with, only through...）或副詞子句（only after, only when, only if...）擺句首時，其後的主詞和動詞需倒裝，動詞若為 Be 動詞，則主詞直接與 Be 動詞倒裝；若有一般動詞，需借該時態的助動詞，再進行倒裝，請看以下例句。

例句：

1. Only when the sun sets *are owls* active again.

   只有在太陽西下，貓頭鷹才再度活躍起來。

2. Only through cooperation *can we two companies reap* the greatest benefit of profits.

   只有透過合作我們兩公司才能獲得對大利益的優勢。

3. Only after I put on two earplugs *could I focus* on my studying. It was too noisy outside.

   只有當我帶上耳塞，我才有辦法專心讀書。外面實在太吵了。

   溫馨提醒：若 only 後所加的為一般名詞，則無須倒裝。

例句：

<u>Only a cup of hot ginger</u> tea can remove the cold feelings from me.

現在只有一杯熱薑茶可以讓我不感到冷。

## 牛刀小試

1. Only with tight airport security _____ the chance of terror attacks.

   只有密不透風的機場安檢我們才可以減少恐攻的機會。

2. Only if more attention is paid to those in need _____ similar tragedies from happening.

   只有如果更多關注投向需要幫助的人身上我們才能阻止類似的悲劇發生。

3. Only by continuous practice _____.

   只有藉由不斷的練習一位籃球手才能使技術完美。（使…完美 perfect）

4. _____ will they realize how precious and warm the family is.

   只有在人們自己獨立生活後，才會了解到家是多麼珍貴和溫暖。

## Answer

1. can we reduce

2. are we able to stop

3. can a basketball player perfect his skills

4. Only after people live on their own

## (4) As…, so…

在 As S+V, so S+V.（正像 ......，...... 也一樣）的句型中，so 後面的句子可倒裝，也可不倒裝。

例句：

1. <u>As</u> a big fish swallows a small fish, <u>so</u> a big company acquires a small one.
   正如同大魚吞食小魚，大公司也會併吞小公司。

2. <u>As</u> you sow, <u>so</u> shall you reap.
   該怎麼收穫，就該怎麼栽。

### 牛刀小試

1. _____ most animals need companions, _____ human beings cannot stay away from the crowd.
   正如大多數的動物需要同伴，人類也一樣無法離群索居。

2. _____ a president rules a country, _____ a principal manages a school.
   正如同總統治理國家，校長經營學校。

### Answer

1. As；so

2. As；so

## (5) so/ nor/ neither

**說明**

表示肯定的「也」，我們可以用 so；而表達否定的「也」，則可以用 nor 及 neither。不管肯定「也」或否定「也」的寫法，皆需倒裝。句子裡的動詞若為 be 動詞，可直接倒裝；但若為一般動詞，則需借該時態的助動詞。

例句：

1. He is a night owl, and so are you. (=you are, too)
   他是個夜貓族，你也是。

2. Most people find cockroaches and mice disgusting, and so does Anna. (=Anna does, too)
   很多人覺得蟑螂和老鼠很噁心，Anna 也是。

3. Many people cannot put up with noise and congestion in a big city. Nor/Neither can I. ( =I can't, either )
   很多人無法忍受大城市的噪音和擁擠，我也不行。

4. Neither can the baby walk nor speak.
   這個嬰兒不會走也不會講話。

### 牛刀小試

1. I am an early bird, and _____ is Eve.
   (A) neither  (B) too  (C) either  (D) so

2. Leo can hardly believe what he just witnessed, and neither _____ we.
   (A) are  (B) can  (C) do  (D) will

3. Most lions hunt at night, _____.
   大部分的獅子都會在夜間狩獵，蛇也是。

4. _____ if it is scanned regularly.

電腦不會當機也不會遭駭客攻擊，假如常掃毒。

## ✔ Answer

1. (D)　　2. (B)

3. and so do snakes

4. A computer neither crashes nor gets hacked

## (6) so 引導的句子

**說明**

在 so... that...（如此 ... 以至於 ...）的句型中，可因為要強調 so 後方的形容詞或副詞，而進行倒裝。同樣地，若是 be 動詞，可直接與主詞倒裝；但若是一般動詞，則需借對應該時態的助動詞。

公式為：So + 形容詞 + be + S + that…

So + 副詞 + 助動詞 + S + V + that…

例句：

1. Anderson's room is so messy that his mother keeps nagging him about it.

   ⇨ So messy is Anderson's room that his mother keeps nagging him about it.

   Anderson 的房間是如此髒亂以至於他媽媽不斷地嘮叨他。

2. Mr. Wang talked so eloquently that many housewives were talked into buying his insurance.

   ⇨ So eloquently did Mr. Wang talk that many housewives were talked into buying his insurance.

   王先生是如此滔滔不絕以至於很多婆婆媽媽都被說服買他的保險。

   溫馨提醒：that 所引導的子句需含主詞及動詞。

1. _____ beautiful is that girl _____ we can't take our eyes off her.

   那女孩是如此的漂亮，以至於我們的目光都離不開她。

2. _____ quietly did the thief sneak into the house _____ people inside didn't notice him.

   小偷是如此安靜地溜進房子內，以至於屋內的人都沒有注意到他。

3. _____ that his business was looking up.

   這餐廳老闆是如此的好客，以至於他的生意逐漸好轉。

4. So diligently did he study _____.

   他是如此地勤奮讀書，以至於能進入理想中的大學。

## Answer

1. So；that

2. So；that

3. So hospitable was the restaurant owner

4. that he entered his ideal university

## (7) such 引導的句子

**說明**

在 such…that…（如此 ... 以至於 ...）的句型中，可因強調 such 後方的名詞，而倒裝句子；有時 such 可直接當名詞使用，後方無須加名詞，意思為「如此」。

公式：

Such + 名詞 + 助動詞 + S + V + that…

Such + 名詞 + Be + S + that…

Such + Be + S + that...

例句：

1. <u>Stan has such various work experience</u> that he can easily stand out among all interviewees.

   ⇨ <u>Such various work experience does Stan have</u> that he can easily stand out among all interviewees.

   Stan 有如此多樣的工作經驗以至於他很容易在眾多面試生中脫穎而出。

2. <u>Copper's magic show was such an amazing performance</u> that he won a thunderous ovation.

   ⇨ <u>Such an amazing performance was Copper's magic show</u> that he won a thunderous ovation.

   Copper 的魔術秀是如此精彩的表演以至於他贏得如雷的掌聲。

3. The restaurant's steak is such that it has become its signature dish.

   ⇨ <u>Such is the restaurant's steak</u> that it has become its signature dish.

   這家餐廳的牛排如此（好），以致於它變成店裡的招牌菜。

## ✏ 牛刀小試

1. _____ an outgoing and easygoing person is Ryan _____ he can easily make friends.

   Ryan 是如此的外向和隨和，以至於他可以很輕易交到朋友。

2. _____ great opponents do we face tonight _____ we will have to play with good teamwork.

   今晚我們面對的是如此棒的對手，以至於我們必須要打出團隊合作來。

3. _____ that he didn't strike a deal with his client.

   Allen 犯了一個如此嚴重的錯誤，以至於他並沒有和客戶達成交易。

4. _____ that it is often crowded with visitors in winter.

   北投是一熱門的溫泉渡假勝地，以致於一到冬天常擠滿遊客。

## ✓ Answer

1. Such；that

2. Such；that

3. Such a serious mistake did Allen make

4. Such a popular hot spring resort is Peitou

## (8) 比較級的倒裝

**說明**

在「形容詞或副詞」比較級的句型中，than 之後除了可以直接放另一個比較的對象外，亦可將 be 動詞或助動詞寫出，此時，可以使用倒裝來變化句子。

例句：

1. Successful people devote more time to work than regular people (do).
   ⇨ Successful people devote more time to work than do regular people.
   成功的人會比一般人投入更多的時間於工作上。

2. Light runs faster than any material (does) so far.
   ⇨ Light runs faster than does any material so far.
   光線跑得比目前任何物質都還來的快。
   另外，在 the same... as 的句型中，亦可倒裝。
   Tom fished the same milkfish as did I.
   Tom 釣到和我一樣的虱目魚。

1. The blue whale is bigger than _____ any other animal in the sea.
   藍鯨比起海中任何動物都還來得巨大。

2. This factory produces better-quality bicycles than _____ others.
   這家工廠生產出比其他工廠品質來的更好的腳踏車。

3. Rich countries, like America, _____

   _____.

   富有國家，如：美國，製造出比貧窮國家還要多的食物浪費。

4. _____ all the other

   companies in Taiwan.

   我們公司已經製造出比台灣其他家公司還要多的智慧型手機。

## Answer

1. are

2. do

3. produced more food waste than did other poor countries

4. Our company has manufactured more smartphones than

## (9) 假設語氣的倒裝

**說明**

if 所引導的假設語氣，可分為「與現在事實相反的假設語氣」及「與過去事實相反的假設語氣」，可省略 if，但其後需要倒裝。特別注意，與現在事實相反的假設語氣只有動詞為 were 時，才可倒裝；與過去事實相反的假設語氣中，則是直接將 had 與主詞倒裝。

例句：

1. If I were on the beach of Hawaii now, I would get a nice suntan.

   ⇨ Were I on the beach of Hawaii now, I would get a nice suntan.

   如果我現在在夏威夷海灘，我可以曬出漂亮的古銅色。

2. If Sam had checked his car before hitting the road, he wouldn't have had a flat tire on the freeway.

   ⇨ Had Sam checked his car before hitting the road, he wouldn't have had a flat tire on the freeway.

   如果當初 Sam 在上路前有檢查車子，他就不會在高速公路上爆胎。

   溫馨提醒：

   與現在事實相反的假設語氣公式：If S+Ved, S+(should/would/could/might)+V

   與過去事實相反的假設語氣公式：If S+had+p.p., S+(should/would/could/might)+have+p.p.

## 🖊 牛刀小試

1. _____ I a bird, I could fly to any place I want.

   (A) Was   (B) Were   (C) Am   (D) If

2. _____ Houston not clicked the unknown link, his computer wouldn't have been infected.

   (A) Has   (B) Does   (C) Have   (D) Had

3. _____, I could go surfing and diving every weekend.

   如果我的房子在海邊的話，我就會周末都去衝浪和潛水。

4. _____, the world would have been in the dark at night.

   如果愛迪生當初沒發明電燈的話，世界晚上還是一片黑。

**✓ Answer**

1. (B)　　2. (D)

3. Were my house on the beach

4. Had Edison not invented the lights

## (10) 全倒裝

**說明**

有時為了強調，我們可將 S + Be 動詞 + 主詞補語的句型中，主詞補語的部份移到句首，來進行倒裝。另外，可於主詞後加一句形容詞子句（關代），來修飾主詞，讓句子更漂亮。

例句：

1. A considerate friend is George.
   George 是一位貼心的朋友。

2. Interesting and cliff-hanging is the novel "Harry Potter" **that** has attracted millions of readers around the global.
   哈利波特是一部有趣並扣人心弦的小說，吸引全球數百萬計的讀者。

3. Barking at the mailman is my dog, Harry.
   正對郵差吠叫是我的狗，哈利。

4. Criticized by the public were the legislators **who** tabled many important energy bills.
   遭民眾批評的是那些擱置重要能源法案的立委。

   溫馨提醒：倒裝後的句子，be 動詞仍需與主詞的單複數一致。

1. _____

   有著現代科技配備的別墅是 James 的家。

2. _____ which hadn't
   been seen for decades.

   生長在懸崖邊的這朵花已經數十年沒被見過。

3. _____, who was
   dumped by her boyfriend.

   站在雨中一個小時的是剛剛被男朋友拋棄的 Mia。

4. _____ that draws thousands
   of worshippers every year.

   坐落於山丘上的一間寺廟，每年都會吸引數以千計的香客到訪。

 Answer

1. A villa equipped with modern technology is James' house.

2. At the edge of the cliff grew a flower

3. Standing in the rain for one hour was Mia

4. Situated on the hill is a temple

# 八、Coordinating 對等的概念

Coordinating 對等的概念（口訣：fan boys 電風扇男孩）

說明：

| 口訣 | 代表字 | 相關片語 | 當連接詞時的用法 |
|------|--------|----------|------------------|
| f | for | X | 連接兩句 |
| a | and | both…and…<br>（是…也是…） | 連接兩句、或詞性對等的字或詞 |
| n | nor | neither…nor…<br>（不是…也不是…） | 連接兩句、或詞性對等的字或詞 |
| b | but | not only…but also…<br>（不但…也…） | 連接兩句、或詞性對等的字或詞 |
| o | or | either…or…<br>（不是…就是…） | 連接兩句、或詞性對等的字或詞 |
| y | yet | X | 連接兩句、或形容詞 |
| s | so | so…that…; so that… | 連接兩句 |

## For

**說明**

for 的意思是「因為」，通常接的該句，是顯而易見或者聽話者已經知道的訊息。另外，because 也是「因為」，但帶出的句子，則是聽話者所不知道的新訊息。

例句：

Mom must be at home, <u>for</u> the lights in the living room are on.

媽媽一定在家，因為客廳的燈是亮著的。

## 牛刀小試

1. It must have been raining, _____ the road is quite wet and slippery now.
   剛才一定有下過雨，因為現在地上又濕又滑。

2. John might do something wrong, _____
   John 可能做錯事，因為他又送 Mary 一束玫瑰花了。

## Answer

1. for

2. for he sent Mary a bouquet of roses again.

## And（both…and）

### 說明

and 常見於 both…and.. 的句型，意思是「既…又…」，所連接的詞性也須對等。若將 not 加入，則有部分否定的意思。

例句：

1. Drugs and guns keep our society from peace.
   毒品和槍枝讓我們的社會無法安詳。（N and N）

2. Jolin is beautiful and talented in music.
   Jolin 既聰明又有音樂天分。（adj and adj）

3. We can often see advertisements on TV, in the movie, and even on the bus bodies.
   我們常可在電視上、電影中、甚至是公車車身看到廣告。（prep and prep）

4. Eric's ex-girlfriend broke his heart and cheated him out of his fortune.
   Eric 的前女友 既傷了他的心，又騙走他全部的財產。（V and V）

5. Jordan was good at stealing, blocking, scoring, and passing.

Jordan 擅長於抄截、火鍋封阻、得分和傳球。（Ving and Ving）

6. Students burned the midnight oil for their finals, and this also compromised their health at the same time.

學生熬夜準備期末考，而這也同時危害到健康。（S+V and S+V）

7. Not both Perry and Terry have a good command of English.

並非 Perry 和 Terry 對英文都有專精。（部分否定）

### 牛刀小試

1. The clown can walk on a ball _____ juggle three balls at the same time.

這小丑可以邊在球上面走動又同時耍三顆球。

2. Japan has been thankful that _____

_____

日本一直很感謝台灣在 311 地震後捐贈金錢和物資。

### Answer

1. and

2. Taiwan donated money and necessities to it after the 311 earthquake occurred.

## Nor（neither…nor…）

説明

> nor 常見於「neither…nor…」的句型，意思是「不是…也不是…」所連接的詞性一樣要對等，特別注意，如果是連接兩個主詞時，動詞是跟與它最近的主詞而定。

例句：

1. Neither Tom nor I *am* to blame.

   不是 Tom 也不是我該被責備。（neither S nor S）

2. Fast food is neither nutritious nor cheap.

   速食非但不營養也不便宜。（neither adj nor adj）

3. The man is neither a thief nor a robber.

   那男子不是小偷也不是強盜犯。（neither N nor N）

### 牛刀小試

1. Your mean joke to me was ＿＿＿＿＿＿＿ funny ＿＿＿＿＿ polite.

   妳那苛薄的玩笑對我而言既不有趣也沒禮貌。

2. ＿＿＿＿＿＿＿＿＿＿＿＿＿＿＿＿＿＿＿＿＿＿＿＿

   to taking care of this orphan.

   不是 Cain 也不是我們有付出足夠時間來照顧這孤兒。

### Answer

1. neither；nor

2. Neither Cain nor we have devoted enough time

## But（not only…but also…）

**說明**

對等連接詞 but 也常出現於「not only…but also…」，意思是「不但…
也…」，特別注意：如果 not only…but also…連接兩個主詞時，動詞的單
複數要以靠近動詞的主詞來決定動詞的單複數。

例句：

1. She was poor but satisfied with her life.
   她雖窮但滿意她的生活。（adj but adj）

2. I ate nothing but fruit, but I still could not shed any weight.
   我都只吃水果，但還是沒辦法減重。（S+V but S+V）

3. Ken not only had a car accident but also came down with a bad cold.
   Ken 不但出了車禍，而且染上重感冒。（not only V but also V）

4. Not only Oliver but also we *make* it a habit to watch Hollywood movies without captions.
   不僅是 Oliver，我們也是看好萊塢電影時都沒有顯示字幕。

## 牛刀小試

1. Success depends on efforts, _____ efforts do not always lead to success.
   成功靠努力，但努力不一定能成功。

2. My new watch not only can keep good time _____
   _____.

   我的手錶不但很時間很準，而且還有 GPS 和監控我睡眠的功能。

 **Answer**

1. but

2. but also has the function of GPS and of monitoring my sleep

## Or（either…or…）

 說明

either…or…意思是「不是…就是…」，如果連接兩個主詞時，動詞的單複數是跟與它最近的主詞而定。

例句：

1. Is (either) <u>he</u> or <u>you</u> a detective?

   他還是你是偵探？（S or S）

2. Ruby didn't either <u>get late</u> or <u>leave early</u>. = Ruby neither <u>got late</u> nor <u>left early</u>.

   Ruby 不遲到也不早退。（either V or V）

---

**補充用法：**（or 也有「否則 / 不然……」的意思）

You had better ask her out as soon as possible, <u>or</u> you will regret someday.

你最好儘快邀她出去，<u>否則</u>你有一天會後悔的。

---

## 牛刀小試

1. A determined person will not fear _____ give up easily when faced with challenges.

   一個有決心的人在面對挑戰時，不會害怕或輕易放棄。

2. It is plain to see that this baby is in need of _____

   _____.

   （diaper 尿布；breastfeed 餵母奶）

   顯而易見的是這嬰兒不是需要換尿布就是餵母奶。

 **Answer**

1. or

2. either having diapers changed or being breastfed

## Yet

**說明**

yet 的意思與 but 相近，不過語氣較強。

例句：

1. They are wealthy <u>yet</u> not healthy.

   他們很富有但不健康。（adj yet adj）

2. John is proficient at table tennis, <u>yet</u> he does not excel in studies.

   John 很專精於桌球，但不擅長於學業。（S＋V yet S＋V）

> **補充用法：（yet 亦可當副詞）**
> I haven't finished my art report <u>yet</u>.
> 我還沒做完美術報告。

**牛刀小試**

1. I always complain about the fact that the road to my office is short _____ congested.

   我總是要抱怨到辦公室的路雖短但卻壅擠。

2. The worker is as busy as a bee, _____

   這工人和蜜蜂一般忙碌，但他的效率卻跟蝸牛一樣慢。

1. yet

2. yet his efficiency is as slow as a snail.

## So

**說明**

so 前後須連接兩個句子；另外，so 亦可用於 so…that… 及 so that 句型中，so… that…，意思為「如此…以至於…」；so that 意思為「以便……」，後接一表目的的句子。

例句：

1. Using Braille is a way to learn for the blind, <u>so</u> they can still enjoy the fun of reading.

   使用點字機對於盲人而言是一種學習的方法，所以他們仍可以享受閱讀之樂趣。（S+V so S+V）

2. Mr. Lin spoke <u>so</u> eloquently <u>that</u> no one could argue with him.

   林先生如此能言善辯，以至於無人可以跟他爭辯。

3. Mr.s Huang is <u>so</u> religious <u>that</u> she recites Buddhist sutras every morning.

   黃太太是如此信仰虔誠的，以至於她每個早上都會唸佛經。

4. The dog peed onto the lamp pole <u>so that</u> it could claim it as its turf.

   那隻狗在路燈柱子尿尿，如此來宣示地盤。

 **牛刀小試**

1. I love you so much, _____ I let you go and pursue your happiness.

   我是如此愛妳，所以我讓妳去追求妳的幸福。

2. Cherry checked her cellphone _____ frequently _____ she wouldn't miss any calls or messages.

   Cherry 察看手機如此地頻繁以至於她不會錯過任何的來電或訊息。

3. Ian tied a red ribbon on the trees along the mountain path _____ _____

   Ian 在山中小徑路上綁上紅帶子，以便他可以找到回家的路。

 **Answer**

1. so

2. so；that

3. so that he could find his way back home.

## 一、含名詞

### (1) One…; the other…

> **說明**
>
> 此句型適用於列舉人 / 事 / 物時，細分如下：
>
> （兩者）One…; the other….
>
> （三者）One…; another…; the other….
>
> （三者以上，沒限定範圍）Some…; others…; still others…
>
> （三者以上，有限定範圍）Some of the/one's…; the others…

例句：

1. Taiwan has *two* major parties. <u>One</u> is DPP; <u>the other</u> is KMT.

   台灣有兩大政黨。一是民進黨；另一是國民黨。

2. There are three types of flowers in my yard. <u>One</u> is the rose; <u>another</u> is the sunflower; <u>the other</u> is the morning glory.

   我院子裡有三種花。一種是玫瑰；一種是向日葵；另一種是牽牛花。

3. Jill has many excuses for being late. <u>Some</u> are about traffic; <u>others</u> are about weather; <u>still others</u> have something to do with his old car.

   Jill 有很多遲到的藉口。有些有關交通；有些有關天氣；還有一些跟他的老爺車有關。

4. <u>Some of the mistakes</u> in your writing were grammatical; <u>the others</u> were word usage.

   你的作文錯誤有些是文法問題；剩下其他是單字用法錯誤。

   溫馨提醒：

   1. 各句型中的分號可用逗點代替，但最後一個列舉前需有連接詞，如：

      One is Latte, another is black coffee, <u>**and**</u> the other is Mocha.

2. another 指「另一個（的）」，沒有限定是哪一個，可當名詞或形容詞。此外，another 後亦可接複數名詞，翻譯為「額外的」。相對於 another，the other 是指「剩下的那一個」，有限定。

3. other 為形容詞，意思是「其他的」; others= other + N，詞性為名詞，並無限定；反觀 the others 則是有限定的，意思是「其他、剩下之人事物」。

## 牛刀小試

1. I have two dream sports cars. _____ is Lamborghini; the _____ is Ferrari.

   我心目中有兩款夢想跑車。一是藍寶堅尼；另一是法拉利。

2. Paul has three roommates. _____ is from Taipei; _____ comes from Tainan; _____ _____ is a Japanese exchange student.

   Paul 有三個室友。一個來自台北；另一個來自台南；最後那一個是個日本交換學生。

3. _____ people like beef; _____ prefer pork; _____ _____ can't eat without fish.

   有些人喜歡牛肉；一些人喜歡豬肉；還有一些人吃飯一定要有魚。

4. _____ of the watermelons are sweet and juicy but _____ _____ are broken and rotten.

   這些西瓜有些又甜又多汁，但剩下的都破了而且爛掉。

## Answer

1. One；other

2. One；another；the other

3. Some；others；still others

4. Some；the others

## (2) The former…and the latter…

the former 代表「前者」；the latter 則是代表「後者」，此句型適用於比較兩者時。至於動詞單複數的選擇，要依前一句所提的兩個名詞單複數來決定。

例句：

1. When it comes to water and oil, <u>the former</u> is more expensive and precious than <u>the latter</u> in some desert countries.

   當談論到水和石油，在某些沙漠國家，前者比後者來的昂貴和珍貴。

2. Dogs and cats are different. <u>The former</u> are friendly; <u>the latter</u> are indifferent.

   狗和貓個性不同。前者友善；後者冷漠。

   溫馨提醒：later 意思是「之後」、late 是「去世的」。

### 牛刀小試

1. Albee and Sandra are our new managers. The _____ is very easygoing; the _____ seldom shows her emotions.

   Albee 和 Sandra 是我們的新經理。前者非常隨和；後者不常顯露她的情感。

2. Harry Potter has two best friends, Ron and Hermione. _____

   _____

   哈利波特有兩個最好的朋友，榮恩和妙麗。前者有點傻傻的但很老實，而後者既聰明又漂亮。

### Answer

1. former；latter

2. The former is a little silly but honest, while the latter is clever and beautiful.

## (3) 虛受詞 it

**說明**

此句型公式為：V+it adj/N to V，it 為虛受詞，其中，真正的受詞為整個不定詞片語（to V）。舉例來說，feel it adj/N to V 意思為「覺得……」，但並非所有動詞都可以套用此句型，常用此句型的動詞如下：

相信：believe

認為：consider, think

讓某事…：make

覺得：feel, find

例句：

1. I believe it necessary to do an annual physical exam, especially when we are old.

   我相信每年做健康檢查是必須的，特別是我們老的時候。

2. Kevin found it an interesting thing to watch all kinds of people passing by in the train station.

   Kevin 覺得在車站看形形色色的人走過去是件有趣的事。

3. Customers' criticism made it possible for our cars to be perfect.

   顧客的批評讓我們的車子完美成為可能。

### 牛刀小試

1. Elsa found _____ impossible _____ communicate with her stubborn father.

   Elsa 發覺和她固執的爸爸溝通是不可能的。

2. Mother considered it _____

   媽媽認為靠吹風機的幫助移除貼紙是個好點子。（sticker 貼紙）

 **Answer**

1. it ; to

2. a smart idea to remove a sticker with the help of a hairdryer.

## (4) that… /those…

說明

that 可代替前面句子所出現的單數名詞，those 則可代替複數名詞；另外，that 與 those 後面可依據語意，替換成各種的介系詞。此句型亦常與比較級句型連用。

例句：

1. Taipei in summer is normally hotter than that in any other place in Taiwan.
   台北夏天天氣一般而言是比台灣其他地方熱。

2. People in North Korea have less contact with the outside world than those in South Korea.
   北韓人民比起南韓人民較少機會與外面世界接觸。

**牛刀小試**

1. The roses in our garden are ＿＿＿＿ beautiful than ＿＿＿＿ in our neighbor's.
   我們花園裡的玫瑰比起鄰居家的更美麗。

2. ＿＿＿＿＿＿＿＿＿＿＿＿＿＿＿＿＿＿＿＿＿＿＿＿＿
   我工作地點的氣氛遠比 Kevin 的來的好多了。（atmosphere 氣氛）

**Answer**

1. more ; those

2. The atmosphere of my workplace is much better than that of Kevin's.

## (5) N + that + S + V

**說明**

名詞可以與 that 子句形成同位語，但並非所有名詞都可以這麼使用，一般都為抽象名詞，常見的名詞有：idea, fact, hope, news, truth, decision, statement（陳述）, opinion（意見）, suggestion（建議）, evidence（證據）, information（資訊）, etc. 另外，請留意：that 不可省略，因為一省略掉，就會變成有兩個句子，但中間沒有連接詞的錯誤。

例句：

We can hardly believe the <u>news</u> <u>that Taiwan's baseball team won the world</u> <u>championship</u>.

我們都很難相信台灣棒球隊贏得世界冠軍的消息。

### 牛刀小試

1. _____ to study in Oxford University.

   我剛剛聽到訊息說我被給予全額獎學金來就讀牛津大學。

2. No one can't deny _____

   _____.

   沒有人會否認過多陽光的曝曬與皮膚癌有關連這個事實。

### Answer

1. I just heard the information that I was given a full scholarship

2. the fact that too much exposure to the sun relates to skin cancer

## 二、含動詞

### (1) suggest that S + (should) + V

**說明**

suggest 意思為「建議…」，所帶出 that 子句，助動詞 should 可以省略，所以會常看到子句內的主詞即便是第三人稱單數，不管時態為何，動詞必須使用原形動詞。

常見類似的動詞如下：(口訣：尖尖要命)

建（建議）：suggest, move, recommend, propose

堅（堅持）：insist, maintain

要（要求）：ask, require, request, demand

命（命令）：order, command

例句：

1. My doctor <u>suggested</u> that I (should) <u>eat</u> more vegetables and fruit.

   醫生建議我要多吃蔬菜水果。

2. The foreman <u>demanded</u> each of us <u>wear</u> helmet before entering the construction site.

   工頭要求我們每個人在進入工地前要戴安全帽。(that 亦可省略)

### ✏ 牛刀小試

1. The restaurant owner _____ that every customer _____ all they had ordered before leaving.

   這餐廳老闆堅持每一個顧客在離開前要吃完所點的東西。

2. _____ after I came to a new workplace.

   Miranda 建議我在到一個新的工作地點要試著融入。(fit in 融入)

## Answer

1. insisted；finish

2. Miranda suggested that I should try to fit in

## (2) would rather V than V

**說明**

此句型意思為「寧願 ...... 也不願 ........」，所連接的兩個動詞，必須為原形動詞，也相當於 prefer to V rather than V 的句型。

例句：

1. The workers <u>would rather</u> take to streets <u>than</u> accept unfair treatment from the government.

   這些工人寧願上街抗議也不願接受政府不公平對待。

2. Mr. Ellinton <u>prefers to</u> wear a wig <u>rather than</u> look bald.

   Ellinton 先生寧願戴假髮也不願看起來禿頭。

## 牛刀小試

1. Mr. Benson _____ rather retire _____ work overtime every day because he was already 60.

   因為 Benson 先生已經 60 歲了，他寧願退休也不願每天加班工作。

2. The parents would rather call the police _____.

   這對爸媽寧願打電話報警，也不願和綁匪談判。

## Answer

1. would；than

2. than negotiate with the kidnappers

## (3) have trouble+ Ving

> **說明**
>
> 此句型意思為「在……有困難」，trouble 可換成 a hard time 或 difficulty。

例句：

Dan <u>had trouble</u> *dancing* to the music and got tripped by his own shoelace.

Dan 要跟上音樂跳舞有困難，還被自己的鞋帶絆倒。

take one's time（慢慢來做…）、waste one's time/money（浪費時間或金錢做…）、have fun, have a good time（玩得很開心）等等，後面亦須加動名詞。

例句：

1. We <u>had fun</u> *playing* the card game during the Chinese New Year.
   我們在農曆新年期間打牌打得很高興。

2. You can <u>take your time</u> *preparing* for your science report.
   你可以慢慢來準備你的科學報告。

3. Don't <u>waste too much time</u> *doing* something meaningless.
   不要浪費時間做一些無意義的事。

### 牛刀小試

1. Tommy's kid has _____ _____ herself on a bike.
   Tommy 的小孩在腳踏車上平衡方面有困難。（balance 平衡）

2. _____
   the director wanted.
   這新的女演員在演出如導演想要的方式上有困難。

1. trouble balancing

2. The new actress had difficulty acting in the way

## (4) have no choice but to V

**說明**

此句型可用於表達「沒有其他選擇，只好……」的意思，其中，choice 可替換成 option, alternative。

例句：

To support his family, Adam <u>has no choice but to</u> moonlight as a dancer.

為了養活全家，Adam 沒有選擇只好晚上去兼差當舞者。

### 牛刀小試

1. The thief said _____

   這小偷說他沒有選擇只好偷別人的皮包。

2. _____

   Richard 沒有選擇只好向高利貸者借錢。（loan shark 放高利貸者）

### Answer

1. he had no choice but to steal people's purses.

2. Richard had no choice but to borrow money from a loan shark.

## (5) wish that S + V

wish 意思為「但願」，需與假設語氣連用，換句話說，與現在事實相反時，that 子句內用過去式；與過去事實相反，that 子句內用過去完成式。另外，as if/as though（彷彿）亦常搭配假設語氣。

例句：

1.  I wish (that) I were a bird.
    我但願我是隻鳥。（與現在事實相反）

2.  He wished he had never gambled away all his money.
    他但願他當初沒有把全部的錢賭光。（與過去事實相反）

3.  She talks as if she won a gold medal in the Olympic Games.
    她講話的感覺彷彿在奧運得了金牌。（與現在事實相反）

4.  You ate as though you hadn't eaten anything for three days.
    你吃的彷彿你已經三天沒吃東西。（與過去事實相反）

    溫馨提醒：若要表達「希望」未來某事發生，且可能發生的事，則需要使用 hope。

    例句：

    I hope (that) I will see you again.

    我希望我可以再見你一面。

 牛刀小試

1.  Musk wishes that _____

    Musk 但願他上個月就有預訂河岸邊的旅館房間。

2.  Mr. Wang wishes that _____

    王先生但願他的兒子沒有被逮捕並關在牢裡。

3. The magician talks as if _____.

這魔術師說的彷彿她有辦法偷到我的皮包而不用碰到我。

1. _____

Ron 行為怪異彷彿他看到外星人或鬼。

## Answer

1. he had reserved the room of the hotel by the riverside last month.

2. his son were not arrested and put in prison.

3. she could steal my wallet without touching me.

4. Ron acted strangely as though he had seen an alien or a ghost.

## (6) not to mention…

**說明**

此句型意思為「更別說 ......」，可等於 let alone, to say nothing of, not to speak of。另外，let alone 後面可接對等的動詞、名詞或動名詞；而其他的片語則都接名詞和動名詞。

例句：

1. The prodigy knows calculus well, not to mention arithmetic.
   這位神童精通微積分，更別說是一般算術了。

2. Peterson can barely make a living, let alone support a family.
   Peterson 連養活自己都有問題，遑論是一個家庭。

 **牛刀小試**

1. Little Carter couldn't tie his own shoestrings, _____ to _____ putting on clothes on his own.

   小 Carter 不會自己綁鞋帶，更不用說自己穿衣服。

2. My grandfather couldn't type, _____ _____ write an app for smartphones.

   我奶奶不會打字，遑論寫智慧型手機的 app。

**Answer**

1. not；mention

2. let alone

## (7) should have + p.p.

**說明** ...........

此句型意思為「過去該去做……但沒去做」，相當於句型：ought to have+p.p.。否定時：shouldn't have+p.p., ought not to have+p.p.。

例句：

1. The cicada <u>should have noticed</u> a mantis behind; it ended up being eaten.

   這隻蟬當初應該注意到一隻螳螂在後面。它最後被吃了。

2. Sam <u>shouldn't have talked</u> so loudly; he woke up the sleeping baby.

   Sam 當初不應該講話這麼大聲的；他吵醒正在睡覺的嬰兒了。

   溫馨提醒：would have+p.p. 則是「原本會……（但沒有去做）」；could have+p.p. 表達「原本可以……」；may/might have+p.p. 可以表達「先前可能做了……」。

 **牛刀小試**

1. Linda regretted that _____

   _____

   Linda 後悔她先前應該在她兒子迷路前去接他的。

2. Ted yelled for help in the bathroom; _____

   _____

   Ted 在廁所大喊需要幫忙；他早應該帶足夠的衛生紙的。

## Answer

1. she should have picked up her son before he got lost.

2. he should have brought enough tissues.

## (8) can't help

**說明**

此句型為「忍不住 ......」，後加名詞或動名詞；試比較：can't (help) but+V 意思為「不得不 ......」。

例句：

1. Many smartphone addicts can't help *sending* messages or checking out FB updates even when driving or walking.

   很多手機成癮的人都會忍不住傳訊息或查看臉書動態更新，甚至是開車或走路時。

2. Shane couldn't help but *go* on a blind date because her parents forced her to do so.

   Shane 不得不去相親，因為她父母逼她的。

 牛刀小試

1. Melody was so touched that _____

   _____

   Melody 是如此的感動，以至於看到她男友求婚忍不住哭出來。

2. Faced with criticism from its people, _____

   _____

   面對人民的批評，政府不得不處理食安問題。

## Answer

1. she couldn't help crying when seeing his boyfriend proposing to her.

2. the government couldn't help but tackle the problem of food safety.

## (9) used to & be used to

### 說明

used to 意思是「過去習慣做……」，後面要加原形動詞 =would，但如果是指過去的一個狀態，則只能用 used to；be used to 則是「現在習慣於……」=get used to=be accustomed to，句型中的 to 為介系詞，所以後面必須接名詞或動名詞。

例句：

1. This place used to *be* a big parking lot; now, it is replaced by a commercial building.

   這地方原本是大停車場，而現在，它被一棟商辦大樓取代了。

2. My mother is used to *doing* yoga every day and she looks younger than she really is.

   我媽媽現在習慣都會做瑜珈，她現在看起來比她真正年紀還年輕。

**牛刀小試**

1. _____

   and seldom fall victim to them.

   現今，人們習慣於電話詐騙，而很少受害。

2. _____,

   but now I turn to Buddhism.

   我過去習慣於向我朋友求助心靈的平靜，但我現在求助於佛教。

**Answer**

1. Nowadays, people are used to phone scams

2. I used to turn to my friends for real peace of mind

## (10) had better

**說明**

此句型的意思是「最好⋯⋯」，常用於給對方建議時，用法上的重點是，後面所接的動詞要用原形；此外，將 not 加於 had better 後面（had better not⋯），則可以表達「最好不要⋯⋯」。

例句：

1. Global warming has caused dramatic climate change, so people had better cut down on the emission of carbon dioxide.

   全球暖化已經造成劇烈氣候變化，所以人們最好減少二氧化碳的排放。

2. You had better not bother Glen because he is in a bad mood now.

   你最好不好煩 Glen，因為他現在心情不好。

1. _____

because it didn't show much originality.

Judy 最好花多點時間在她的藝術作品，因為它並沒有甚麼原創性。

2. _____ which can

be reused and recycled.

你最好不要丟掉這些可以重複使用及回收的紙張。

## Answer

1. Judy had better spend more time on her art work

2. You had better not throw away the paper

## (11) have…to do with

**說明**

此句型意思是「與……有關」，have 與 to do with 中間可加一些詞，讓句子語意更清楚，例如：anything, nothing, something, a lot (a great deal), little, etc.

例句：

1. Michael's success had a lot to do with his perseverance and a little luck.
   Michael 的成功和他的毅力與一點運氣有很大關聯。

2. Did this mountain accident have anything to do with the insurance claims?
   這場山難意外與保險賠償金有任何關聯嗎？

3. Your facial expression seemed to tell me you had nothing to do with this.
   你的臉上表情似乎告訴我你跟此事一點關係都沒有。

 **牛刀小試**

1. The reason that Mr. Wang went broke _____

   _____（virtual currency 虛擬貨幣）

   王先生破產的原因和他投資虛擬貨幣有很大的關係。

2. _____

   the recent motorcycle accidents.

   據說這些流浪狗和最近機車意外有一些關聯。

## Answer

1. had a lot to do with his investment in virtual currency.

2. It is said that the stray dogs have something to do with

# 三、含形容詞

## (1) 形容詞比較級

**說明**

形容詞比較級是在形容詞（單音節或雙音節）字尾加「-er」，或者，形容詞為多音節，前加「more」以形成比較級，如：taller, bigger, nicer, lazier, better; less, more interesting。

例句：

1. The blue whale is <u>bigger than</u> any other animal in the sea.

   藍鯨比海裡任何動物都還來得巨大。（＝…than all the other animals…）

2. People nowadays are <u>more willing</u> to purchase eco-friendly home appliances than before.

   比起以前，現在人們更樂意於購買對生態有利的家電產品。

溫馨提醒：

(1) 強調形容詞比較級可用：even, far, much, a lot (informal), very much, a little, a bit (informal), any, no, twice (three times⋯)。

例句：

My current work environment is *much* worse than that of my previous job.

我現在的工作環境比起我之前的工作糟很多。

(2) 反面的比較級，可用 less 後加形容詞，此時則不用管形容詞是否為單音節或多音節，意思為「較不⋯」。

例句：

To me, English is less difficult than any other subject.

對我而言，英文比起其他科目來的不困難。

## 牛刀小試

1. Alice looks ＿＿＿＿＿＿ ＿＿＿＿＿＿＿ than she was two years ago.
   Alice 看起來比起她兩年前來的更加瘦了。

2. Writing on the paper is ＿＿＿＿ time-consuming ＿＿＿＿ typing with a computer.
   寫在紙上比起用電腦打字來的更耗時。

3. Working the graveyard shift is ＿＿＿＿＿＿＿＿＿＿＿＿＿＿＿＿＿＿
   上大夜班比起上日班來的不健康。

## Answer

1. much thinner

2. more；than

3. less healthy than working the day shift.

## (2) 形容詞最高級

**說明**

最高級形容詞使用上是在形容詞（單音節或雙音節）的字尾加「-est」或多音節形容詞前加「most」如：tallest, biggest, nicest, laziest, best, least, most interesting。

例句：

1. Taipei 101 is <u>the tallest</u> building in Taiwan.
   台北 101 是台灣最高的建築物。

2. Tracy is <u>the most inefficient</u> person that I've ever worked with.
   Tracy 是我工作過最沒效率的人。（最高級常跟完成式連用）
   溫馨提醒：強調形容詞最高級可用 very, much, nearly, by far 等等。
   例句：
   Billy's new villa seems <u>by far the most luxurious</u> one of all time.
   Billy 的別墅是有史以來最奢華的。

### 牛刀小試

1. Professor Cliff can use ＿＿＿＿ ＿＿＿＿＿＿ words to explain a complex physics idea.
   Cliff 教授可以用最簡單的字來解釋一個非常複雜的物理概念。

2. The typhoon which is coming to Japan is ＿＿＿＿＿＿＿＿＿＿＿＿＿＿＿＿

   ＿＿＿＿＿＿＿＿＿＿＿＿＿＿＿＿＿＿＿＿＿＿＿＿＿＿＿＿＿＿

   即將要登陸日本的颱風被預測是 50 年來最有破壞性的。（destructive 破壞性的）

Answer

1. the simplest

2. predicted to be the most destructive one in 50 years.

## (3) The + 比較級, the + 比較級.

說明

此句型中文意思為「越……越……」，the 後面所以加的比較級，可以是比較級形容詞或比較級副詞，如果句意清楚，則可省略後方的主詞及動詞。

公式為：

The + 比較級形容詞 / 副詞 +（S+V）, the + 比較級形容詞 / 副詞 +（S+V）

例句：

1. The hotter it is, the more impatient I will be.
   天氣越熱，我越不耐煩。

2. The more energy you consume, the more food you will need to eat.
   你消耗越多能量，你就必須吃更多食物。

3. The earlier you book train tickets, the more likely you can have seats.
   你越早訂火車票，你就越可能有位子坐。

有時我們也可用「反面」的比較級（less）來表達反面的意思。

例句：

The less money you spend, the more money you are able to save.
你花越少錢，你就越能存到錢。

1. The more good novels people read, _____

   人們讀越多好的小說，就會越有想像力。

2. The fatter you are, _____
   such as diabetes.

   你越胖的話，你就會有越多的健康問題，如：糖尿病。

## Answer

1. the more imaginative they can be.

2. the more problems of health you will have,

## 四、含介系詞

### (1) with N adj

**說明**

with 本身沒有額外的意思，功用是為了帶出後面受詞的狀態（受詞補語），受詞補語可為現在分詞、過去分詞、形容詞、或介系詞片語。

例句：

1. To ventilate the room, I opened all windows with the door open.（形容詞）

   為了讓房間空氣流通，我打開所有窗戶而且讓門保持開啟。

2. Feeling really cold, I went to everywhere with my hands in my pocket.（介系詞片語）

   覺得實在很冷，我去哪裡都手插口袋。

3. We lay on the grass and enjoyed the winter sun with our eyes closed.（p.p.）

   我們躺在草地上享受冬天的太陽，眼睛並闔上。

4. The dog stared at the fried chicken <u>with</u> its mouth <u>watering</u>.（Ving）

這隻狗狗盯著炸雞，口水直流。

### 牛刀小試

1. My father is very angry with me now _____

我爸爸現在對我非常生氣，雙臂還交叉著。

2. My parents stood on the platform _____

我爸媽站在月台上，手揮舞著跟我說再見。

### Answer

1. with his arms crossed.

2. with their hands waving goodbye to me.

## (2) To one's 情緒名詞, S + V

### 說明

此句型意思為「令人感到……」，常見情緒名詞有：sadness, sorrow, surprise, regret, horror, delight, amazement, satisfaction, disappointment, relief, etc. 可應用於敘述文中或描寫文中。

例句：

<u>To my delight</u>, the sparrow I saved has recovered from injury.

令我高興的是，我救的那隻麻雀已經從受傷中復原差不多了。

溫馨提醒：可於情緒名詞前加 much 或於名詞前加 great 來加強語氣。

例句：

<u>Much to my surprise</u>/<u>To my great surprise</u>, the kung fu master broke the stone in half with bare hands.

讓我驚訝的是，這功夫大師徒手將石頭劈成兩半。

1. _____, the girl turned down my invitation again.

   讓我很失望的是，這女孩又拒絕我的邀請。

2. _____

   _____

   讓每個人大大欣慰的是，颱風轉向遠離台灣了。

 Answer

1. To my disappointment

2. Much to everyone's relief, the typhoon changed its moving direction away from Taiwan.

## (3) As for N, S + V

說明

as for 意思為「至於 / 關於 ......」，後面可加名詞或動名詞，相似片語還包括：as to, as far as N is concerned, regarding, concerning, as regards, with respect to, etc.

例句：

1. <u>As for</u> money, Dickson thinks it outweighs love.

   至於金錢而言，Dickson 認為錢更勝愛情。

2. <u>As for</u> making smart investments, Mrs. Kim is second to none.

   至於做聰明投資，Kim 女士最懂了。

牛刀小試

1. All the workers will take to streets for better wages. _____

_____

所有的工人將為了更好的工資而上街抗議。至於 Eason，他也不例外。

2. _____

至於油電車而言，他們減少對環境的汙染。( hybrid car 油電車 )

Answer

1. As for Eason, he is no exception.

2. As far as hybrid cars are concerned, they reduce pollution to the environment.

## (4) Like/Unlike N, S + V

**說明**

此句型適用於比較兩者間的相同及相異點時，該特別注意的是：句型中的 N 要與後面句子中的主詞同性質，如：城市與城市相比；氣候與氣候相比等等。

例句：

1. Like Jordan, Kobe had his own remarkable partners, O'Neil and Gasol, on the road to NBA championships.

就像 Jordan 一樣，Kobe 在 NBA 冠軍之路有他自己得力隊友— O'Neil 和 Gasol。

2. Unlike most far-sighted general manager, Richard would rather be an opportunist.

不像大多數有遠見的總經理，Richard 寧願當個投機者。

 **牛刀小試**

1. _____ a meteorite, a shooting star burns up before it reaches the earth.

   不像隕石，流星在到達地球之前就燒光了。

2. _____

   像日本一樣，台灣易受颱風和地震的威脅。（be prone to 易受…的傷害）

**Answer**

1. Unlike

2. Like Japan, Taiwan is prone to the threats of typhoons and earthquakes.

## (5) instead of

**說明**

instead of 意思是「而不是……/ 代替……」，後須接動名詞或名詞。試比較：instead，意思則是「反而 / 相反地」，為副詞。請注意：instead of 後接的東西，是主詞不會去做的事；而 instead 後面的句子，則是會去做。

例句：

The girl on a diet only eats vegetables and fruit, <u>instead of</u> a balanced meal.

= The girl on a diet doesn't eat a balanced meal; <u>instead</u>, she only eats vegetables and fruit.

這正在減肥的女生只有吃蔬菜水果，而不是均衡的一餐。

**牛刀小試**

1. I didn't quite enjoy my sister's singing; _____

   我沒有很喜歡我妹妹唱歌；相反地，她的歌聲快逼瘋我了。

2. The defendant admitted his guilt, _____

   被告承認他的罪刑，而不是堅持他無辜清白。

 **Answer**

   1. instead, it nearly drove me nuts.

   2. instead of insisting on his innocence.

## (6) 譬喻法

**說明**

我們於描寫文或記敘文中，為了使文章句子更生動活潑，可利用隱喻、明喻或擬人法的手法來書寫。

例句：

1. The whole world is facing a financial tsunami.
   全世界正面臨金融海嘯。（隱喻）

2. My love for you is like fire.
   我對你的愛就像烈火。（明喻，含有 like）

3. Every flower is smiling at me.
   每朵花都在對我微笑。（擬人法）

## 牛刀小試

   1. To find my missing key is _____ finding a needle in the sea.
      要找到我丟掉的鑰匙就像在大海撈針。

   2. A massive landslide suddenly _____ the villa.
      一巨大的土石流突然吞噬的這棟別墅。

**Answer**

1. like

2. swallowed

## 五、含副詞

### (1) too…to V

**說明**

本句型意思為「太……而不能……」，too 後面可接形容詞或副詞。如果動詞為 be 動詞或連綴動詞（remain, taste, go,..., etc），則 too 後接形容詞；而動詞為一般動詞時，則 too 後接副詞。另外，加入 for，可以來表達「對於某人 / 某物而言」。

例句：

1. It is never <u>too</u> old <u>to</u> learn.
   學習永遠不會太晚。（活到老學到老）

2. The lung cancer spread <u>too</u> fast *for doctors* <u>to</u> treat the patient.
   肺癌擴散太快而醫生無法醫治病人。

**牛刀小試**

1. Stinky tofu is _____ smelly _____ some foreigners _____ give it a try.
   臭豆腐對於一些外國人而言太臭了而無法嘗試。

2. _____
   這條河被汙染太嚴重而魚無法存活。（severely 嚴重地）

 **Answer**

    1. too；for；to

    2. This river was polluted too severely for fish to live in.

## (2) not A, but B

 說明

此句型意思為「⋯不是 A，而是 B」，A 與 B 的詞性需對等，如：名詞對名詞，動詞對動詞，甚至可以對等兩個子句等。

例句：

1. What I do after work is not watching TV and playing with smartphones, but reading novels.
   我下班後做的不是看電視滑手機，而是看小說。( not Ving but Ving )

2. I love Ron not because he is rich, but because he is kind and considerate.
   我愛 Ron 不是因為他有錢，而是因為他心地好而且體貼。( not because⋯but because⋯ )

🖊 **牛刀小試**

    1. Who is to blame is _____ me, but all of the decision makers.
   該怪罪的不是我，而是那些做決定的人。

    2. _____
   我現在需要的並不是一朵玫瑰花，而是你的關心。

 **Answer**

    1. not

    2. What I need right now is not a rose, but your concern.

## (3) 副詞比較級 / 副詞最高級

**說明**

副詞比較級 / 副詞最高級形成方式大部分字為：字首加 more 或 most，來分別形成，只有一些例外，如：early, late, hard, fast, deep, long, near, high, soon 等等，這些字則在字尾加 -er 或 -est。

例句：

1. The girl acted <u>more courageously than</u> the man.
   這女孩表現得比這男子還要來的勇敢。

2. Bradly jumped <u>higher than</u> Tim.
   Bradly 跳得比 Tim 高。

3. Vicky ate up all the hamburgers <u>the most quickly</u> in the competition.
   Vicky 在比賽中是最快吃完漢堡的。

### 牛刀小試

1. In my opinion, a spider can wait for its prey _____ patiently _____ any other animal.
   依我之見，蜘蛛可以比任何其他動物更有耐心地等待它的獵物。

2. The newest bullet train in Japan can run _____ _____ any trains that you know.
   日本最新的子彈列車跑得比你所知道的火車都還來的快。

3. _____
   Rubecca 在她的班上是閱讀最廣泛地。

 **Answer**

1. more；than

2. faster than

3. Rubecca reads the most extensively in her class.

## (4) as…as

 說明

此句型意思為「像 …… 一樣 ……」，若句子的動詞為 be 動詞或連綴動詞，as...as 中間用形容詞；但若為一般動詞，則用副詞，因為副詞修飾動詞。

例句：

1. Our new principal is <u>as</u> *busy* <u>as</u> a bee.
   我們的新校長和蜜蜂一樣忙碌。

2. Don't expect Randle do everything <u>as</u> *carefully* <u>as</u> you.
   不用期待 Randle 做事跟你一樣仔細。

   溫馨提醒：as... as 可用於肯定句與疑問句，當用於否定句時，可用 not so...as 替換。

   例句：

   To some people, marriage is <u>not so</u> sweet and happy <u>as</u> a love story says.
   對於一些人而言，婚姻並非像愛情故事裡那麼的甜蜜與快樂。

## 牛刀小試

1. For elephants, their trunks are _____ useful _____ humans' hands.
   對於大象而言，他們的鼻子和人們的雙手一樣好用。

2. Miller ran his new company _____

Miller 把他的新公司經營得如同一家賺錢的大公司一樣有競爭力。
（profittable 競爭力的）

3. _____

自己創業並且很成功並非像我想的這麼簡單。

## Answer

1. as；as

2. as competitively as a big profittable company.

3. Starting a business and making it successful is not so easy as I think.

## (5) not…until…

**說明**

此句型意思為「直到……才……」，until 後面可以加一個時間片語或句子，請注意：如果時間是設定在未來，則 until 當句的時態，需用現在式代替未來式。

例句：

1. If I work overtime, I usually won't leave my office until 11pm.
   如果我需要加班，我通常到晚上 11 點才能下班。

2. We can't use this super computer until we are authorized.
   我們直到授權，才可以使用這台超級電腦。

not…until…可換成：

Not until…be+S+…/ Not until…助動詞 +S+V（使用倒裝句句型）

It is not until…that…（使用強調句句型）

例句：

1.  It was not until this afternoon that the power in our neighborhood was restored.

    = Not until this afternoon was the power in our neighborhood restored.

    直到下午，我住家鄰近地區的電才恢復供電。

2.  It was not until Joseph's computer crashed several times that he knew it was infected.

    = Not until Joseph's computer crashed several times did he know it was infected.

    直到 Joseph 的電腦當機幾次後，他才明瞭電腦中毒了。

### 牛刀小試

1.  _____ until midnight.

    Brian 直到午夜才回我 Line 的訊息。

2.  _____ that all the players stopped competing.

    直到哨聲響起所有的球員才停止競賽。

3.  _____ did the tiger jump through the burning loop.

    直到訓練員給出跳躍的手勢，這隻老虎才跳過火圈。

 **Answer**

1. Brian didn't reply to my Line messages

2. It was not until the whistle was blown

3. Not until the trainer gave a jumping gesture

## (6) twice as…as

**說明**

在講「倍數」比較時，我們可利用以下公式：

倍數 + as …as

倍數 + 比較級 + than

倍數 +the N of

例句：

1. The adult is <u>twice</u> <u>as tall as</u> the child.

   = The adult is <u>twice</u> <u>taller than</u> the child.

   = The adult is <u>twice</u> <u>the height of</u> the child.

   那位大人是這位小孩的兩倍高。

2. A rhino weighs <u>five times</u> <u>heavier than</u> a tiger.

   犀牛是老虎的 5 倍重。★註：3 倍以上，利用 time（次數），來形成倍數

   溫馨提醒：

   (1) 在「倍數 + the N + of」句型中，尺寸用 size；價格用 price；重量用 weight；高度用 height；寬度用 width；長度用 length；數量用 amount 或 number, etc.

   (2) 倍數也可能是幾分之幾，如：one fourth (1/4)；four fifths (4/5)

 **牛刀小試**

1. The distance from my home to my office is _____

   _____

   我家到辦公室的距離是我家到火車站的 5 倍的距離。

2. Hank's luxurious car is _____

   Hank 的奢華車是我家的 3 倍貴。

3. The pig fed for the festival was _____

   為了這節慶所飼養的豬是一般豬的兩倍重。


**Answer**

1. five times as long as it to the train station.

2. three times more expensive than my house.

3. twice the weight of a normal one.


## (7) not so much A as B

**說明**

此句型用於表達「與其說是 A，不如說是 B」= more B than A = B, rather than A。

例句：

Jack Sparrow is <u>not so much</u> frightened <u>as</u> excited when seeing a bunch of pirates.

= Jack Sparrow is <u>more</u> excited <u>than</u> frightened when seeing a bunch of pirates.

= Jack Sparrow is excited, <u>rather than</u> frightened, when seeing a bunch of pirates.

當 Jack Sparrow 看到一群海盜時，與其說他很驚恐，不如說他很興奮。

溫馨提醒：在 more B than A 句型中，若 A 與 B 皆為名詞，則須多加 of，請看例句。

例句：

Mr. Justin is <u>more of</u> a businessman <u>than of</u> a lawmaker.

與其說 Justin 先生是立委，不如說他是生意人。

### 牛刀小試

1. Lee is not so ＿＿＿＿＿＿ disappointed ＿＿＿＿ devastated.

   與其說 Lee 失望，不如說他是身心交瘁的。

2. Ms. Glen was not ＿＿＿＿＿＿＿＿＿＿＿＿＿＿＿＿＿＿＿＿

   與其說 Glen 小姐小氣，不如說她是太窮而無法捐贈任何東西。（stingy 小氣的）

### Answer

1. much；as

2. so much stingy as too poor to donate anything.

## (8) as…as possible

### 說明

此句型意思為「盡可能……」。請注意：第一個 as 後面需接形容詞或副詞。

例句：

1. To make a good impression on your new boss, you have to be <u>as sincere as possible</u>.

   為了讓新老闆留下好印象，你必須越誠懇越好。

2. The seafood needs to be put into a refrigerator <u>as soon as possible</u>.

這些海鮮都需儘快放入冰箱。

### 🖊 牛刀小試

1. The boss wanted his employees to do their work _____

_____

這老闆要的他員工工作時越有效率越好。

2. _____

士兵們被訓練成越順從和勇敢越好。（obedient 順從的）

### ✔ Answer

1. as efficiently as possible.

2. Soldiers are trained to be as obedient and brave as possible.

### (9) 雙重否定

> 說明

雙重否定的句型中，會有兩個否定詞（如：not, no, none, never, hardly…），再加上另一個否定詞（如：but, without…）來形成，語意上，因為兩個否定，所以會變成肯定。

例句：

1. There are <u>no</u> parents <u>but</u> love their own children.

沒有不愛自己小孩的父母。（but 後面用肯定寫）

2. It <u>never</u> rains <u>but</u> it pours.

從不下雨，除了傾盆大雨（禍不單行）。

3. He <u>never</u> performs <u>without</u> singing off key.

他每次表演都會走音。

### 牛刀小試

1. There are _____ mosquitoes _____ bite me because I have a higher body temperature.

因為我體溫較高，所以蚊子幾乎都會叮我。

2. My family never watches Conan's talk show _____

我的家人每次看 Conan 的脫口秀節目都會笑破肚皮。（split ones' sides 笑破肚皮）

### Answer

1. few；but

2. without splitting our sides.

## 六、含連接詞

### (1) 關係副詞（where, when）

**說明**

關係副詞 where, when，原本是由介系詞 + 受格關代轉換而來，使用判斷上，如果先行詞為地點，用 where；如果先行詞為時間，則用 when。

例句：

1. This is the farm <u>on which</u> a UFO was said to land.

=This is the farm <u>where</u> a UFO was said to land.

這是幽浮據説降落的地方。

2. Tomorrow is the day <u>on which</u> our school meets will be held.

= Tomorrow is the day <u>when</u> our school meets will be held.

明天是我們學校運動會舉行的日子。

溫馨提醒：如果先行詞是「獨一無二、地名、專有名詞等等」，則需要在 where, when 前面加一個逗點。

例句：

Paris, <u>where</u> I had my wedding ceremony, is famous for its fashion design.

我在巴黎舉行婚禮，而它以時尚設計出名。

## 牛刀小試

1. This is the season _____

   這是鮭魚會逆游而上產卵的季節。

2. The Lins usually go to the countryside _____

   _____

   林氏一家人經常去鄉間，在那裏他們才可以覺得放鬆和恢復精神。

3. Tainan_____

   is also known for its historic buildings.

   台南，有著各式各樣的可口小吃，也以歷史悠久的建築而聞名。

## Answer

1. when salmon will swim upstream to lay their eggs.

2. where they are able to feel relaxed and refreshed.

3. , where there are a wide variety of tasty snacks,

## (2) 複合關係代名詞

**說明**

所謂的複合關係代名詞，簡單來說，長相上，很像是名詞子句，公式：
5W1Hever+S+V；功能上，可當一個句子的主詞、受詞；或當兩個句子
的連接詞。意思上，舉 whatever 為例，有 anything that（所有⋯⋯的任
何東西）及 no matter what（不論什麼事/東西）。

例句：

1. We should severely punish whoever (anyone who) drives under the influence.

   我們應該嚴懲任何酒駕者。（當主詞）

2. Whenever (Any time when) the suspect leaves the apartment or wherever (any place where) he goes is under the police's surveillance.

   不管嫌犯何時離開公寓或不管他去哪裡，都在警方的監控中。（當主詞）

3. However (No matter how) you spend money and however expensive things are, think about the whole family you have to support.

   不管你怎麼花錢及不管東西多貴，你都應該想想你還有一個家要養。（當連接詞）

4. Whatever (No matter what) happens, remember you always have us to back you up.

   不管發生甚麼事，你都有我們當你的後盾。（當連接詞）

## 牛刀小試

1. _____, she is always protected by two strong bodyguards.

   不管這巨星去到哪裡，她總是被兩個強壯的保鑣保護著。

2. _____

deserved everyone's praise.

不管你用甚麼方法實現成為機師的夢想都值得每個人的讚美。

3. This secret agent _____.

這特務不准與她所認識的任何人連絡。

## Answer

1. Wherever the superstar goes

2. However you realized your dream of becoming a pilot

3. wasn't allowed to contact whomever she knew

### (3) 準關係代名詞：as, but, than

說明

準關係代名詞的用法非常類似關代的用法，即主格關代（後加動詞）與受格關代（後加主詞、動詞），相較於關代，這三個準關係代名詞，只可以搭配固定的字才能使用，公式如下：

the same/such/as…＋as…

否定詞…＋but…

比較級…＋than…

例句：

1. This is the same smart camera as I have.

這智慧相機和我的一樣。

2. Try not to buy such cheap batteries as may explode if the temperature is too high.

試著不要去買那些溫度過高可能會爆炸的便宜電池。

3. There is no rule but has exceptions.

   凡是規則都有例外。

4. Swimming is more difficult than I thought.

   游泳比我預期的還要難。

   溫馨提醒：準關係代名詞後加動詞之單複數，需與前面的名詞單複數一致。（如：例句 3 中，rule 和 has 的關係）

### 牛刀小試

1. Don't bite off _____

   不要咬超過你能咀嚼的食物。（量力而為）

2. I don't blame you because _____ .

   我不怪你因為我剛剛也犯你和你一樣的錯誤。

3. There were no contracts _____

   沒有一個合約是內容細節裡不藏著魔鬼的。

### Answer

1. more than you can chew.

2. I just made the same mistake as you did.

3. but have some devils in the detail.

## 七、含句子

### (1) It is... (for sb) to V/that S + V

**說明**

此句型是虛主詞 it，所引導的句子，真正的主詞為後面的不定詞（to V）或 that 子句；be 動詞後面可以放形容詞或名詞當補語，而這補語其實是在修飾真主詞。

例句：

1. <u>It is</u> illegal *for* people under 18 years old <u>to</u> drive or ride scooters in Taiwan.
   在台灣，18 歲以下開車或騎車的人是非法的。

2. <u>It was</u> a big surprise <u>that</u> I met my former homeroom teacher on the honeymoon trip.
   我在蜜月旅行中遇到以前的導師真是很驚訝。
   溫馨提醒：it is... 後方的補語如果是修飾人，則介系詞需用 of。

3. <u>It was</u> generous <u>of</u> Freddy <u>to</u> dish out gifts and candy to children in the neighborhood on Xmas.
   聖誕節當天 Freddy 發送禮物和糖果給社區小孩真是很慷慨。

### ✏️ 牛刀小試

1. _____ is inappropriate _____ Ford _____ wear red clothes to his friend's funeral.
   對於 Ford 而言，穿紅衣服去他朋友的婚禮實在不適當。

2. _____ whom he hadn't seen for years.
   對於 Eric 而言，巧遇他多年不見的老朋友真是一大樂事。

3. _____

   那男子那樣虐待他的狗真是很殘忍。

1. It；for；to

2. It was a joy that Eric ran into his old friend,

3. It was really cruel of the man to abuse his dog like that.

## (2) It is necessary that S + (should) + V

說明

虛主詞 it 所帶出的句型中，necessary 意思為「必須的」，that 子句中助動詞 should 可以省略。此類形容詞，用法與上一類動詞雷同。

急（急迫的）：urgent

適（適當的）：advisable, proper

必（必要的）：necessary, essential, imperative

重（重要的）：vital, important

例句：

It is *necessary* that we (should) <u>stay</u> home if the PM 2.5 level is too high.

如果 PM2.5 太高，我們必須待在家。

1. _____

   to clean up the oil spills.

   政府採取行動清理漏油是必要的。

2. _____

if they want to lose weight.

如果人們想減肥，三餐前先喝湯是適當的。

 **Answer**

1. It is imperative that our government take action

2. It is advisable that people eat soup before meals

## (3) It is time…

說明

此句型意思為「該是……的時候」，It is 後可加 that 子句或用 to V 來書寫。在 that 子句內，因為某人該去做某事，即暗示著某人尚未去做，所以需用假設語氣或用 should。此外，我們可以在 time 的前面，加 high 或 about 來強調語氣。

公式：

It is time that S+Ved.

It is time that S+should+V.

It is time for S to V.

例句：

1. It is time that we watered the flowers in our backyard.
   我們該為後院的花澆水了。

2. It is (high) time that Janet should stop gossiping and spreading rumors about us.
   該是 Janet 停止八卦並亂傳關於我們的謠言的時候了。

3. It is (about) time for the hunter to escape because a bear is approaching.
   該是這獵人逃跑的時候了，因為一隻熊正逼近。

 **牛刀小試**

1. It is time that you _____ on your costume and _____ trick-or-treating.
   該是你穿上服裝並去"不給糖就搗蛋"的時候了。

2. It is time _____ the police _____ crack down on those gangsters.
   該是警方取締那些幫派分子的時候了。

3. _____
   if you want to walk without pain.
   如果你想走起路來不痛的話,該是你去接受膝蓋開刀了。

**Answer**

1. put;went

2. for;to

3. It is high time that you should have knee surgery

## (4) Whether S… or …, S + V

**說明**

此句型意思為「不管……或……」,or 前後所列的詞性需對等,即:動詞 or 動詞;副詞 or 副詞,也就是說會有兩個選項,但如果只有一個選項,會變成 Whether S+V…or not, S+V. 的句型。另外,如果 whether 子句的動詞為 be 動詞,則可換成 Be S…or…, S+V 的句型。

例句:

1. Whether it rains or shines, we can see mailmen delivering letters and packages.
   不管下雨或大太陽,我們都可以看到郵差先生遞送著信件和包裹。

2. Whether you buy our products online or not, you can get a 10% discount.
   不管你是否線上購買我們的商品,你都可以得到 10% 的折扣。

3. <u>Whether</u> it is history <u>or</u> geography, I cannot master it at all.

⇨ <u>Be</u> it history <u>or</u> geography, I cannot master it at all.

不管是歷史或地理，我都無法專精。

**牛刀小試**

1. _____,

I would never forgive her.

不管 Sandy 不斷道歉或根本甚麼都沒說，我都不會原諒她。

2. _____, children are

often attracted by them.

不管是漫畫書或卡通，小孩常常會被吸引。

**Answer**

1. Whether Sandy kept saying sorry or saying nothing at all

2. Be it comic books or cartoons

## (5) What with…and what with…

**說明**

此句型意思為「一半因為……一半因為……」，第二個 what with，因為有對等連接詞 and，所以可以省略。

公式為：

What with N and what with N, S+V.

= Partly because of +N and partly because of+N, S+V.

= Partly because S+V and partly because S+V, S+V.

例句：

1. What with loss of habitats and what with illegal hunting, this kind of rhinos are facing extinction.

   一半是因為棲息地減少，一半是因為非法獵捕，這種犀牛正面臨絕種。

2. Partly because she isn't used to the new job and partly because she is short of money, Kelly suffered from insomnia.

   部分是因為她不熟悉新工作，部分因為她缺錢，Kelly 飽受失眠之苦。

### 牛刀小試

1. _____,

   Olivia burst out crying at work today.

   一半因為壓力，一半因為疲倦，Olivia 今天工作時突然大哭起來。

2. _____,

   Nina shivered and couldn't speak on stage.

   一半因為緊張，一半因為沒演戲經驗，Nina 在台上發抖並講不出話來。

### Answer

1. What with pressure and what with tiredness

2. What with nervousness and what with no experience of acting

## (6) adj as/though + S + V

説明

as 與 though 皆可引導出讓步語氣的句子，句子意思為：「雖然…但是…」。若要表達強調語氣，我們可以將名詞、副詞、形容詞，甚至是動詞提到句首。

例句：

1. Though Watt looks muscular, he is actually afraid of cockroaches very much.

   ⇨ _Muscular_ <u>though</u> Watt looks, he is actually afraid of cockroaches very much.
   （adj）

   雖然 Watt 看起來很有肌肉，但他卻怕蟑螂怕得要死。

2. <u>Bachelor</u> <u>as</u> he is, he seems to lead a happy life.（若為單數名詞，冠詞 a/an 省略）

   他雖然是單身漢，但他日子似乎還是過得很開心。

3. _Hard_ <u>though</u> Pan blew the trumpet, he still couldn't make any sound.（adv）

   Pan 儘管努力吹奏喇叭，但他仍然無法吹出任何聲音。

4. _Bark_ <u>as</u> these puppies might, the cat still kept eating their dog food.（V）

   儘管小狗們吠叫，但這隻貓仍然繼續吃著它們的狗飼料。

## 牛刀小試

1. _____ though Shane was, she didn't focus too much attention on her studies.

   雖然 Shane 很聰明，但她並沒有放太多注意力在課業上。

2. _____, she has defeated many men in the arm-wrestling game.

   即便她是個女人，但至今在比腕力比賽中已經打敗許多男人。

3. _____,
   it still slipped from his hand.

   雖然他試著很快地抓住正掉落的玻璃杯，它仍然從他的手滑出。

4. _____, he was caught by some brave pedestrians.

   這嫌犯雖可能逃跑，但還是被勇敢的路人所抓住。

**Answer**

1. Clever

2. Woman as she is

3. Fast though he tried to catch the falling glass

4. Escape as the suspect might

## (7) 感嘆句

**說明**

what 與 how 所引導出來的句子，稱為「感嘆句」，如果主詞與動詞顯而易見，則可以省略不寫，請注意，句尾需用驚嘆號。用法差別以例句說明：

例句：

How hot (it is today)!

今天天氣真熱！（how 後加形容詞）

How fast the panther ran!

那隻豹跑真快！（how 後加副詞）

How cute a baby (he is)!

他真是個可愛的嬰兒！（how 後加形容詞 + 單數名詞）

What a stinky durian (it is)!

這榴槤真臭！（what 後加名詞）

What dirty water!

水真髒！（what 後加不可數名詞，how 無此用法）

What busy employees!

多麼忙的員工啊！（what 後加複數名詞，how 無此用法）

1. _____ ! He saved several people from a burning apartment!

多麼勇敢的一位消防員！他從一著火的公寓中搶救數人。

2. _____ !

你是多麼的貼心啊！

**Answer**

1. What a courageous firefighter

2. How thoughtful you are

## (8) All S has to do is V

說明 ⋯⋯⋯⋯⋯⋯⋯⋯⋯⋯⋯⋯⋯⋯⋯⋯⋯⋯⋯⋯⋯⋯⋯⋯⋯⋯⋯
此句型意思為「某人該去做的是……」。其中 all 可換成 what，請注意：
be 動詞後所接的動詞，常用原形動詞。

例句：

All we have to do is elect a president who views people's welfare as the top priority.

我們所該做的是選出一個視人民福利為第一優先的總統。

 牛刀小試

1. _____ to get vitamin D.

Wesley 該做的是曬曬太陽來得到維他命 D。( bask in the sun 曬太陽 )

2. _____

as an easy prey for its prey.

這隻響尾蛇該做的就是利用它的尾巴來當作它獵物上鉤的獵物。

（rattlesnake 響尾蛇）

 Answer

1. All Wesley has to do is bask in the sun

2. All this rattlesnake has to do is use its tail

## (9) 強調句

說明

「強調句」的句型公式為 It is…that…，我們可以在 It is 與 that 中間放入，所要強調的東西，例如：名詞、時間、地點，甚至是副詞子句。

例句：

Elsa found a love letter in her schoolbag yesterday.

Elsa 昨天在她的書包內發現一封情書。

⇨ It was *Elsa* that found a love letter in her schoolbag yesterday.（若強調為人，that 可換成 who，這句子的 that 功能很像主格關代）

⇨ It was *a love letter* that Elsa found in her schoolbag yesterday.（強調受詞）

⇨ It was *in her schoolbag* that Elsa found a love letter yesterday.（強調地點）

⇨ It was *yesterday* that Elsa found a love letter in her schoolbag.（強調時間）

⇨ It was *when Elsa opened her schoolbag* that she found a love letter yesterday.（強調副詞子句）

1. _____ was Brent _____ was almost hit by a car because he was using his phone.

   就是 Brent 差點被車撞到，因為他當時正在使用手機。

2. _____ air tickets are relatively more expensive.

   正是在暑假期間機票相對都比較貴。

3. _____ you need to take if you want to feel better.

   正是這咳嗽藥你必須服用，如果你要舒服一點的話。

4. _____

   正是等到悲劇一再發生，立法委員才開始修法。（amend 修改…）

## Answer

1. It；that/who

2. It is during the summer vacation that

3. It is the coughing medicine that

4. It was after tragedies occurred again and again that lawmakers started to amend the law.

## (10) It is thought that S + V

說明

本句型亦為虛主詞 it 所變化出的句型，that 子句為真正主詞，be 動詞後採被動寫法，目的為客觀陳述事實。另外，that 後的主詞也可以移到句首來做改寫，請見例句。

例句：

1.  It is thought that second-hand smoking does as much damage as smoking itself.

    一般認為吸二手菸和吸菸本身造成一樣傷害。

2.  It was thought that the tennis player quit the match because of the knee injury.

    = The tennis player was thought to have quit the match because of the knee injury.

    一般認為這網球選手因為膝傷而退出比賽。

    溫馨提醒：除了 thought 以外，我們亦可利用其他字來書寫：said, expected, believed, rumored, decided, reported, etc.

    例句：

    It is rumored that the TV host lost one million dollars overnight in a casino in Hong Kong.

    謠傳這位電視節目主持人在香港一夜之間輸掉一百萬。

### 牛刀小試

1.  _____ the gas price will rise next week.

    據報導油價下禮拜會上漲。

2.  _____;

    that's why we have seldom explored it.

    謠傳外星人住在月球上，這就是之所以我們很少去探索它。

### Answer

1.  It is reported that

2.  It was rumored that aliens lived on the moon

## (11) There is no + Ving

說明

此句型在表達「某事不可能⋯⋯」，相當於 It is impossible to V.

例句：

<u>There is no accouting</u> for taste; that's why some love lamb very much, while others find it disgusting and smelly.

每個人的品味是無法解釋的；這就是之所以有些人超愛羊肉，但有些人覺得它又噁心又臭。

### 牛刀小試

1. _____ your ex-boyfriend will change his mind and come back to you.

   不用去希望你前男友會改變心意並回到妳身邊。

2. _____

   不能否認的是恐怖份子與全世界的戰爭不會輕易或很快結束。

### Answer

1. There is no hoping that

2. There is no denying that the war between terrorists and the world will never end easily or soon.

## (12) It occurs to sb that…

此句型意思為「某人突然想起 ......」，類似句型為 It flashes through one's mind that... ; It dawns on sb that... ; It strikes sb that...。請注意，that 後需接一句子。主詞若要換成以人當主詞時，則動詞要換成 realize。

例句：

1. It occurred to the tourist that she forgot to take a picture with that famous statue.

   這觀光客突然想起她忘記和那有名的雕像拍照。

2. It stroke Eve that she was riding the scooter without wearing a helmet.

   Eve 突然想起她騎車忘記戴安全帽了。

3. Cathy realized that money couldn't buy everything after she lost her mother.

   Cathy 在失去媽媽後，才了解到錢並不能買到每樣東西。

### 牛刀小試

1. _____ yesterday was my 10th wedding anniversary.

   我突然想到昨天是我 10 周年的結婚紀念日。

2. _____

   這女人突然想到她在高速公路上逆向行駛。

### Answer

1. It occurred to me that

2. It occurred to the woman that she was driving in the wrong direction on the freeway.

## (13) Those who…

此句型意思為「那些 …… 的人」，可替換成 People who...，請注意：those who 可放於句首或句中，而且關代 who 前面不可有逗點。

例句：

1. God helps <u>those who</u> help themselves.
   天助自助。

2. <u>Those who</u> have high body temperature are prone to mosquito bites.
   體溫比較高的那些人容易被蚊子叮。

 牛刀小試

1. _____

   can re-contact many long-lost friends.

   那些善用臉書的人可以再度聯絡上長久失聯的朋友。

2. Samuel looked down on _____

   _____

   Samuel 看不起那些還靠爸媽而不找工作的人。

Answer

1. Those who make good use of Facebook

2. those who depended on their parents without finding a job.

# Chapter 3

# Topic sentence
# 主題句

 說明

關於主題句（topic sentence）必須要有以下的認識：

1. 主題句是一個概括性的概念，而不是一個特定明確的狹小概念。所以在寫主題句的時候，要能用一句話把整段所要闡述的總概念開宗明義的跟讀者講。等於說，主題句就是這一段的大意。

2. 一段只能有一句主題句，在該段內的每一句都應繞著主題句來發展，簡單的說，該段內每一句都是依主題句概念去詳說，或提供證據來說明。一旦主題句確立，整段寫作方向便不會偏離。

3. 主題句大多出現在一段的第一句。當然，也有可能出現在一段中間或一段的尾巴，不過通常以第一句為常見。像中文作文中的開門見山法。建議讀者還是將主題句寫在第一句，等到寫作功力已經成熟，再去做變化。

4. 寫主題句時，應盡量以肯定句書寫。不宜用疑問句或立場觀點不堅定的方式來寫。

# 如何寫主題句？

各種文體的書寫方式稍稍不同，但大致來說：

- 偏論說的文章，對於該議題的觀點，需要清楚、言簡意賅的表明堅定的立場，所以建議用簡單句書寫，因為如果使用太過複雜的句子書寫則顯不出強而有力的感覺。

- 而記敘文的主題句，因為是敘述一個事件或經驗，如同講故事般，所以可以善用 5W1H 將整件事的人 who、事 what、時 when、地 where、如何發生 how、為何發生 why，寫入主題句內。

- 當遇到描寫文時，因為描寫文主要是描寫人物、物品、地方，所以主題句應該一針見血般的點出該篇文章要描寫的主角（人、物品或地方），輔以簡單敘述主角特徵，可用 5W1H 來簡易描述。

例子：

### 論說文

Topic: On Drunk Driving

Topic sentence: Drunk driving not only endangers the driver's life but also poses a threat to anyone using the road.

酒駕不僅危害駕駛生命還會對用路人造成威脅。

### 記敘文

Topic: My Most Unforgettable Experience with a Dentist

Topic sentence: Having my decayed molar pulled out last Sunday almost tortured me to death.

上禮拜天拔臼齒幾乎把我折磨到死。

### 描寫文

Topic: My Favorite Teacher

Topic sentence: Ronnie, my favorite teacher, looks rough but has a kind heart and a good sense of humor.

Ronnie 是我最喜愛的老師，雖然看起來很粗曠，但他有顆善良的心和幽默感。

1. Topic: Eating at Home or Dining out（論說文）

   Topic sentence: _____

   _____

2. Topic: Sun Moon Lake（描寫文）

   Topic sentence: _____

   _____

3. Topic: A Lie to My Parents（記敘文）

   Topic sentence: _____

   _____

## Answer 僅供參考

1. I prefer to eat at home in light of health, hygiene, and strengthening family bonding.

2. Sun Moon Lake, located in Nantou County, is famous for its scenic resources, gondola rides and bird-watching.

3. A lie about my poor math grades to my parents led to harsh punishment.

# Chapter 4

# Supporting ideas &
# Paragraph development
# 段落發展及支持的論點

**說明**

Topic sentence 提供一個概括性的概念，而 supporting ideas 則是在該段內提供一些細節，如：事實、例子或論點來支持主題句。在寫 supporting ideas 的時候必須繞著主題句去發展，不可提到新的論點。

如何寫 supporting ideas 呢？各文體的段落發展原則都不盡相同，本書第 6 章節有更詳盡的解說，在此僅舉記敘文為例，目的只為告訴讀者 supporting ideas 的概念。

一般非論說文的文章，其實只要善用 5W1H 就可寫出一完整的段落。

舉例來說，題目為（My First Trip Abroad）審題完後，判斷應為一篇記敘文，接下來只要順著事件發生的順序，透過 5W1H，一一敘寫整個旅程所發生之事即可。

Topic: My First Trip Abroad

Topic sentence: I had a great time on the Bali beach.

在腦中構思或於白紙上寫上關鍵字，如下：

Who：Who went to the Bali beach with me?

When：When did I take the trip abroad?

What：What did I do on the beach?

Why：Why did I take a trip to the Bali beach?

Where: Where did I visit or have fun?

How：How did I feel about the trip and how did it affect my future trip plan?

**I had a great time on the Bali beach.** Last summer vacation, my family and I took a trip to the beautiful Bali beach, a paradise for fun-seekers. The reason for this family trip was that I entered a national university and Father received a promotion. Feeling so excited about my first trip abroad, I arranged all the itinerary of the four-day journey. On the first day of the trip, we took a bus to cruise the whole island and also tasted a variety of local snacks and sea food…. On the third day, never would we miss the thrilling water sports, including skin diving, banana boating, etc…. We all got a suntan and enjoyed ourselves on this attractive island. This is the most memorable trip that I have ever had. I hope that I can pay a visit to this fantastic island again.

中譯：

　　我在巴里島玩得很開心。去年暑假，我和家人到玩樂者的天堂：巴里島旅行。我們家旅遊的原因是我進入到一所國立大學，而爸爸也剛升遷。因為對於我第一次出國太興奮了，我一手規劃了四天的旅遊行程。在一天時，我們搭公車遊覽整個島並品嚐了當地的各式各樣的小吃和海鮮…在第三天時，我們絕不會錯過刺激的水上運動，包含浮淺、香蕉船…我們都曬成古銅色並且在這島嶼玩的很盡興。這是我最難忘的旅行。我希望下次還可以再來這超棒的島嶼。

# Chapter 5

# Cohesion & Coherence
# 連貫及緊密

## Sentence cohesion

> 說明
>
> cohesion 是指前後兩句，因為兩句中的關鍵字有關聯，以達到句子與句子的連貫性，目的使文章不至於渙散，有以下的技巧：

**A** Repetition（重複法）：在第二句重複上一句的一個關鍵字。

例句

(1) Tom shot down a bird with his BB gun. The bird turned out to be a rare cardinal bird according to the encyclopedia.

Tom 用 BB 槍擊落一隻小鳥。根據百科全書，這隻鳥結果是一隻罕見的憤怒鳥。

(2) The thief bumped into a pedestrian and fell down. The pedestrian happened to be a police officer on leave and arrested him on the spot.

那個小偷撞到了一名路人並跌倒。這名路人剛好是休假中的警官，當場將他逮捕。

**B** Pronoun（代名詞法）

(1) Can you think of anyone who is more suitable for me than Catherine? She is the one. Tomorrow I am going to propose to her.

你能想出比 Catherine 更適合我的人嗎？她就是我的真命天女。明天我要跟她求婚。

(2) Ben's father got married to another woman after divorce. She turned out to be Ben's ex-girlfriend. How ironic!

Ben 的爸爸離婚後娶了另一名女人。她結果是 Ben 的前女友。多諷刺！

**C** Synonymy（同義字法）

(1) Mr. Chang is the one who brings the bacon home. However, the money he earns is not enough to support his family with his wife and five children.

張先生是他們家會賺錢的人。但，他所賺的錢不足以養活全家人，含老婆和四個小孩。

(2) The minister passed away last night in his own house. It was reported that he died from a drug overdose. However, the police are still finding the real cause of his death.

這名部長昨晚在自家身亡。據報導他是死於藥物過量。然而，警方還在找他真正的死亡原因。

**D** Antonym（反義字法）

(1) The wealthy mogul has everything he wants. Nevertheless, he is like a pitiful beggar spiritually. Never will he read anything.

這富有的大亨擁有他想要的任何東西。但，心靈上他就像是個可憐的乞丐。因為他從不閱讀。

(2) Mia's father always tells her to <u>put her feet on the ground</u>. Therefore, when starting to pursue her dream, she <u>seldom builds castles in the air</u>.

Mia 的爸爸總是叫她要腳踏實地。因此，當她開始追求夢想時，她很少做白日夢。

**E** Enumeration（列舉法）

**例句**

(1) <u>First</u>, you stood me up. <u>Second</u>, you lied to me. <u>Third</u>, you flirted with another girl. How am I supposed to trust you?

首先，你放我鴿子。第二，你對我說謊。第三，你和其他女生調情。我是要如何能相信你？

(2) There are two advantages of riding bicycles to work. <u>For one thing</u>, it saves money and produces no carbon dioxide. <u>For another</u>, you can build up your muscles.

騎腳踏車去上班有兩個好處。一方面而言，可以省錢且不會製造二氧化碳。另一方面，你可以鍛鍊肌肉。

**F** Collocation（搭配字詞法）

**例句**

(1) I have two doubts right now. <u>One</u> is what to do. <u>The other</u> is how to do it.

我現在有兩個疑問。一個是要做甚麼。另一個是如何做。

(2) <u>The more</u> movies you watch, <u>the easier</u> you can tell good movies from bad ones.

你看越多電影，你就越容易辨別出好電影與壞電影。

# Sentence coherence

Coherence（連貫性）乃指文章的發展，務必各段相連貫。一段之內，句與句之間連接得自然，可透過轉承詞（transitional words）及連接詞（conjunction）的方法，使整篇的組織架構完整、邏輯緊密，讀者會容易了解句與句間的意義，並透過邏輯，預期接下來文章會如何發展。

連貫方式，可以分為：

**A** 時間連貫（**time order** 由時間上的先到後或由後到先）

例子：In mid July, Mr. Boxer was diagnosed with lung cancer. Soon afterwards, he sought medical treatment. One year later, his health improved. At last, with a regular life and a balanced diet, he became healthier and healthier....

（時間由先到後：in mid July ⇨ soon afterwards ⇨ one year later ⇨ at last）

**B** 空間連貫（**space order** 由空間上的小到大或由大到小）

例子：Taiwan is a beautiful country. I live in Taipei. Taipei is the most convenient and prosperous city around the island. In Da'an District, there are some famous universities, such as National Taiwan University and National Taiwan University of Science and Technology. In fact, I just live beside the NTU....

（空間由大至小：Taiwan ⇨ Taipei ⇨ Da'an District ⇨ NTU）

**C** 或以邏輯連貫（**logical order** 由邏輯上的原因到結果或由結果到原因）

例子：I have made my mind to enter a national senior high school. However, my teacher does not think my grades are good enough to achieve my goal. Therefore, I have to make the best use of every minute because the test is eight months away. Hopefully, my dream can come true.

（邏輯由：however ⇨ therefore ⇨ hopefully）

運用這三種連貫的原則，可避免文意前後倒置，雜亂無章。另外除了句與句要有連貫性外，字與字之間也要有連貫性，要達到此目的，便需作出適當排序，如果一段落內句子不「統一」，則即使有「連貫性」也沒用，反之，若沒有連繫的句子亂成一團，就算全部與主旨有關，也是令讀者看不懂，所以，unity、cohesion及 coherence 三者缺一不可。而下一章節「轉承詞與連接詞」，便是令一段落有連貫性的關鍵。

# Chapter 6

## Transitions & Conjunctions
### 轉承詞與連接詞

**1 Transitions 轉承詞**

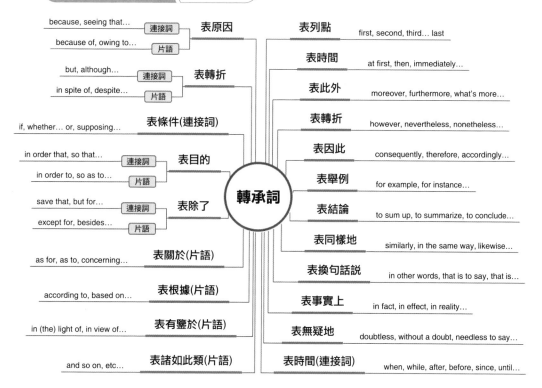

| 功能 | 轉承詞 |
|---|---|
| 表列點<br><br>論說文適用 | 第一點，第二點，第三點…最後：<br>1. first, second, third… last<br>2. firstly, secondly, thirdly…, finally<br>3. the first, the second, the third…, the last<br>4. in the first place, in the second place, in the third place…, lastly<br>首先：<br>5. to begin with, to start with, first and foremost<br>此外：<br>6. in addition, additionally, furthermore, besides, moreover, what's more<br>更重要的是：<br>7. above all, more importantly<br>最後：<br>8. most important of all, finally, last but not least<br>適用於兩點的情況：一方面…，另一方面…：<br>9. on (the) one hand, on the other hand<br>10. for one thing, for another (thing) |

例句：

1. My colleagues and I make it a habit to have fun at the KTV. For one thing, the KTV provides comfortable space to sing and relax. For another thing, it also serves desserts and drinks.

   我同事和我習慣去 KTV 找樂子。一方面而言，KTV 提供舒適的唱歌和放鬆空間。另一方面，它也提供點心和飲料。

2. Please follow the following steps to operate the washing machine. Firstly, put the laundry and detergent into the tub. Secondly, select the water level button according to your volume of laundry. Thirdly, set the time for washing. Finally, push the start button.

   請依照下面步驟操作洗衣機。首先，將髒衣物及清潔劑放入洗衣槽。第二，依衣物多寡選擇水量。第三，選擇清洗時間。最後，按下開始鍵。

| 功能 | 轉承詞 |
|---|---|
| 表時間<br><br>記敘文適用 | 1. 起初：at first, in the beginning<br>2. 然後：then, later, later on, afterwards, soon afterwards<br>3. 在那時候：at that time<br>4. 馬上：immediately, at once, right away, in no time, instantly<br>5. 不久：before long, shortly, soon<br>6. 同時：at the same time, meanwhile, in the meantime<br>7. 突然：suddenly, all of a sudden, all at once<br>8. 從現在起：from now on, in future<br>9. 從那時起：from then on<br>10. 隔天：(the) next day<br>11. 在未來：in the future, in the near future<br>12.（3 天）前：(three days) ago<br>13. 再（一個禮拜）：in (one) week<br>14. 到目前為止：so far, to date<br>15. 暫時：temporarily, for the time being<br>16. 有時候：from time to time, every now and then, at times, once in a while, occasionally, on occasion<br>17. 總是：all the time, at all times<br>18. 有一次：at one time, once<br>19. 最近：recently, lately, of late<br>20. 最後：finally, eventually, at last, in the end, in the long run<br>21. 在過去：in the past<br>22. 將來有一天：some day, someday, one day |

例句：

1. Seeing a police car on the roadside, Jack took a sharp turn at once because he was drunk. Then, luckily he came home safe and sound.

   Jack 看到路邊有警車，馬上急轉彎，因為他酒駕。之後，幸運地，他平安到家。

2. From now on, I will never ever leave my child alone in the car again in the future.

   從現在開始，我以後再也不會將小孩獨自留在車內。

3. My grandfather has been addicted to using Facebook recently.

   我爺爺最近迷上臉書。

| 功能 | 轉承詞 |
|------|--------|
| 表此外 | moreover, furthermore, what's more (informal), in addition, additionally, besides, also, as well |

例句：

1. Today is not Miss Lin's day. She got laid off; moreover, she left her purse on the bus.

   林小姐今天非常不順。她先是被解雇，此外，她還把錢包遺留在公車上。

2. This digital camera has the highest resolution. Also, users can upload pictures through its built-in WiFi function.

   這台數位相機有最高的解析度。此外，使用者還可透過內建的無線網路功能上傳照片。

| 功能 | 轉承詞 |
|------|--------|
| 表轉折 | however, nevertheless, nonetheless, yet, still, though, on the contrary, in contrast, by contrast, on the other hand, |

例句：

1. Gorge has many shortcomings; however, Mary is still madly in love with him.

   George 有很多缺點；然而，Mary 還是深深地愛著他。

2. Taking the MRT to work is not only fast but also inexpensive for me. By contrast, driving costs more and traffic congestion always annoys me.

   搭捷運上班不但快速且不貴。相反地，開車就花費高且塞車相當惱人。

| 功能 | 轉承詞 |
|---|---|
| 表因此 | consequently, in consequence, as a consequence, therefore, accordingly, as a result, thus, hence |

例句：

1.  I didn't get the passing grade in history; therefore, I have to sit a make-up test.
    我歷史這科沒及格，所以，我必須參加補考。

2.  China has become the world factory from shoes to 3C products. As a result, many western countries are joining the Chinese-learning bandwagon.
    大陸已經變成世界工廠，不管從鞋子到 3C 產品。因此，許多西方國家都搶搭學中文的熱潮。

| 功能 | 轉承詞 |
|---|---|
| 表舉例 | for example, for instance, e.g., take N, take…for example/instance. |

例句：

1.  For instance, it is better to make a checklist before shopping and reduce the desire of buying something we don't need.
    舉例來説，我們最好在購物之前先列清單，並減低買一些不必要東西的慾望。

2.  Taiwan is facing many social problems. Population ageing can never be overlooked, for example.（放句尾）
    台灣正面臨許多社會問題。舉例來説，人口老化絕對不能輕忽。

3.  Take myself (for example). I had inadequate sleep during my military service, which caused pimples to pop up one by one/one after another.
    舉我自己為例。當兵時睡眠不足，造成臉上痘痘一顆接一顆冒。

| 功能 | 轉承詞 |
|------|--------|
| 表結論 | to sum up, to summarize, to conclude, in conclusion, in sum, in summary, in brief, to be brief, in short, all in all, in a nutshell, in one word, in a word, |

例句：

1. <u>To conclude</u>, stress from life and malnutrition resulted in the woman's breakdown.

   總結來説，生活壓力和營養缺乏導致這女人的崩潰。

2. <u>In a nutshell</u>, what people dream about at night has something to do with sub-consciousness and pressure from life.

   總之，人們晚上做的夢和淺意識及生活壓力有關。

| 功能 | 轉承詞 |
|------|--------|
| 表同樣地 | similarly, in the same way, likewise, by the same token, in the same/similar way |

例句：

1. The atmosphere of this restaurant is enjoyable. <u>Likewise</u>, every dish is absolutely delicious.

   這家餐廳的氣氛佳，同樣地，每道菜也都很美味。

2. Drug abuse endangers people's health in this city. <u>In the same way</u>, illegal gun possession poses a threat to their safety.

   毒品濫用危害市民健康，同樣地，非法持有槍枝也對市民人身安全構成威脅。

| 功能 | 轉承詞 |
|---|---|
| 表換句話說 | in other words, that is to say, that is, to put it differently, i.e. |

例句：

1. The curfew was lifted. In other words, people can stay outside until midnight.

   宵禁解除。換句話說，人們可以在外待到午夜。

2. Our mission is to storm the den of the terrorists, that is, to arrest them and to rescue all the hostages.

   我們的任務是要攻堅恐怖份子的巢穴，也就是說，逮捕他們並順利救出人質。

| 功能 | 轉承詞 |
|---|---|
| 表事實上 | in fact, in effect, in reality, as a matter of fact, actually (informal) |

例句：

1. Mrs. Chen considered his husband loyal to her. In fact, he is preparing for a divorce.

   陳太太一直都認為先生是忠於她。事實上，他正準備離婚。

2. Teresa excels at karate. In reality, she just won the championship this week.

   Teresa 空手道了得。事實上，她這禮拜才贏得冠軍。

| 功能 | 轉承詞 |
|---|---|
| 表無疑地 | doubtless, without a doubt, needless to say, unquestionably, undoubtedly |

例句：

1. Doubtless, you are my true love.

   無疑地，你是我的真愛。

2. This gang, without a doubt, is the most notorious one in Japan.

   這幫派，無疑地，是日本最惡名昭彰。

## ② Conjunctions　連接詞

| 功能 | 連接詞 |
|---|---|
| 表時間 | when, while, after, before, since, until, by the time, once, as soon as, = hardly/scarcely…when, = no sooner…than, = the instant, = the moment, = the second, =the minute |

例句：

1. The moment/The minute/The second/As soon as I saw you, I knew I love you.
   我一看到你，我就知道我已經愛上你了。

2. The class had no sooner been quiet down than the teacher came in.
   老師一進來，這班級同學馬上安靜下來。

3. By the time the tiger approached, all the rabbits had already escaped for life.
   老虎接近之前，所有兔子都早已逃命。

| 功能 | 連接詞 | 片語 |
|---|---|---|
| 表原因 | because, seeing that, since, now that, because, as, in that, for（for 不可擺句首） | because of, owing to, thanks to, due to, on account of, as a result of |

例句：

1. Since it is freezing cold outside, let's do indoor activities today.
   既然外面冷得要命，我們今天就做室內活動就好。

2. Owing to the ankle sprain, I have to walk on crutches.
   由於腳踝扭傷，我必須用拐杖行走。

| 功能 | 連接詞 | 片語 |
|---|---|---|
| 表轉折 | but, although, though, even though, even if, while, whereas, yet | in spite of, despite, regardless of, notwithstanding |

例句：

1. <u>Even though</u> the communist government has brainwashed its people for decades, quite a few intellectuals still staged protests and trumpeted for freedom.

   <u>即使</u>這共產國家一直在對人民洗腦，仍有不少知識分子發起抗議行動鼓吹自由。

2. <u>Despite</u> repeated setbacks, Andy stuck to his goal and succeeded at last.

   <u>即使</u>連續受挫，Andy 仍堅持目標，最後成功了。

| 功能 | 連接詞 |
|---|---|
| 表條件 | if, whether… or, supposing, suppose, providing, provided, on condition that |

例句：

1. <u>Supposing</u>/<u>Suppose</u>/<u>Providing</u>/<u>Provided</u> (that) you won the jackpot, what would you spend this windfall?

   <u>假使</u>你中了頭彩，你會怎麼使用這筆意外之財？

2. <u>Whether</u> I report you to the police, <u>or</u> you turn yourself in.

   <u>要不</u>我向警方檢舉你，要不你自己自首。

3. The child cannot decide <u>whether</u> to eat ice cream <u>or</u> to drink soda first.

   這小孩無法決定<u>是否</u>先吃冰淇淋<u>還是</u>喝汽水。

| 功能 | 連接詞 | 片語 |
|------|--------|------|
| 表目的 | in order that, so that, so | 1. (in order to, to, so as to)＋V<br>2. (with a view to, with the view to, with the intention of, with the object of, with an eye to) ＋Ving |

例句：

1. In order to/To catch the girl's attention, I tried to impress her by cracking jokes.
   為了引起那女孩的注意，我試著在她面前講笑話。

2. The party bombarded people with election advertisements with a view to winning votes and ridding the vote-buying image.
   這政黨用選舉廣告轟炸民眾，為了贏得選票和擺脫買票形象。

3. Kobe practices shooting for hours each day in order that he can sink every ball in every game.
   Kobe 每天練習投籃數小時為了能在比賽中投進每一球。

4. The global warming problem deteriorates day by day, so some tropical fishes even appear in cold waters off the coast of U.K.
   全球暖化問題日趨嚴重，所以一些熱帶魚竟跑到英國沿岸的海域。

| 功能 | 連接詞 | 片語 |
|------|--------|------|
| 表除了 | save that, but for, but that | 1. except for, except, excepting＋N（沒包括 N）<br>2. in addition to, besides＋N（有包括 N）<br>3. aside from, apart from＋N（可包括或沒包括 N） |

例句：

1. Except/Except for some off-key notes, Gary, though an amateur, sang quite a good song.
   除了一些走音外，Gary 雖然業餘，的確是唱了一首好歌。

2. Save that you must pay off the debt, there is no way you can keep the house.
   除了你必須還債外，目前是無法保住你的房子。

另外：

| 功能 | 片語 |
|---|---|
| 表關於 | as for, as to, concerning, regarding, in regard to, with regard to, as regards, speaking of, talking of, when it comes to, respecting, with respect to, in respect to, as far as…is concerned, in terms of |

例句：

1. <u>As for</u> Hualien, it is its amazing scenic spots that set it apart from others.

   <u>至於</u>花蓮，就是景點讓它與其他縣市不同。

2. <u>When it comes to</u> the Red Dot award, creativity and originality abound in each work.

   <u>當談論到</u>紅點獎，每件作品都富有創意和原創性。

| 功能 | 片語 |
|---|---|
| 表根據 | according to, based on |

例句：

1. <u>According to</u> the latest weather forecast, the super typhoon is three hundred kilometers in radius.

   <u>根據</u>最新的氣象預報，超級颱風半徑就有 300 公里。

2. <u>Based on</u> what Jimmy said, speed walking burns more calories than jogging.

   <u>根據</u> Jimmy 所言，快走消耗的卡路里比慢跑多。

| 功能 | 片語 |
|---|---|
| 表有鑒於 | in (the) light of, in view of, considering, given |

例句：

1. In light of the tragic air crash, the New Year fireworks show was cancelled this year.

   有鑑於這悲劇性空難，今年的新年煙火取消。

2. Given you are on a tight budget, we can share the apartment and meals.

   有鑑於你的預算吃緊，我們可以共享公寓和三餐。

| 功能 | 片語 |
|---|---|
| 表諸如此類 | and so on, etc, and the like, and so forth |

例句：

1. Alice grew many flowers in her backyard, such as lilies, roses, cherries, and so on.

   Alice 在後院種了許多花，如百合、玫瑰、櫻花等等。

2. During the trip to Changhua, we visited many tourist attractions, such as Tianwei Highway Garden, Bagua Mountain, Lukang, etc.

   彰化之旅中，我們去了許多景點，如田尾公路花園、八卦山、鹿港等等。

# Chapter 7

# Summary
# 結論

> **說明** ........................................................................
> 任何文章都需結論段,上面章節也已經交代了各文體的結論段書寫方式
> 及所引導出的轉承詞,在此,筆者再為讀者稍稍複習一番:
> ........................................................................

1. 論說文及說明文:通常採前後呼應法,寫法為將之前各段的 topic sentences 做一個濃縮,用不同文字或比喻法將相同概念表達出來,以達畫龍點睛的功效,不過就是不要將 topic sentences 重抄,因為這樣了無新意。

    題目為:Corporal Punishment(體罰)

    中心論點為反對體罰

    Topic sentence 1:

    Corporal punishment makes learning itself not a joy, but a horrible thing.

    Topic sentence 2:

    Because of corporal punishment, students may deem violence a solution to every problem.

Topic sentence 3:

Replacing spanking with praise and encouragement brings out students' better learning effect.

結論可以使用 wielding the stick 來取代體罰的説法：

Wielding the stick and scolding not only stifle the learning happiness, but also convey a misleading concept to students—violence is a master key. As an alternative for corporal punishment, compliment and confidence-giving work better for both learning and teaching.

2. 記敘文及描寫文：常採自然結束法或書寫一些對此一事件的感想。

題目為：An Experience of Seeing a Dentist

結論就可採把整個看牙醫的尾聲是整篇最精彩的部份就可作為結論，比如説：醫生拔錯牙之類的。如果拔牙結果順利，也解決牙痛的問題，那就可以寫一些感想，如：要吃完甜食或三餐後刷牙，定期檢查是否有蛀牙之類的話。

(1) After having my tooth pulled out, I still felt a toothache. I asked the dentist to re-check my decayed tooth. To my surprise, the dentist pulled the wrong tooth.

(2) After having my decayed tooth pulled, I felt no more ache inside my mouth. I had better follow the doctor's suggestion to brush teeth after eating if I want to enjoy tasty food in the future.

切記：不管是書寫哪一種體裁，皆不可再提出新的觀點（idea）或論點（argument）。

# Chapter 8

## Composition genres
## 作文類型

**① Letter**　書信文

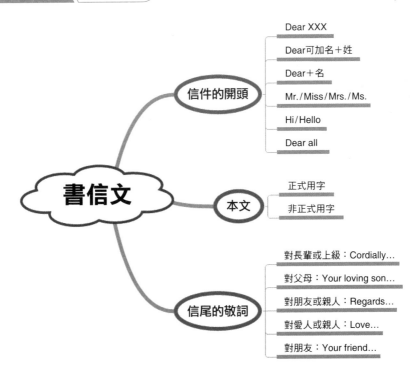

書信文

信件的開頭
- Dear XXX
- Dear可加名＋姓
- Dear＋名
- Mr./Miss/Mrs./Ms.
- Hi/Hello
- Dear all

本文
- 正式用字
- 非正式用字

信尾的敬詞
- 對長輩或上級：Cordially…
- 對父母：Your loving son…
- 對朋友或親人：Regards…
- 對愛人或親人：Love…
- 對朋友：Your friend…

| | |
|---|---|
| 信件的開頭 | 一般書信，右上角會寫上日期，但如果是 email 當然不用寫。<br><br>Dear XXX 幾乎可適用於各種情況，Dear 可加名＋姓（用於不熟時）；Dear ＋名（用於熟識時）。但如果你知道對方的婚姻關係，可另加 Mr.（為先生，不管已婚或未婚）；Miss（為小姐，用於未婚）；Mrs.（為太太，用於已婚）；Ms.（用於女性婚姻狀態不清楚時）。另外，如果是比較熟識的對象，email 時，我們常用 Hi/Hello 來開頭，在加對方的名字。倘若寫信對象為一個團體 / 一群人，則可用 Dear all。 |
| 本文 | 依照寫信對象、目的而書寫。一般而言，寫給長輩或上級或外國客戶，用字要比較正式；相反的，若寫給親人或朋友，則可使用非正式用字，如：口語、俚語、縮寫等等。 |
| 信尾的敬詞 | 對長輩或上級，常用：Cordially; Respectfully; Yours respectfully 等等；<br>對父母：Your loving son; Your loving daughter<br>對一般朋友或親人：Regards; Best regards; Kind regards; Warm regards; Best wishes; All the best 等等。<br>對愛人或親人間：Love; Yours ever; Yours always。<br>對朋友間：Your friend; Cheers; Take care; Ciao; Later 等等。 |

**說明**

請依以下提示寫一封英文 email，長度約 120 字（8 至 12 句子）。作文可以是一個完整的段落，也可以分段。（評分重點包括內容、組織、文法、用字遣詞、標點符號、大小寫。）

提示：你的朋友 Angela 正為了考慮畢業後，要不要出國打工度假（working holiday）而困擾。請寫一封英文 email 給她，信的內容必須包括以下兩點：

1. 分享打工度假可能遇到的困難。
2. 給她幾個建議。

## 腦力激盪擬大綱

| | |
|---|---|
| 主題句 | I can give you something that you have to know and prepare for. |
| 支持句 1 | solving the problem of language |

| 支持句 2 | worrying about the safety |
|---|---|
| 支持句 3 | tiring work on the farm; doing "dirty" work in a meat-processing factory |
| 支持句 4 | a good employer; make good preparations for any emergency; learning some useful English conversation |
| 結論句 | Take good care and keep in contact with me every day if possible. |

## 範文

Dear Angela,

How have you been? I've heard that you've felt bothered by whether to go on a working holiday in Australia or not. I googled some information about it and as your best friend, I can give you something that you have to know and prepare for.

Going on a working holiday is never as easy as people think. I know the pay is good but have you ever thought of the following things? Frist, you've got to solve the problem of language. If I remember correctly, you don't like English much, do you? Second, I know you will go alone and don't you worry about the safety of yourself? Third, about the work you'll do over there, you may need to stand for over eight hours to pick fruit or take care of the poop the animals have left on the farm. It's extremely tiring. And you probably have to do "dirty" work in a meat-processing factory. How disgusting and stinky it is! And many more....

So, I suggest you thoroughly consider what I've mentioned above. If you still want to do it, please make sure that you must find a good employer online first, make good preparations for any emergency that may happen, and do learn some useful English conversation before you get on the plane. Last but not least, take good care and keep in contact with me every day if possible.

Your best friend,

Ben

| 參考單字： | | |
|---|---|---|
| poop 大便 (U) | process 加工 (vt) | emergency 緊急狀況 (C) |
| extremely 極度地 (adv) | disgusting 噁心的 (adj) | |

親愛的 Angela：

　　近來好嗎？我聽說妳最近因為是否要去澳洲打工度假而感到困擾。我 google 了一些資訊，身為妳最好的朋友，我想我可以給妳一些該知道且準備的事。

　　打工度假絕非人們想的這麼簡單。我知道薪水不錯但妳有曾考慮過以下這些事嗎？第一，妳必須解決語言問題。如果我沒記錯，妳好像不太喜歡英文吧？其次，我知道妳要單獨前往，妳不會擔心個人安全嗎？第三，有關妳的工作內容，妳可能需要站超過八小時摘取水果，或者清理農場動物的大便。這是極度辛苦的。妳很可能要在肉品加工廠做一些髒活。這光想就很噁心和惡臭！還有很多很多…

　　所以，我建議妳仔細考慮我上面所提。如果妳還是要前往，請確認妳先在網路上找到一位好雇主、並做好緊急事件發生的萬全準備，並在上飛機前學些實用的英文對話。最後，好好照顧自己並且，可能的話，每天與我保持聯絡。

妳最好的朋友
Ben

## 文章分析

1. 主題句：I can give you something that you have to know and prepare for.

   （雖然說這是一封 email，無法遵從像一般文章制式的寫法，但我們可以在第一段時，安插一句本文所要發展的主題句並不一定要放第一句，但卻是內文發展的依據。）

2. 結論句：Take good care and keep in contact with me every day if possible.

   （溫馨提醒與關心）

3. 口語用法：因為是朋友間的 email，所以大部分句子都比較以口語類為主，甚至出現許多問句、附加問句、省略句、感嘆句。

開頭問候：

> Good morning. How are you? 早安，你好嗎？
>
> Good evening. How are you doing? 晚上好，你好嗎？
>
> Hi, how have you been? 嗨，近來好嗎？
>
> I guess you must be doing well/OK. 我猜你應該過得不錯。

## 結尾用語

- **表感謝**

    Thanks in advance. 先謝謝您。

    Thank you for your time and attention. 感謝您的時間和關注。

    Thank you for your cooperation. 感謝您的合作。

    Thank you for your patience. 感謝您的耐心。

    Thank you for your help/assistance. 感謝您的協助。

- **期待回覆**

    I'm looking forward to seeing you. 期待再相會。

    I'm looking forward to hearing from you. 期待再有您的消息。

    I'm looking forward to your (prompt) reply. 期待您的（快速的）回覆。

- **祝福**

    Have a nice/wonderful day. 祝您有個美好的一天。

    Have a nice afternoon. 祝您有個美好的下午。

    Have a lovely weekend. 祝您有個美好的周末。

    Have a happy trip. 祝您旅途愉快。

    Have a happy summer vacation. 祝您有個愉快的暑假。

1. 題目：

【提示】一天你去圖書館，發現一位身障人士，因為無障礙設施不夠完善，導致進入圖書館困難重重，請寫一封 email 告訴館方：
(1) 當天所見的細節 (2) 你的建議

 

2. 題目：

【提示】你的朋友 Jeff 正為了體重過重而困擾，甚至不敢出門，社交活動幾乎不參加，正需要你的幫助，請寫一封 email，內容必須包含：
(1) 安慰他的話 (2) 減重建議

## ❷ Expository Essay 説明文

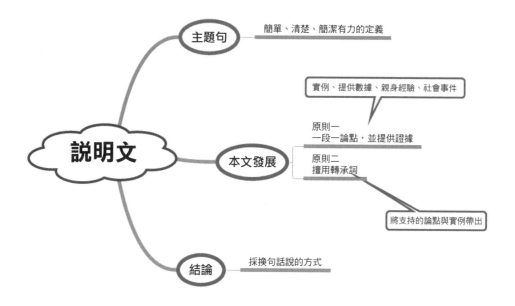

| 主題句 | 原則 | 為主題下一個簡單、清楚、簡潔有力的定義。 |
|---|---|---|
| 本文發展 | 原則一 | 一段一論點，並提供證據。 |
| | 説明 | 本文中必須説明理由或舉實例、提供數據、親身經驗、社會事件，甚至是以假設狀況來對主題句的延伸説明等等，來支持論點。但注意：所有列的論點，必須與主題句的邏輯一致，不可偏離。 |
| | 原則二 | 擅用轉承詞。 |
| | 説明 | 因為説明文，很重邏輯與條理，為了讓讀者了解情況、明白事理、知道真偽，所以建議讀者應該多多利用上面章節中的轉承詞，一一將支持的論點與實例帶出。如：firstly, secondly, therefore, in light of, for example 等等。 |
| 結論 | 原則 | 寫法很簡單，就上面段落的主題做一融合，採換句話説的方式呈現。 |

請依下面所提供的文字提示寫一篇英文作文,長度約 120 字(8 至 12 個句子)。作文可以是一個完整的段落,也可以分段。

提示:許多人沉迷於智慧型手機上的遊戲,玩到廢寢忘食,例如:之前的糖果粉碎(Candy Crush)、神魔之塔(Tower of Saviors)、到最近的寶可夢(Pokemon)等等。請說明玩這些遊戲的優點與缺點,並給這些人一些建議。

## 腦力激盪擬大綱

| 主題句 | Playing games on smartphones has its pros and cons. |
|---|---|
| 支持句 1 | relieve their pressure<br>provide entertainment and excitement |
| 支持句 2 | do harm to people's eyes |
| 支持句 3 | ignore something vital<br>inefficiency at work and sleepiness at school |
| 支持句 4 | sacrifice precious time with their family and friends |
| 結論句 | Playing games on smartphones can serve as an outlet for our stressful life as long as we manage our time of having fun well. |

## 範文

**Playing Games on Smartphones**

**Playing games on smartphones has its pros and cons.** On one hand, it can not only help people relieve their pressure from work and life, but it also provides them with entertainment and excitement. On the other hand, being addicted to these games brings quite a few harmful effects. First, it does harm to people's eyes if they stare at the phone screens for too long. Medically speaking, more and more people were reported to suffer from eye problems, such as bad eyesight. Second, spending too much time on games, people probably ignore something vital they should do first. What's worse, staying up to use their smartphones leads to inefficiency at work and sleepiness at school. Finally, with a majority of time and attention on phone games, people tend to sacrifice precious time with their family and friends. Take my friend, Eddy, for example. He has seldom talked to and played sports with us since he began playing games on his smartphone. Moreover, Eddy has been seen dozing off in class and his grades went from bad to worse.

In my opinion, **playing games on smartphones can serve as an outlet for our stressful life as long as we manage our time of having fun well**. In other words, only if we strike a balance between life and these phone games can we really have a "smart" life and a "smart" phone.

| 參考單字： | | |
| --- | --- | --- |
| pros and cons 利弊 (C) | addicted 上癮的 (adj) | sacrifice 犧牲 (vt) |
| relieve 減輕 (vt) | harmful 有害的 (adj) | outlet 出口 (C) |
| pressure 壓力 (U) | vital 重要的 (adj) | |
| entertainment 娛樂 (U) | inefficiency 沒效率 (U) | |

### 範文翻譯

　　玩手機遊戲有其利弊。一方面來說，它不但可以減輕人們工作和生活的壓力，而且也可以提供娛樂和刺激。另一方面而言，對手機遊戲成癮會帶來不少的壞影響。首先，如果盯著手機螢幕太久，這會傷害眼睛。醫學上而言，越來越說人被報導有眼睛方面的問題，例如：視力差。第二，花太多時間在遊戲上，人們可能會忽略很重要的事。更糟糕的是，熬夜玩遊戲會導致工作上沒效率及上課想睡覺。最後，大部分的時間和注意力都擺在遊戲，人們會犧牲掉和家人朋友相處的寶貴時光。舉我朋友 Eddy 為例。他自從開始玩手機遊戲，就很少和我們講話或運動。此外，Eddy 常被發現上課打瞌睡，成績也一落千丈。

　　依我所見，只要我們管理好玩樂時間，玩手機遊戲可以是我們充滿壓力生活的出口。換句話說，只有在我們於生活和手機遊戲間取得平衡，我們才能擁有"智慧"生活和"智慧"手機。

1. 主題句：Playing games on smartphones has its pros and cons.

   （開宗明義說明：玩手機遊戲有利有弊，開啟本文的發展，可就優點與缺點加以說明。）

2. 結論段：Playing games on smartphones can serve as an outlet for our stressful life as long as we manage our time of having fun well.

   （根據題目給予手機遊戲成癮的人意見，並綜合通篇的利弊，利用換句話說的方式下一簡潔結論。）

3. 轉承詞：on one hand; on the other hand; first, second, finally; what's worse; moreover; in my opinion; in other words

4. 舉例：Medically speaking, more and more people were reported to suffer from eye problems, such as bad eyesight.

   Take my friend, Eddy, for example.

5. 多利用同義字字典：relieve their pressure from work and life ≒ an outlet for our stressful life; being addicted ≒ spending too much time; sleepiness ≒ dozing off

6. 句型多變：除了一般的 S＋V 直述句外，另外，亦使用動名詞當主詞的句型；副詞連接詞連接兩句；被動句；分詞構句；倒裝句等等。

## 溫馨提醒

如何引經據典及舉例：

★ According to ..., S＋V.（根據）

   ⇨ According to the survey, eighty percent of the citizens oppose the new parking regulation.

   根據調查，百分之八十的市民都反對新的停車規定。

★ Based on ..., S+V.（根據）

⇨ Based on the research, the mass disappearance of honeybees can lead to a food crisis.

根據研究，大規模蜜蜂消失會引起糧食危機。

★ As the report says, S+V.（如同報導所説……）

⇨ As the report says, some lawmakers are involved in the bribery and under investigation.

如同報導所説，一些立法委員涉入賄賂案件，並接受調查中。

★ As the experiment shows, S+V.（如同實驗所顯示……）

⇨ As the experiment shows, use of smartphones before bedtime affects the quality of sleep.

如同實驗所顯示，睡前使用智慧型手機會影響睡眠品質。

★ As the proverb goes, ....（俗話説）

⇨ As the proverb goes, the early bird catches the worm.

俗話説：早起的鳥兒有蟲吃。

★ As an old saying goes, ....（俗話説）

⇨ As an old saying goes, where there is a will, there is a way.

俗話説：有志者事竟成。

★ A recent study shows that S+V.（最近一項研究顯示……）

⇨ A recent study shows that 60% office workers prefer online shopping due to their busy life and its convenience.

最近一項研究顯示，有百分之六十的上班族偏愛網路購物，原因是因為生活忙碌和其便利性。

★ Research conducted by ... has shown that S+V.（…所做的研究顯示…）

⇨ Research conducted by Swiss scientists has shown that certain symtoms of depression can raise the risk of suicide.

一項瑞士科學家所做的研究顯示某些憂鬱症症狀會提高自殺風險。

★ It is reported that S+V.（報導指出……）

⇨ It is reported that the movie star has two children before marriage.

報導指出這位電影明星在結婚前就已經有兩個小孩了。

★ Research indicated that S+V.（研究顯示……）

Research indicated that 75% of employees are not satisfied with their year-end bonuses.

研究顯示百分之七十五的員工不滿意他們的年終獎金。

★ It is proved that S+V.（證實……）

⇨ It is proved that nutrtition are significantly linked to a baby's brain development.

小孩的營養和其大腦發展緊密相關已被證實。

★ It is well-known that S+V.（眾所皆知……）

⇨ It is well-known that sedentary work has a lot to do with obesity and bad blood circulation.

眾所皆知的是久坐的工作和血液循環不好有很大的關係。

★ Take ... for example.（舉……為例）

⇨ That food is so strange. Take Russel for example. He is a born-and-bred American but has never heard of it.

那食物實在太奇怪了。舉 Russel 為例。他是個土生土長的美國人，但從未聽過。

★ Take ... for instance.（舉……為例）

⇨ Many people in Taiwan are addicted to smartphones. Take myself for instance. I usually spend three hours a day on it.

很多台灣人都對智慧型手機上癮。舉我自己為例。我通常每天花 3 個小時在手機上。

★ S, for example, V.（舉……為例）

⇨ Edison, for example, takes pleasure in making fun of others.

舉例來説，Edison 以取笑別人為樂。

★ S+V, for example.（舉……為例）

⇨ Compared with students in Taiwan, South Korean students face much more pressure of entering a good university, for example.

舉例來說，比起台灣學生，南韓學生所面臨的升上好大學壓力大多了。

**牛刀小試** 請依據所給的題目與主題句發展一篇文章，並請將文章上傳至本書前言中所列之作文評改網站

1. 題目：A Day without Cellphones

   主題句：A day without cellphones can be a nightmare for most people nowadays.

   【提示】

   第一段論點：As far as the inconvenience of communication is concerned

   第二段論點：In terms of the entertainment

   結論：綜合全部論點，用換句話說方式寫出


   A day without cellphones can be a nightmare for most people nowadays. __

   _____

   _____

   _____

   _____

   _____

   _____

   _____

   _____

2. 題目：Work and Play

主題句：It is important to strike a balance between work and play. As the proverb goes, "All work and no play makes Jack a dull boy."

【提示】

第一段論點：Play can relieve one's pressure and improve work efficiency

第二段論點：Without play, people will feel work tiring and it is not good for their health.

結論：綜合全部論點，用換句話說方式寫出


It is important to strike a balance between work and play. As the proverb goes, "All work and no play makes Jack a dull boy." _____

_____

_____

_____

_____

_____

_____

_____

_____

# ③ Argumentative Essay　議論文

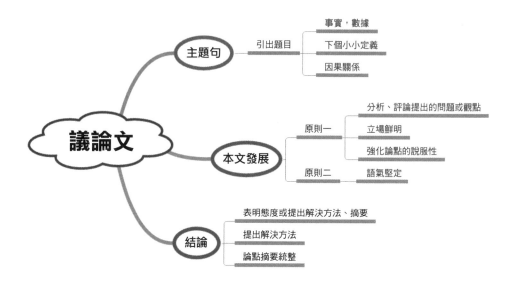

| 前言 | | 議論是對事物或問題進行推斷、論證、發表評論、提出作者的論點及主張，為了印證觀點的正確，而使人有所信服。 |
|------|------|------|
| **主題句** | 原則 | **引出題目** |
| | 說明 | 1. 透過已熟知的事實、數據。<br>2. 對題目下個小小定義。<br>3. 藉其他主題的因果關係，利用類比技巧導入題目。 |
| **本文發展** | 原則一 | **分析、評論提出的問題或觀點** |
| | 說明 | 選擇正方或反方的立場，請記得：立場一定要鮮明，不可游移不定。接下來開始列支持所選立場的觀點、理由，輔以事實來強化論點的說服性，如：實例、數據、引經據典、親身經歷。本文各段皆須照此原則：論點＋論證（證據、例子）。 |

| | 原則二 | 語氣堅定，但不武斷、教條說教及浮誇 |
|---|---|---|
| 本文發展 | 說明 | 避免以下用字：People always...；Everyone...；We all...；You should...；You must；People certainly...；People definitely..., etc. 而是應該用：People usually...；We often...；Most of us...；Most people...；We had better...；People had better..., It is better for people that..., etc. |
| | 原則 | 對提出的問題、觀點表明態度或提出解決方法，亦或對正文的論點做一摘要 |
| 結論 | 說明 | 在表明態度這點，務必和文章最開始的立場一致，絕不可產生矛盾，亦不可模擬兩可，立場不堅定。其次如果採用提出解決方法來做結論，可善用倒裝句，如：Only when...；Only by...。至於，若要對整篇論點做一摘要統整，不要再把正文裡的主題句原封不動的照抄，而是應該就已有的觀點，利用 variety 章節內各式句型公式，重新改寫，如此會讓讀者會心一笑。 |

**說明**

請依下面所提供的文字提示寫一篇英文作文，長度約 120 字（8 至 12 個句子）。作文可以是一個完整的段落，也可以分段。

提示：電視是人們在家最主要的娛樂管道，即便是今日亦然，有人認為電視對人們有負面影響，有人覺得正面，現在請就你和電視的關係及它對你的影響寫一篇作文。

## 腦力激盪擬大綱

| 主題句 | It is not too much to say that TV plays a vital role in people's daily entertainment and information communication. |
|---|---|
| 支持句 1 | the main source of entertainment |
| 支持句 2 | keeping me abreast with the times |
| 結論句 | With TV, I can taste the flavor of every culture and keep up with the times. |

範文

On TV

**TV plays a vital role in people's daily entertainment and information communication**. In fact, people's life is intimately connected with TV and constantly affected by it from consuming, to fashion and even to thoughts. As far as I am concerned, TV influences me positively.

TV provides me with the main source of entertainment. After going through one tiring day, I rely on TV programs, especially variety shows, to get rid of the stress by laughing heartily at artists' performances. Oftentimes, I feel refreshed and relieved after laughing out loud to no end.

TV keeps me abreast with the times. It offers the latest information around the world at a lightning speed. Through these instant news reports, I can practically witness every big event around the globe. In addition, TV makes it easy to sample various cultures and customs of different regions with the remote control.

**With TV, I can taste the flavor of every culture and keep up with the times.** Never can I imagine leading a life without the company of TV. The charm of TV is unstoppable to me.

| 參考單字： | |
|---|---|
| intimately 緊密地 (adv) | to no end 不間斷 (adv) |
| consume 消費 (vt) | keep abreast with 了解……最新（訊息） |
| positively 正面地 (adv) | at a lightning speed 快速地 (adv) |
| refreshed 恢復精神的 (adj) | sample 體驗 (vt) |

範文翻譯

電視在提供娛樂和資訊傳遞上扮演重要的角色。事實上，人們的生活都緊密地和電視連接在一起，同時也不斷受其影響，從消費、時尚、甚至是想法。就我個人而言，電視對於我的影響是正面的。

電視提供了我主要的娛樂。在疲累的一天後，我依賴電視節目，特別是綜藝節目，看藝人們的表演來開懷大笑解除壓力。我總是在不停大笑後，覺得身心舒暢並放鬆。

電視讓我能與時俱進。它快速提供全世界各地的資訊。透過這些即時的新聞報導，我彷彿親眼目睹各地的重大事件。此外，電視也讓我體驗各風俗文化變得簡單，只需按按遙控器。

有了電視，我可以體驗各文化，並接收最新消息。我絕無法想像沒有電視陪伴的生活。電視對我的魅力無法擋。

## 文章分析

1. 主題句：

   第一段主題句：TV plays a vital role in people's daily entertainment and information communication.

   （這句主題句點出了整篇文章的大意，並引出題目。）而 TV influences me positively.（則表明了立場。）

   第二段主題句：TV provides me with the main source of entertainment.

   第三段主題句：TV keeps me abreast with the times.

   （第二三兩段主題句皆是跟著第一段主題句而發展延伸。）

2. 結論段：With TV, I can taste the flavor of every culture and keep up with the times. Never can I imagine leading a life without the company of TV. The charm of TV is unstoppable to me.

   （以換句話說方式將論點再次重述，並帶出個人感想。）

3. 轉承詞：in fact, as far as ... concerned, oftentimes, in addition

4. 多利用同義字字典：keep abreast with ≒ keep up with; sample different cultures ≒ taste the flavor of every culture; laughing heartily ≒ laughing out loud to no end; provide ≒ offer; various ≒ different

結論段常用句型：

- It is (about) time for us to ... .（該是……的時候了）

  ⇨ It is time for us to take measures to stop littering in the school.

  該是我們採取行動遏止校園中亂丟垃圾了。

- It is (high) time that we (should) ... .（該是……的時候了）

  ⇨ It is high time that we should put our ideas into action.

  該是我們將點子付諸行動的時候了。

- It is our duty to ... .（這是我們的責任去……）

  ⇨ It is our duty to protect citizens any forms of intrusion into their privacy.

  這是我們的責任去保護市民免於任何形式的侵犯隱私。

- We should spare no efforts to ... .（我們應該不遺餘力去……）

  ⇨ We should spare no efforts to find the suspects of this crime.

  我們應該不遺餘力找出這犯罪的嫌疑犯。

- We had better strive to ... .（我們最好努力去……）

  ⇨ We had better strive to cut down on the use of fossil fuel; moreover, we need to seek more alternative green power.

  我們最好努力去減少使用化石染料，此外，我們須尋求替代性綠能。

- It is essential/necessary/imperative/important that S + V.（這是必須的 / 重要的……）

  ⇨ It is important that we bring enough food and necessary supplies when going mountainclimbing for several days.

  如果我們一連爬山好幾天，攜帶足夠食物和任何必需品是重要的。

- Only when S + V + 倒裝句（只有當……）

  ⇨ Only when the sun almost sets does the tired farmer get ready to go home.

  只有太陽快下山的時候，這疲憊的農夫才會踏上歸途。

- Only by Ving + 倒裝句（只有藉著……）

  ⇨ Only by putting our brains together can we work out the solution to this deficit problem.

  只有藉著集思廣益我們才能找出赤字問題的解決方法。

- Not only + 倒裝句 , but S also V.（不但……，而且……）

  ⇨ Not only did he turn down my invitation, but he also asked me not to see him again.

  他不只拒絕我的邀請，他還叫我不要再和他見面。

- Not until S + V + 倒裝句（直到……，……才……）

  ⇨ Not until I heard "Happy April Fool's Day" did I realize I was fooled again.

  直到我聽到愚人節快樂我才意識到我又被耍了。

- Not until N + 倒裝句（直到……，……才……）

  ⇨ Not until the eleventh hour will Johnson start to get packed.

  不到最後一刻 Johnson 才開始要打包。

- If we can ..., ... .（如果我們能……，……）

  ⇨ If we can care more about the underprivileged, our world will be a better place.

  如果我們能多關懷弱勢族群，我們的世界會變得更好。

- If we want to ..., we need to... .（如果我們要……，我們就須……）

  ⇨ If we want to travel around the world, we need to try to save more and spend less.

  如果我們要環遊世界，我們就需設法存多點並花少一點。

- We will not ... without ... .（我們沒……就不……）雙重否定

  ⇨ We will not stop protesting without seeing social welfare improved.

  我們沒看到社會福利改善前，是不會停止抗議的。

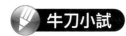 **牛刀小試** 請依據所給的題目與主題句發展一篇文章，並請將文章上傳
至本書前言中所列之作文評改網站

1. 題目：On Nuclear Power Plants

   主題句：Nuclear power plants solve some problems of power shortage but they also bring negative impacts.

   【提示】

   論點 1：potential leak of radiation

   論點 2：difficulty in disposing of nuclear waste

   論點 3：possible attack target for enemies

   Nuclear power plants solve some problems of power shortage but they also bring negative consequences. _____

   _____

   _____

   _____

   _____

   _____

   _____

   _____

   _____

   _____

2. 題目：On Corporal Punishment

   主題句：Corporal punishment, in my opinion, brings more harm than good.

   【提示】

   論點 1：In terms of learning motivation,

   論點 2：As far as students' self-respect is concerned,

   論點 3：Misconception that violence can solve problems

   Corporal punishment, in my opinion, brings more harm than good. _____

   _____

   _____

   _____

   _____

   _____

   _____

   _____

   _____

## ❹ Narrative Essay 記敘文

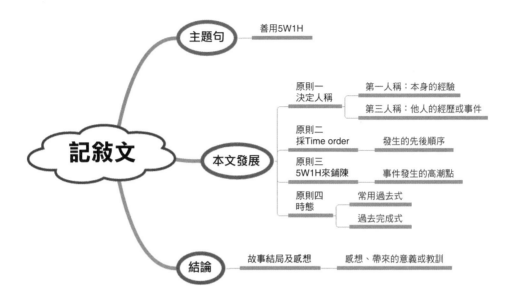

| 主題句 | 原則 | 善用 5W1H 將事件的（人、事、時、地、物、發生原因），用一句話大概敘寫。 |
|---|---|---|
| 本文發展 | 原則一 | 決定人稱（第一人稱或第三人稱） |
| | 說明 | 記敘文可以視為說故事的方式來敘寫，所以可能是敘寫本身的經驗（第一人稱），亦可能敘述他人的經歷或事件（第三人稱）。特別注意：如果採取第一人稱敘寫，不可每一句開頭都是 I，這樣的句子便會過於單調，該用換句話說的方式，且替換主詞，來表達一樣概念。 |
| | 原則二 | 採 Time order |
| | 說明 | 基本上整篇寫作的順序，採整件事情、故事發生的先後順序來書寫即可。但注意：不可將文章中的句子，不管發生的時間先後，隨意穿插，因為這樣會干擾讀者理解文章。 |

| | | |
|---|---|---|
| | 原則三 | 使用 5W1H 來鋪陳，使讀者清楚整篇文章的來龍去脈 |
| 本文發展 | 說明 | 用 5W1H 來交代整個故事，包含 who（何人？）、what（何事？）、when（何時發生？）、where（發生地點？）、how（如何？若有發生問題是如何化解？）、why（為何發生？）。寫作原則，不外乎詳實表達，並安排一事件發生的高潮點（亮點）。 |
| | 原則四 | 時態常用過去式 |
| | 說明 | 因為是敘寫過去經驗或事件，所以時態選擇上當然是過去式為主，但也可以穿插過去完成式。另外，在結論段，表達整件事帶來的影響或感想，可用現在式或未來式表達。 |
| | 原則五 | 應用之前幾章的寫作原則 |
| | 說明 | 前幾章的寫作原則須牢記，並在下筆時，要時時提醒自己，文章如何布局架構、句子如何多變化等等。 |
| 結論 | 原則 | 故事結局及感想 |
| | 說明 | 在結論段中，除了帶出故事結局外，另外可以提及整個事件的感想、帶來的意義或教訓等等。 |

**說明**

請依下面所提供的文字提示寫一篇英文作文，長度約 120 字（8 至 12 個句子）。作文可以是一個完整的段落，也可以分段。

提示：不少人都害怕看牙醫，還有人視其為夢魘，而不願去看牙齒，非等到痛不欲生才勉強自己就醫。現在，請你以自己的經驗為例，描述一次看牙醫的過程，並從中得到的感想。

## 腦力激盪擬大綱

| 主題句 | I hate seeing a dentist but the ache of the decayed tooth beat my fear for dentists. |
|---|---|
| 支持句 1 | dentist tried to relax me<br>sound of the machine, frightening |

| 支持句 2 | unendurable sour feelings<br>fixed my cavity |
|---|---|
| 支持句 3 | lasted around ten minutes<br>decayed tooth removed |
| 結論句 | Since then, I have made it a habit to brush my teeth after meals and stayed away from candy as much as I can. |

 範文

Seeing a Dentist

**I hate seeing a dentist but the ache of the decayed tooth beat my fear for dentists.** My fear for dentists has existed since my childhood because of the unbearable sour feelings and terrifying sound from the dentist's drill.

Waiting for treatment in the clinic was frightening enough. Before long, my nightmare started. The nurse asked me to lie down on the dentist's chair. Then, the dentist sat next to me and tried to relax me with a friendly conversation. Apparently, I must have acted like an ant on a hot pan. As soon as I opened my mouth, the horrible sound of the dentist's drill went into my ears, stimulating my nerves. As I was thinking about how to stand this sound, the dentist had already begun to fix my cavity. The unendurable sour feelings from the decayed tooth came up in no time. At that time, what I hoped for was a quick end to this torture. The whole treatment lasted around ten minutes. Finally, the dentist had the decayed tooth removed from my mouth. What a relief! **From this experience, I have made it a habit to brush my teeth after meals and to stay away from candy as much as I can.**

| 參考單字： | |
|---|---|
| decayed tooth 蛀牙 (C) | cavity 蛀牙 (C) |
| dread 害怕 (vt) | unendurable 無法忍受的 (adj) |
| unbearable 無法忍受的 (adj) | torture 折磨 (C) |
| nightmare 惡夢 (C) | remove 移除 (vt) |
| horrible 恐怖的 (adj) | relief 鬆一口氣 (C) |
| apparently 明顯地 (adv) | made it a habit to 想成習慣去 …… |
| stimulate 刺激 (vt) | stay away from 遠離 …… |

## 範文翻譯

我討厭看牙醫但是蛀牙的疼痛戰勝我對牙醫的恐懼。我從小時候就害怕去看牙醫，因為那令人無法忍受的酸感和牙鑽傳來令人害怕的聲音。

診所內等待治療本身就已經夠恐怖了。不久後，我的噩夢便開始了。護士叫我躺上牙醫椅。之後，醫生坐在我身邊，並嘗試用友善的談話讓我放輕鬆。很顯然地，我一定表現得像熱鍋上的螞蟻。我一躺下時，牙鑽令人驚嚇不已的聲音傳入耳裡，刺激著我的神經。當我還在想如何忍受這聲音時，牙醫已經開始幫我修補蛀牙。那從蛀牙所產生的無法忍受的酸感馬上湧上。在那時候，我唯一希望的是快點結束這折磨。整個治療持續大約十分鐘。最後，牙醫師把蛀牙從我口中移除。總算鬆了一口氣！從這次經驗，我養成餐後刷牙的習慣，並盡可能遠離甜食。

## 文章分析

1. 主題句：I hate seeing a dentist but the ache of the decayed tooth beat my fear for dentists yesterday.

   （Tips：who: I; what: seeing a dentist; why: ache of the decayed tooth; how: fear）

2. 結論段：From this experience, I have made it a habit to brush my teeth after meals and stayed away from candy as much as I can.

   （Tips：what I have learned: brushing teeth regularly; staying away from candy）

3. 本文中的轉承詞：before long, then, apparently, at that time, finally，串起整個看牙醫的過程，遵循 time order 來發展，依序將故事娓娓道來。

4. 譬喻：I must have acted like an ant on a hot pan.（比喻焦急如熱鍋上的螞蟻）；torture（比喻整個治療過程）

5. 多利用同義字字典：terrifying ≒ horrible; unbearable ≒ unendurable; cavity ≒ decayed tooth

6. 句型多變：除了一般的 S+V 直述句外，另外，亦使用動名詞當主詞的句型；副詞連接詞連接兩句；分詞構句；名詞子句；感嘆句等等。也因為善用句型變化，才不至於讓整篇都是以 I 來開頭，避免單調性，畢竟這是一篇敘述個人經驗的作文，是很多考生會落入的寫作缺點。

1. 轉承詞：因為記敘文強調事件因時間推移而發展，所以轉承詞的使用格外重要，像似關節般串起整篇文章。

| 起初 | at first, in the beginning, in the first place |
|---|---|
| 然後 | then, later, later on, afterwards, soon afterwards |
| 在那時候 | at that time, at that moment |
| 馬上 | immediately, at once, right away, in no time, instantly, without delay, promptly |
| 不久 | before long, shortly, soon |
| 同時 | at the same time, meanwhile, in the meantime, simultaneously |
| 突然 | suddenly, all of a sudden, abruptly, all at once |
| 從現在起 | from now on, in future |
| 從那時起 | from then on |
| 隔天 | (the) next day, the following day |
| 在未來 | in the future, in the near future |
| （3天）前 | (three days) ago |
| 再（一個禮拜） | in (one) week |
| 到目前為止 | so far, to date, up to now, until now, till now |
| 暫時 | temporarily, for the time being |
| 有時候 | from time to time, every now and then, at times, once in a while, occasionally, on occasion, now and again |
| 總是 | all the time, at all times |
| 有一次 | at one time, once |
| 最近 | recently, lately, of late |
| 最後 | finally, eventually, at last, in the end, in the long run |
| 在過去 | in the past |
| 將來有一天 | some day, someday, one day |

2. 本文部份：請多多利用 variety 章節中所列的各種句型，讓文章的句子活潑多變，特別是副詞連接詞以及轉承詞，因為整個事件是以時間先後順序發展。

3. 結論句

★ It turned out that S＋V.（結果是……）

⇨ It turned out that my new boss was my ex-wife.

結果是我的新老闆是我的前妻。

★ As it turned out, S＋V.（結果是……）

⇨ As it turned out, caning was proved to be an effective method to lower the crime rate.

事情結果是鞭刑證實為降低犯罪率很有效的工具。

★ I learned a lesson that S＋V.（我學到一課……）

⇨ I learned a lesson that honesty was not always the best policy.

我學到一課：誠實未必是上策。

★ Never will I ....（我再也不會……）

⇨ Never will I buy Eason's words. He is a horrible liar.

我再也不會相信 Eason 的話了。他是個糟糕騙子。

★ From this experience, S＋V.（從這次經驗中，……）

⇨ From this experience, I will never ever plug in any electronic appliances with my hand wet.

從這次經驗中，我再也不會手濕濕地插任何電器產品。

★ From now on, I will/had better/should ....（從現在開始……）

⇨ From now on, I had better keep within the speed limit even if I am in a hurry.

從現在開始，我最好保持速限，即便是很趕。

★ Not only did I ..., but I also ....（我不但……，我也……）

⇨ Not only did I learn the importance of punctuality, but I also realized how to arrange my schedule well.

我不但學習到守時的重要性，我也了解到如何妥善安排我的行程。

★ Next time, if I ..., I will (not)....（下次，我如果⋯⋯，我一定⋯⋯）

⇨ Next time, if I attend any wedding banquet, I will never drive under the influence of alcohol.

下次，我如果再參加婚宴，我一定不會再酒後駕車。

★ I wish that S＋had＋Ved ....（但願我當初可以⋯⋯）

⇨ I wish that I had booked the hotel rooms earlier.

但願我當初可以早點定飯店房間。

★ In retrospect, I ....（回想起來⋯⋯）

⇨ In retrospect, I think I should apologize to Anita and try my best to compensate for her loss.

回想起來，我應該跟 Anita 道歉，並盡最大努力彌補她的損失。

★ Thinking back, I ....（回想起來⋯⋯）

⇨ Thinking back, I should have kept a close eye on my belongings on the train.

回想起來，我當初應該在火車上好好盯緊個人隨身物品。

 **牛刀小試** 請依據所給的題目與主題句發展一篇文章，並請將文章上傳至本書前言中所列之作文評改網站

1. 題目：My most Embarrassing Experience

   主題句：I had the most embarrassing experience when I ....

   【提示】

   What was the experience?

   When did it happen?

   Where did it happen?

   How did it happen?

   Why did it happen?

   Who else was involved in it?

   How did I feel about it and what was the reflection?

   I had the most embarrassing experience when I _____

   _____

   _____

   _____

   _____

   _____

   _____

   _____

   _____

   _____

2. 題目：A Trip with my Family

主題句：My family and I went on a trip to _____ last summer vacation.

【提示】

Where did I go on the trip?

When did I have the trip?

With whom did I go on the trip?

What did I do during the trip?

What was the highlight of the trip?

How did I feel after the trip?

My family and I went on a trip to _____ last summer vacation.

_____

_____

_____

_____

_____

_____

_____

_____

# ⑤ Descriptive Essay 描寫文

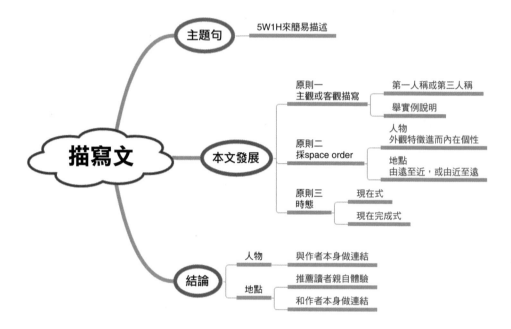

主題句 ── 5W1H來簡易描述

本文發展
- 原則一 主觀或客觀描寫
  - 第一人稱或第三人稱
  - 舉實例說明
- 原則二 採space order
  - 人物 外觀特徵進而內在個性
  - 地點 由遠至近，或由近至遠
- 原則三 時態
  - 現在式
  - 現在完成式

結論
- 人物 ── 與作者本身做連結
- 地點
  - 推薦讀者親自體驗
  - 和作者本身做連結

| 主題句 | 原則 | 描寫文可能描寫人物、物品、或地點，所以應該一針見血般的點出該篇文章要描寫的主角（人或物品或地點），輔以簡單敘述主角特徵，可用 5W1H 來簡易描述。同樣地，盡量用一句話表達即可。 |
|---|---|---|
| 本文發展 | 原則一 | 主觀或客觀描寫 |
| | 說明 | 可用第一人稱或第三人稱來描寫，力求具體生動，擅用形容詞及譬喻法（隱喻及明喻）並舉實例說明，目的使讀者能在閱讀文章時，腦中能浮現該主題的影像。描寫人物時，能刻畫人物的肖像、言語、行為、心理活動及生活細節；而描寫地點時，可透過感官去描寫刻劃出畫面。 |
| | 原則二 | 採 space order |
| | 說明 | 就描寫順序而言，描寫人物時，可由人物的外觀特徵進而描寫人物的內在個性、特殊習慣（癖好）等等，或由內在特點描寫進而描寫外在特點；至於描寫風景／地點時，可由遠至近，或由近至遠，及由局部著手慢慢擴大範圍。特別注意：在描寫時，需挑值得一讀的特點來陳述，而不是類似流水帳一樣，或樣樣都要寫到。 |
| | 原則三 | 現在式 |
| | 說明 | 時態選擇上，盡量以現在式（現在簡單式或現在完成式）為主，但如果有舉以前發生的事情為例，來加強讀者印象，則可以輔以過去式。 |
| 結論 | 原則 | 若是描寫人物，可於結論段與作者本身做連結，如：影響、情感等的敘寫；若是描寫地點，可就此一地點（景點）值得一遊之處，推薦讀者不仿親自體驗，或是將此一地點和作者本身情感上、影響上做連結等等。 |

請依下面所提供的文字提示寫一篇英文作文，長度約 120 字（8 至 12 個句子）。作文可以是一個完整的段落，也可以分段。

提示：幾乎每個人都有一位最好的朋友，你對他／她想必也相當了解，現在請就你這位最好朋友的外表加以描寫，之後，再對其內在特質做一番陳述。

## 腦力激盪擬大綱

| 主題句 | Ronnie is my best friend, who looks like an athlete and has many good personality traits. |
|---|---|
| 支持句 1 | has short spiky hair<br>is near-sighted<br>has a big nose<br>a health-conscious person; takes regular exercise |
| 支持句 2 | optimistic and easygoing<br>ready to help<br>has a talent for cooking |
| 結論句 | I like to hang around with Ronnie, due to his good sense of humor, excellent cooking, and most important of all, his kindness. |

## 範文

### My Best Friend

**Ronnie is my best friend, who looks like an athlete and has many good personality traits.** My best friend has short spiky hair which he has to style every morning. Near-sighted as he is, Ronnie seldom wears glasses; therefore, he often mistakes people. His big nose makes his face more striking. As a health-conscious person, Ronnie likes to take regular exercise at his leisure time, such as basketball and tennis, to keep in good shape. It is because he loves outdoor activities that his tanned skin earns him a nickname "Sunny Boy."

Ronnie is always willing to lend a helping hand. For example, whenever I get into trouble, he helps me out. Besides, he is humorous and good at cooking. We often laugh out loud because of his jokes and eat too much due to the hearty meals he prepares for us. In my opinion, he does have a talent for cooking. I always say half-jokingly that his fabulous cooking skills have already won many girls' hearts, not to mention his gentleness in getting along with people. **I like to hang around with Ronnie due to his good sense of humor, excellent cooking, and most important of all, his kindness.**

參考單字：

| | |
|---|---|
| personality 個性 (C) | striking 明顯的 (adj) |
| trait 特質 (C) | health-conscious 注重健康的 (adj) |
| spiky hair 刺蝟造型頭髮 (U) | nickname 綽號 (C) |
| near-sighted 近視的 (adj) | hearty 豐盛的 (adj) |

### 範文翻譯

　　Ronnie 是我最好的朋友，他看來像一位運動員並有許多好的特質。我的最好朋友他有短短的刺蝟頭，每天早上都需造型一番。雖然他近視，但 Ronnie 不太常戴眼鏡；因此，他常認錯人。他的大鼻子讓他的五官更明顯。很注重健康的他，喜歡在空閒時規律運動，如：籃球和網球，來保持身材。就是因為他喜歡戶外活動，他的古銅色的皮膚為他贏得「陽光男孩」的綽號。

　　Ronnie 總是樂意幫人。每當我陷入麻煩，他總是幫忙脫困。除此之外，他也很幽默並善於煮菜。我們常因為他的笑話而哈哈大笑，也因為他煮的豐盛大餐而常吃太多。他真的對烹飪有很天分。我總是半開玩笑地說他的好廚藝已經贏得許多女孩的心，更不用說是他對人的親切。我喜歡和 Ronnie 一起，因為他的幽默感、好廚藝，更重要的是，他的好心腸。

1. 主題句：Ronnie is my best friend, who looks like an athlete and has many good personality traits.

   （以 athlete 運動員來大概形容外表；內在則寫出他有許多好的人格特質）

2. 結論句：I like to hang around with Ronnie due to his good sense of humor, excellent cooking, and most important of all, his kindness.

   （感想：呼應主題句，並綜合整篇大意，用換句話說的方式做結論）

3. 轉承詞：therefore, for example, besides , in my opinion

4. 寫作脈絡：由外至內

   由外：（從上到下）從頭髮 ⇨ 眼睛（近視）⇨ 鼻子 ⇨ 臉上膚色 ⇨ 綽號

   至內：熱心、幽默、烹飪技術、和善客氣

5. 主題句與段落發展呼應實例：

   以 short spiky hair、likes to take exercise、tanned skin 、Sunny Boy 來支持主題句（Ronnie looks like an athlete）。

   以 lend a helping hand, ready to help me out, humorous, talent for cooking, gentleness 來支持主題句（He has many good personality traits.）

6. 多利用同義字字典：lend a helping hand ≒ help me out; jokes ≒ humorous/a good sense of humor; fabulous ≒ excellent; gentleness ≒ kindness; get along with ≒ hang around

7. 實例使讀者印象深刻，不流於空談：

   Ronnie seldom wears glasses ⇨ he often mistakes people.

   a health-conscious person ⇨ take regular exercise

   humorous ⇨ we often laugh out loud

   a talent for cooking ⇨ we eat too much

以下提供描寫人事物常用的形容詞：

| | |
|---|---|
| 人的外表 | good-looking, gorgeous, beautiful, pretty, handsome,「長得好看」；attractive「吸引人的」=appealing；cute, lovable, adorable「可愛的」；elegant「優雅的」；slim, slender「瘦的」；skinny, bony「骨瘦如材的」；chubby「嬰兒肥的」；swarthy「黝黑的」；fair「皮膚白皙的」；curly「捲髮的」；blonde「金髮的」… |
| 人的個性 | kind「仁慈的」；generous「慷慨的」；honest「誠實的」；mean「尖酸刻薄的」；stingy「小氣的」；active「積極的」；positive「正向積極的」；negative「消極的」；extrovert「外向的」；introvert「內向的」；quiet「沉默的」；talkative「多話的」；outspoken「直言無諱的」；energetic「精力充沛的」；ambitious「有野心的」；easygoing「隨和的」；creative「有創造力的」；humorous「幽默的」；funny「好笑的」；patient「有耐心的」；diligent/hard-working「努力勤勉的」；optimistic「樂觀的」；pessimistic「悲觀的」；naughty「頑皮的」… |
| 人的情緒 | sad「傷心的」；frustrated/depressed「沮喪的」；disappointed「失望的」；surprised/ amazed/stunned「驚訝的」；confused「困惑的」；tired/exhausted「疲累的」；embarrassed「尷尬的」；satisfied「滿意的」；dismayed/frightened/horrified「嚇壞的」；worried「擔心的」；annoyed/upset/furious/outraged「憤怒的」… |
| 價格 | expensive/exorbitant/costly/overpriced「昂貴的」；inexpensive「不貴的」；cheap「便宜的」；priceless/valuable/invaluable「無價的」；worthless/valueless「沒價值的」… |
| 天氣 | hot/scorching (hot)「炎熱的」；warm「溫暖的」；mild「和煦的」；cool「涼爽的」；cold/freezing/chilly「寒冷的」；breezy「有微風的」；hazy「煙霧迷漫的」；damp/humid「潮濕的」；muggy「悶熱的」；stuffy「悶的」；windy「多風的」；cloudy「多雲的」；snowy「多雪的」；rainy「多雨的」… |
| 交通 | congested「壅擠的」；smooth「順暢的」；slow「慢的」；heavy「流量大的」… |

| 食物料理方式 | steamed「蒸的」；stir-fried「炒的」；deep-fried「炸的」；boiled「水煮的」；smoked「煙燻的」；baked「烘培的」；barbecued「烤的」；marinated「滷的」；pickled「醃漬的」；roasted「（烤箱）烤的」；stewed「燉煮的」… |
| --- | --- |
| 食物味道 | spicy「辣的」；sweet「甜的」；bitter「苦的」；sour「酸的」；tasty/delicious「美味的」；tasteless「沒味道的」；salty「鹹的」；juicy「多汁的」；greasy「油膩的」… |
| 景色 | breath-taking/amazing「驚人的」；beautiful, picturesque, fantastic, splendid, impressive, attractive, appealing, marvelous「漂亮的 / 壯麗的」 |
| 建築物 | splendid/magnificent/imposing「壯麗的」；century-old/ancient「古老的」；historic「歷史上有意義的；古老的」；unique「獨特的」；memorial「紀念的」；high-rise「高聳的」；modern「現代的」；shabby/crumbling「破爛的」；jerry-built「偷工減料的」… |
| 植物 | evergreen「常綠的」；verdant「翠綠的」；withered「枯萎的」 |
| 名氣 | be famous for/be renowned for/be well-known for/ be distinguished for「出名的」；notorious/infamous「惡名昭彰的」；unsung hero「無名英雄」；mediocre「平庸的」… |
| 速度 | fast, speedy, rapid, swift「快速的」；snail-paced, sluggish, dilatory, tardy「慢的」 |
| 值得 | be worth＋N/Ving, be worthy of N, It is worthwhile that S＋V/to V |

以下提供描寫事物常用的動詞：

| 坐落於… | 主動寫法：stand, lie, sit；被動寫法：be located/situated ＋介系詞（in, at, on…） |
| --- | --- |
| 認為 | be regarded as, be viewed as, be referred to as, be thought of as；be seen as, be considered (to be), be thought ＋補語 |
| 扮演…的角色 | play a/an (vital/crucial/significant/key/important/essential) role/part in |
| 吸引 | attract, appeal to, captivate, enchant, enthrall |
| 命名 | be named；be recognized as「公認為」 |

| （因）導致（果） | lead to, bring about, give rise to, result in, contribute to |
|---|---|
| （果）起於（因） | result from, arise from, be derived from, |
| 以…為特色 | feature；characterize；represent；be typical of（為…典型） |

以下提供描寫人常用的動詞：

| 各種吃 | gobble「狼吞虎嚥」=pig out；gulp「大口喝或吃」；nibble「小口吃」；eat in「在家吃」；eat out「外出吃」；chew「咀嚼」；eat like a bird「胃口小」 |
|---|---|
| 各種看 | see「一般的看（無刻意看）」；watch「看動態的人或物」；look at=stare at=gaze at「盯著看」；glance/glimpse「匆匆一瞥」；peep/peek「偷看」；glare「瞪眼看」；glower「怒目而視」；disdain「輕蔑地看」；scrutinize「仔細地察看」；leer「色迷迷地斜眼看」 |
| 各種笑 | smile「微笑」；laugh「大笑」；simper「傻笑」；giggle「咯咯地笑」；smirk「得意地笑」；roar「哄堂大笑」；chuckle「輕笑」；guffaw「狂笑」；grin「露齒而笑」 |
| 各種哭 | weep「無聲地流淚」；snivel「邊哭邊吸鼻涕」；whine「哀鳴」；lament「慟哭哀悼」；blubber「又哭又鬧」；sob「嗚咽」；wail「哀嚎、慟哭流涕」 |
| 各種走 | hobble「因為腳傷而吃力地走」= limp；wander「漫無目的地走」；swagger「大搖大擺，很驕傲地走」= strut；clump「大力踩地並發出聲響地走」；tiptoe「躡手躡腳地走」；wade「涉水（泥）而走」；stroll, amble, saunter「散步」 |
| 各種跑 | run「快跑」；jog「慢跑」；dart, dash「衝」；scamper「奔馳」；scuttle, sprout「急速移動」 |
| 各種喝 | drink「一般的喝」；sip「啜飲」；guzzle「暴飲暴食」，與 gulp 意思相近；imbibe 則是一正式用字，通常是指「喝酒」，亦可用於幽默用語。 |
| 各種睡 | fall asleep「睡著」；feel sleepy「想睡」；take a nap「午睡」；doze off=nod off=drowse「打瞌睡」；sleep like a log/baby「睡的很熟」 |
| 各種偷 | steal「偷」；rob「搶」；pick one's pocket「扒竊」；burglarize/break into「進屋行竊」；swindle=defraud「詐騙」；shoplift「商店行竊」… |

| 各種運動 | surf「衝浪」; go snorkeling「浮潛」; ski「滑雪」; roller-skate「溜直排輪」; rock-climb「攀岩」; do yoga「瑜珈」; play basketball/baseball/tennis/table tennis/badminton/golf/soccer/snooker |
|---|---|
| 各種寫／畫 | scribble「潦草地書寫」; outline「寫出大綱」; jot down「快速寫下」; sketch「畫草圖」; oil paint「油畫」 |

以下提供描寫人常用的名詞：

| 職業 | doctor「醫生」; lawyer「律師」; teacher「老師」; professor「教授」; civil servant「公務員」; businessman「商人」; entrepreneur「企業家」; mailman「郵差」; soldier「士兵」; police officer「警察」; truck driver「卡車司機」; taxi driver「計程車司機」; chef「主廚」; cook「廚師」; bank clerk「銀行行員」; worker「工人」; artist「藝術家」; politician「政客」; (fruit) famer「農夫」; sculptor「雕刻家」; scientist「科學家」; actor「演員」; athlete「運動家」; miner「礦工」; magician「魔術師」; vet「獸醫」; manager「經理」; writer「作家」; cashier「出納人員」; fashion designer「時尚設計師」; vendor「小販」; firefighter「消防員」; mechanic「技師」; model「模特兒」; coach「教練」; accountant「會計師」; critic「評論者」; reporter「記者」 |
|---|---|
| 社會階級 | middle-class「中產階級」; upper class「上流社會」; the underprivileged「下層社會」; blue collar「藍領階級」; white collar「白領階級」; pink collar「粉領階級」 |
| 毛髮 | straight hair「直髮」; curly hair「捲髮」; flattop/crew cut「平頭」; perm「燙髮」; central parting「中分」; side parting「旁分」; dyed/colored hair「染髮」; highlights「挑染」; bang「瀏海」; bald「禿頭」; wig「假髮」; goatie「山羊鬍」; mustache「鬍子（人中）」; beard「鬍子（下巴）」; sideburns「鬢角」 |
| 個性 | genius「天才」; geek/nerd「書呆子」; neat freak「潔癖者」; oddball「怪胎」; otaku「宅男」; coward「膽小鬼」; dog-lover「愛狗人士」; prodigal「揮霍者」; miser「吝嗇鬼」 |

| | |
|---|---|
| 疾病<br>（症狀） | cold「感冒」；running nose「流鼻水」；fever「發燒」；cough「咳嗽」；sneeze「打噴嚏」；itching skin「皮膚癢」；indigestion「消化不良」；hypertension「高血壓」；headache「頭痛」；migraine「偏頭痛」；asthma「氣喘」；diabetes「糖尿病」；chest pain「胸痛」；mouth ulcer/canker「嘴破洞」；backache「背痛」；sprained ankle「扭到腳」；diarrhea「拉肚子」；stroke「中風」；heart attack「心臟病」；blister「水泡」；constipation「便祕」 |
| 興趣 | 室內：movie-watching「看電影」；yoga「瑜珈」；flower arranging「插花」；ice skating「溜冰」；drawing, painting「繪畫」；calligraphy「書法」<br>室外：bird-watching「賞鳥」；cycling「騎腳踏車」；kayaking「皮艇」；canoeing「獨木舟」；mountaineering「登山」；paintball「漆彈」；scuba diving「淺水」；surfing「衝浪」；snorkeling「浮淺」；windsurfing「風帆衝浪」 |

※ 以上僅列出一般常見的字詞，若讀者想查詢中文字詞的英文怎麼說，可善加利用 google，除了一般線上英漢字典會有解答外，網誌或部落格也會有機會找到需要的英文說法。

步驟：

❶ 鍵入中文，例如："雙眼皮" ＋ 翻譯；"雙眼皮" ＋ 英文；或 "雙眼皮" ＋ English。

❷ 如果有找到英文，請於具權威的英英字典或英漢字典，做確認。

❸ 倘若，以上方法找不到，我們可以在中文後加一些英文關鍵字，例如：鼻屎 ＋ nose（因為與鼻子相關）；迷彩服 ＋ uniform（因為迷彩服為軍人的制服）等等。

❹ 相同地，一找到可能的英文說法，都需要再次確認其正確性。

 **牛刀小試** 請依據所給的題目與主題句發展一篇文章,並請將文章上傳
至本書前言中所列之作文評改網站

1. 題目:The Best Gift that I Have ever Received

   主題句:The best gift I have ever received is _____ as my eighteenth birthday gift from _____.

   【提示】

   What is the gift?

   Who gave it to me?

   Why did I receive the gift?

   What is the appearance of it?

   What are the functions of it?

   Did anything unforgettable happen with it?

   What does it mean to me?

   The best gift I have ever received is _____ as my eighteenth birthday gift from _____. _____

   _____

   _____

   _____

   _____

   _____

   _____

   _____

   _____

   _____

2. 題目：My Senior High School

主題句：My senior high school is _____, which is located in
_____ and famous for its _____.

【提示】

What is my senior high school?

Where is it?

Begin to describe it from the school gate, playground, buildings, Student Activity Center, etc.

Describe some personal memorable experiences with it.

My senior high school is _____, which is located in _____
and famous for its _____. _____

_____

_____

_____

_____

_____

_____

_____

_____

_____

## 6 Compare or contrast 比較性文章

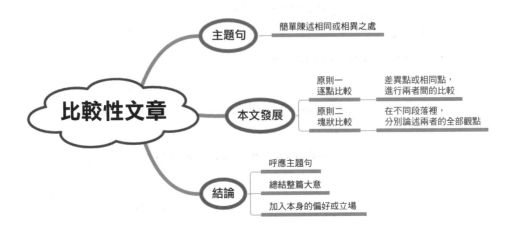

| 前言 | | 在寫主題句之前，先要弄清楚何謂 compare？何謂 contrast？所謂的 compare 是在比較兩者間的相同或類似之處；contrast 則是比較兩者間的差異之處。因此，第一步驟的審題就格外重要。比較時，可以將不同的人與人相比、不同的物與物相比、不同的事件與事件相比；或者，同一個人、物、事件的不同面向相比。不過，通常以不同的人、事、物相比的文章比較常見。 |
|---|---|---|
| 主題句 | 原則 | 開場白需達吸引讀者的功能，簡單陳述內文要比較的兩個人（或事或物）在哪些方面的相同或相異之處。 |
| | 說明 | 茲以「智慧型手機」與「傳統型手機」相比：<br>There are three differences between smartphones and traditional cellphones, that is, functions, sizes and shatterness. |

| | | |
|---|---|---|
| 本文發展本文發展 | 原則一 | 逐點比較：針對所列的差異（或相同點），進行兩者間的比較。 |
| | 說明 | 如：<br><br>| functions | smartphones<br>vs.<br>traditional cellphones |<br>| sizes | smartphones<br>vs.<br>traditional cellphones |<br>| shatterness | smartphones<br>vs.<br>traditional cellphones |<br><br>在 functions 這段裡，敘述智慧型手機和傳統型手機的功能上的差異；以此類推，尺寸、耐摔論點中，討論兩者的差異。 |
| | 原則二 | 塊狀比較：在不同段落裡，分別論述兩者的全部觀點。 |
| | 說明 | 如：<br><br>| smartphones | functions |<br>| | sizes |<br>| | shatterness |<br>| traditional cellphones | functions |<br>| | sizes |<br>| | shatterness |<br><br>在智慧型手機這段，將功能、尺寸、耐摔的特點全部敘述；同樣道理，在傳統型手機這段，論敘其功能、尺寸、耐摔。 |
| 結論 | 原則 | 結論段可呼應主題句、總結整篇大意，或加入本身的偏好或立場。 |

請依下面所提供的文字提示寫一篇英文作文,長度約 120 字(8 至 12 個句子)。作文可以是一個完整的段落,也可以分段。

提示:現代人幾乎人手一機,年輕人偏愛智慧型手機,但老一輩的人,有些還是選擇傳統型手機,有接聽電話功能即可,現在請就智慧型手機與傳統型手機作一比較。

## 腦力激盪擬大綱

| 主題句 | There are three differences between smartphones and traditional cellphones, that is, functions, sizes and shatterness. |
|---|---|
| 支持句 1 | smartphones feature far more functions... |
| 支持句 2 | traditional cellphones'smaller sizes... |
| 支持句 3 | traditional cellphones can bear much more impact... |
| 結論句 | In a nutshell, even with the repair cost and handiness drawbacks, I, as a smart user, still prefer smartphones due to their wide varieties of functions and entertainment. |

## 範文

### Traditional Cellphones and Smartphones

**There are three differences between smartphones and traditional cellphones, that is, functions, sizes and shatterness.**

First, unlike traditional cellphones mainly used to make a phone call, smartphones feature far more functions such as Internet, flashlight, GPS, map, and even remote control. People regard the smartphone as a small personal computer and download any applications they need. Second, traditional cellphones' smaller sizes make them easy to put in the pocket and handy to use. By contrast, smartphones, nowadays, boast larger screen sizes for video watching and Internet browsing. Bigger sizes though they have for entertainment, they can take up too much space and most of the time have to be put in the bag. Last, as for shatterness, it is commonly known that the traditional cellphone can bear much more impact than its counterpart. More specifically, smartphones are easy to break and, what is worse, the repair fee is often costly. It turns out that users may replace it with a new one.

**In a nutshell, even with the repair cost and handiness drawbacks, I, as a smart user, still prefer smartphones due to their wide varieties of functions and entertainment.**

---

參考單字：

| | |
|---|---|
| function 功能 (C) | entertainment 娛樂 (U) |
| shatterness 耐摔 (U) | impact 撞擊 / 衝擊 (C) |
| feature 以⋯為特色 (vt) | counterpart 與⋯對比之物或人 |
| application 行動裝置的應用程式 (C) | drawback 缺點 (C) |
| boast 擁有⋯為豪 | |

---

### 範文翻譯

　　智慧型手機和傳統型手機有三個不同點，也就是：功能、尺寸、和耐摔度。首先，智慧型手機，不像傳統型手機主要用來打電話，有著更多的功能，例如：網路、手電筒、衛星定位、地圖，甚至是遙控。人們將智慧手機視為是一台小型個人電腦，並下載所需之應用程式。第二，傳統型手機的小尺寸讓其輕易地放入口袋並輕便使用。對比之下，當今的智慧型手機擁有利於觀賞影片及上網的大尺寸螢幕。雖然它們有用來娛樂的大尺寸，但是他也占掉太多空間，大部分時間也只能放在包包內。最後，至於耐摔性，一般都認為傳統型手機比起對手還耐摔。更明確而言，智慧型手機容易壞，更糟糕的是，維修費還不便宜。最後使用者往往乾脆換一支新手機。

　　總而言之，即便是維修費用高及體積大不方便，但，身為一個聰明使用者，我還是會因為智慧型手機的多功能和娛樂性而選擇它。

### 文章分析

1. 主題句：There are three differences between smartphones and traditional cellphones, that is, functions, sizes and shatterness.

（主題句即開門見山點出智慧型手機與傳統型手機在於功能、尺寸、耐摔度上的差別。）

2. 結論段：In a nutshell, even with some drawbacks, I, as a smart user, still prefer smartphones due to their wide variety of functions.

（結論段點出作者的偏好和偏好的原因。）

3. 轉承詞：that is, first, second, by contrast, nowadays, last, as for, more specifically, what is worse, in a nutshell

4. 實例：

功能上，智慧型手機優於傳統型：Internet, flashlight, GPS, and even map

尺寸上：傳統型方便攜帶；智慧型娛樂為主

耐摔上：傳統型很耐摔；智慧型不耐摔，且維修貴

---

溫馨提醒

比較與對比時，常用之片語及句型

| Compare | Contrast |
|---|---|
| Both A and B ... | Unlike A, B ... |
| Just as A ..., so B ... | A is different from B |
| A ... and so ... B. | A differs from B |
| A ... and B ..., too. | A is not as ... as B ... |
| Like A, B ... | In contrast, B ... |
| A is similar to B | A has ...; however, B has |
| A is as ... as B | A is more ... than B |
| A vt/vi as ... as B | By contrast, A ... |
| B also has ... | On the contrary, A ... |
| A ...; similarly, B ... | Neither A nor B has ... |
| A ...; likewise, B ... | Although A ..., B ... |
| A is the same as B | A ..., but B ... |
| There are some similarities between A and B. | A ... whereas/yet B ... |
|  | A ...; on the other hand, B ... |
|  | There are some differences between A and B. |

★ Just as A ..., so B .... （正如……，……亦……）

    ⇨ Just as some animals are social amimals, so human beings need friends and family.

正如一些動物是群居動物，人也一樣，需要朋友和家人。

★ A ... and so ... B. （A……，B 也是……）

    ⇨ I hate people who don't clean up after their dog, and so does Watt.

我討厭那些不幫自己的狗清理大便的人，Watt 也是。

★ Like A, B .... （正如 A 一樣，B 也……）

    ⇨ Like Apple, which has its Apple Store, Android has Play for users to download applications.

正如蘋果有 Apple Store，安卓也有 Play 商店給使用者下載 app。

★ A is as ... as B. （A 與 B 一樣……）

    ⇨ A tiger cub is sometimes as ferocious as an adult one.

小老虎有時也會和成年老虎一樣兇猛。

★ A vt/vi as ... as B. （A 與 B 一樣……）

    ⇨ This supercar can run as fast as a bullet train.

這台超跑可以跑得和子彈列車一樣快。

★ A is similar to B. （A 和 B 相似）

    ⇨ Carl is similar to his brother in many ways, such as the way they eat and sleep.

Carl 和他哥哥有很多相似點，例如吃飯和睡覺方式。

★ A ...; likewise, B .... （A……；相同地，B……）

    ⇨ Alisa didn't feel happy after the breakup; likewise, her ex-boyfriend felt depressed.

Alisa 在分手後不快樂；相同地，她前男友也很沮喪。

★ There are some similarities between A and B.（A 和 B 有一些相似點）

⇨ There are some similarities between birds and airplanes, for example, the way they glide.

鳥類和飛機有些相似點，例如他們在空中滑翔方式。

★ Unlike A, B ....（不同於 A，B……）

⇨ Unlike most animals, primates can use tools to do many things.

不同於很多動物，靈長類動物會用工具做很多事。

★ A differs from B.（A 不同於 B）

⇨ Living with parents greatly differs from living on one's own.

與父母同住是相當不同於自己獨自生活。

★ In contrast, B ....（對比之下，B……）

⇨ My father is a quiet person; in contrast, my mother is talkative.

我爸是個沉默寡言的人，對比之下，我媽就顯得愛講話。

★ Neither A nor B has ....（A 與 B 皆不……）

⇨ Neither Athen nor Billy lived up to their boss' expectations, so they couldn't get the bonus this year.

Athen 與 Billy 皆沒有達到老闆期望，所以他們今年沒有獎金可領。

★ A ... whereas/yet B ....（A……然而 B……）

⇨ Criticizing others is one thing, whereas offering constructive suggestions is another.

批評別人是一回事，但能夠提出有建設性的建議又是另一回事。

★ A ...; on the other hand, B ....（A……；另一方面，B……）

⇨ Living in a big city is convenient; on the other hand, the cost of living is one thing that you should take into consideration.

住在大都是很便利沒錯，但另一方面而言，生活費也是你該列入考慮的。

 **牛刀小試** 請依據所給的題目與主題句發展一篇文章，並請將文章上傳至本書前言中所列之作文評改網站

1. 題目：Living in Cities vs. in the Country

   主題句：There are three differences between living in cities and in the country: convenience, job opportunities, and air quality.

   【提示】

   論點 1：from convenience and inconvenience

   論點 2：from the number of job opportunities

   論點 3：from good and bad air quality

    

   There are several differences between living in cities and in the country: convenience, job opportunities, and air quality. _____

   _____

   _____

   _____

   _____

   _____

   _____

   _____

   _____

   _____

   _____

2. 題目：My Best Friend and I

   主題句：There are some similarities between my best friend and me.

   【提示】

   論點 1：Speaking of personality,

   論點 2：When it comes to interests,

   論點 3：Besides, we share the same religion.

   There are some similarities between my best friend and me. _____

   _____

   _____

   _____

   _____

   _____

   _____

   _____

   _____

## ❼ Picture Writing  看圖寫作

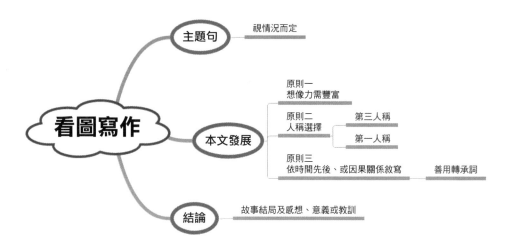

| 前言 | | 圖片寫作可分為：(1) 單張圖片寫作、(2) 三張連環漫畫、(3) 四張連環漫畫，但第四張為空白，須自行想像故事結局。主題句的提供與否不一定，但整篇故事基本上都是以記敘文或描寫文書寫，另外，有時題目會要求第二段對此事件論述，此時就可用議論文的寫作原則來書寫。 |
|---|---|---|
| **主題句** | 原則 | **視情況而定** |
| | 說明 | 當題目有提供時，最好不過；但若題目沒有提供，此時就使用記敘文主題句的寫作原則：5W1H 精簡表達此事件或故事的人物、地點、時間等等。 |
| **本文發展** | 原則一 | **想像力需豐富** |
| | 說明 | 想像力在圖片寫作中扮演相當重要的角色，盡量用豐富想像力，很有邏輯地將圖片中的細節交代清楚，從最開始的開頭，到故事中間發展（需有高潮點），至結尾，要求故事前後連貫。 |
| | 原則二 | **人稱選擇** |
| | 說明 | 可為故事主角命名，此時為第三人稱敘寫；亦可用第一人稱，讓讀者有身歷其境的感覺。 |

| 本文發展 | 原則三 | 依時間先後、或因果關係敘寫 |
|---|---|---|
| | 說明 | 依照圖片發展的先後順序，將故事的情節依續發展；有時故事會比較偏重於因果關係的發展，但不管是哪種方式，都需要善用轉承詞，特別是：「時間方面」的轉承詞和「因此」系列的轉承詞。 |
| 結論 | 原則 | 故事結局及感想 |
| | 說明 | 在結論段中，除了帶出故事結局外，另外可以提及整個事件的感想、帶來的意義或教訓等等。 |

**說明**

請依下面所提供的文字提示寫一篇英文作文，長度約 120 字（8 至 12 個句子）。作文可以是一個完整的段落，也可以分段。

提示：請觀察以下三張漫畫，依故事先後發展並有邏輯地並寫成一篇文章，可給予故事中人物名字。

## 腦力激盪擬大綱

| 主題句 | One day, Bella, as usual, said goodbye to his son and then started to do the housework. |
|---|---|
| 支持句 1 | enjoy the lovely afternoon |
| 支持句 2 | telephone rang; frightened; pay the ransom |
| 支持句 3 | wire the kidnappers the ransom<br>enjoy ice cream with his classmates |
| 結論句 | From this experience, Bella learned a precious lesson that she has to think twice before doing anything important and be cautious of any suspicious calls from fraudsters. |

請根據以下三張連環漫畫，描述故事主角所經歷的過程，並提供合理解釋與結局。

1                2                3

**範文**

**One day**, **Bella, as usual, said goodbye to his son and** then **started to do the housework.** In the afternoon, she brewed herself a cup of coffee, reading magazines and enjoying the lovely afternoon. All of a sudden, the telephone rang. Answering the phone, she was frightened to death because the man said, "We kidnapped your son. If you want him back, pay the ransom right away and never call the police…." Bella easily believed what the man said because she heard a boy crying in the background and yelling, "Mom, help me! It hurts so badly."

Without making sure if her son was really taken, Bella went to the nearest ATM, ready to wire the kidnappers the ransom. As soon as she finished the money transferring, much to her surprise, she saw her son walking by and enjoying ice cream with his classmates. Bella immediately ran to her son, telling what had happened today.

**From this experience, Bella learned a precious lesson that she has to think twice before doing anything important and be cautious of any suspicious calls from fraudsters.**

| 參考單字： | | |
| --- | --- | --- |
| kidnap 綁架 (vt) | background 背景 (C) | suspicious 可疑的 (adj) |
| ransom 贖金 (C) | wire 匯款 (vt) | fraudster 詐騙者 (C) |

**範文翻譯**

有一天，Bella 一如往常般和她兒子說再見後，開始做家事。下午時，她幫自己泡了杯咖啡，看看雜誌，享受悠閒的下午時光。突然間，電話鈴響了。接了電

話後，她嚇死了，因為對方說：「我們綁架了妳的兒子。如果妳想要他平安回去，就必須付贖金，不准報警……」。Bella 輕易地相信對方說的話，因為她在背景聽到小孩哭聲並大叫：「媽媽救我。痛死我了」。

沒有確認是否兒子遭綁架，Bella 跑去最近的自動提款機，準備匯贖金給歹徒。正當她匯完款，讓她十分驚訝的是，她看到她兒子和同學邊走邊吃冰淇淋。Bella 馬上跑去她兒子那邊，並告訴他今天所發生的一切。

從這次經驗，Bella 學到了寶貴的一課，也就是：在做任何重要事之前，要三思而後行，並且小心任何詐騙集團的可疑電話。

## 文章分析

1. 主題句：One day, Bella, as usual, said goodbye to his son and then started to do the housework.

   （這句主題句點出了整篇文章的人物、時間、地點。）

2. 結論段：From this experience, Bella learned a precious lesson that she has to think twice before doing anything important and be cautious of any suspicious calls from fraudsters.

   （提及整個事件所帶來的教訓、和意義。）

3. 轉承詞：one day, then, in the afternoon, all of a sudden, much to her surprise

4. 直接引述增加讀者臨場感："We kidnapped your son. If you want him back, pay the ransom and never call the police...." 及 "Mom, help me! It hurts so badly."

5. 多利用同義字字典：ransom ≒ money; right away ≒ immediately; kidnapped ≒ taken; money transferring ≒ wiring the money

## 溫馨提醒

直接引述句型：（請注意標點符號的使用）

1. Derek said, "When will you pay my money back?"

2. "Step aside, "yelled Gill, "or you'll get hurt."

3. The leaflet reads, "Buy two and get one free."

4. "Ten passengers had been dead before the ambulance came to the scene," says the police.（故事、新聞常用）

5. "Get my armor and horse ready," the prince said.

6. The weather bureau warned, "There is going to be a super typhoon coming toward Taiwan tomorrow evening."

 請依據所給的題目發展一篇文章，並請將文章上傳至本書前言中所列之作文評改網站

1.

_____

_____

_____

_____

_____

_____

_____

_____

_____

2. 請自行想像故事發展的結局

1

2

3

4

?

_____

_____

_____

_____

_____

_____

_____

_____

## ⑧ Autobiography 自傳

| 前言 | | 1. 言簡意賅（最好不要超過一張 A4）<br>2. 從實陳述（不可誇大不實）<br>3. 仔細校稿 |
|---|---|---|
| 第一段 | 內容 | 1. 生長背景<br>2. 家庭成員<br>3. 個性、興趣（凸顯積極向上） |
| 第二段 | 內容 | 大學課內表現：<br>1. 求學階段學業表現<br>2. 專長（專業能力）<br>3. 特殊表現（得獎事蹟） |
| 第三段 | 內容 | 大學課外表現：⇨ 連結未來職場工作<br>1. 社團經驗與收穫和成長<br>2. 幹部經驗與收穫和成長<br>3. 打工經驗與收穫和成長 |
| 結論 | 內容 | 個人短期、長期的生涯期許及展望。 |

**說明**

請依下面所提供的文字提示寫一篇英文作文，長度約 120 字（8 至 12 個句子）。作文可以是一個完整的段落，也可以分段。

提示：假設你／妳現在是大學剛畢業的新鮮人，想找一份工作，根據大學所學、各項表現，並設定對方的公司或工廠，寫一份自傳。

Dear Mr. Huang:

My name is Liu Yixuan. I was born into a family and my parents run a shoes factory in Taichung. Therefore, since my childhood, I have developed a growing interest in business; besides, because of my outgoing personality, I am also good at public relationship.

I graduated from the Department of Business Administration, National Taiwan University of Science and Technology. During my college years, I always stayed in top three academically and graduated with honors. In addition to my major, English was chosen as my minor because it is an essential communication tool in my future business career. Taking part in the national English speech contest, I won third prize, which greatly boosted my confidence in English.

As for extracurricular activities, I joined a fund-raising contest, in which participants had to design a project to raise as much money as possible. I finished first. Furthermore, serving others or lending a helping hand is always much fun for me. I was elected as the leader of the student's union and volunteered for some charities.

To sum up, with all mentioned above, I deeply believe I can make contributions to your company as a staff member if I have the honor to be employed. More importantly, I will certainly work as hard as I possibly can and go after the master's degree in MBA in my free time.

Yours sincerely,

Liu Yixuan

參考單字：

| | |
|---|---|
| outgoing 隨和的 (adj) | minor 輔修 (C) |
| academically 學業上地 (adv) | extracurricular 課外的 (adj) |
| graduate with honors 以優異成績畢業 | fund-raising 募款 (adj) |
| major 主修 (C) | contribution 貢獻 (C) |

敬愛的黃先生

我的名字是劉憶萱。我出生於台中，我爸媽經營一家鞋子工廠。因此，從我小時候，我便培養出商業的興趣，此外，也因為我的外向個性，我對公共關係方面很在行。

我畢業於台灣科技大學商管系。大學期間，我的成績總是可以保持前三名，並且以優等成績畢業。除了我的主修外，我也輔修英文，因為英文是我以後商業生涯的重要溝通工具。我曾參加全國的英文演講比賽，並得到第三名，這大大提升我對英文的信心。

至於我的課外活動，我參加過募款比賽，在這比賽中，選手們必須設計一個方案，並盡可能募越多款越好。我得了第一名。另外，服務人群或幫助別人對於我而言一直是非常有趣的。我曾被選為學生會會長，並參與一些慈善團體的義工活動。

總而言之，就上面所提，我深深相信如果我幸運錄取貴公司，一定能做出貢獻。更重要的是，我會盡全力努力工作並且在空閒時間攻讀 MBA 學位。

劉憶萱 敬上

文章分析

1.

| | | |
|---|---|---|
| **第一段** | 姓名 | Liu Yixuan |
| | 家庭 | shoes factory in Taichung |
| | 興趣 | business |
| | 個性 | outgoing |
| **第二段** | 畢業科系學校 | Department of Business Administration, National Taiwan University of Science and Technology |
| | 在學表現 | in top three and graduated with honors |
| | 輔修 | English |
| | 比賽成績 | 3rd place in national English speech contest |

| | | |
|---|---|---|
| 第三段 | 課外活動表現 | 1^st place in a fund-raising contest；leader of the student's union & volunteered for some charities |
| 結論段 | 強調自己未來之貢獻及展望 | make contributions to your company as a staff member；the master's degree in MBA |

2. 善用轉承詞：therefore, since my childhood, besides, in addition to, furthermore, to sum up, more importantly

## 溫馨提醒

1. 常用單字及片語

| 家庭 | extended family（大家庭）, nuclear family（小家庭）, single-parent family（單親家庭）, adoptive family（收養家庭）… |
|---|---|
| 興趣 | painting（繪畫）, hiking（健行）, mountain-climbing（登山）, fishing（釣魚）, gardening（園藝）, singing karaoke（唱卡拉ok）, playing the violin（拉小提琴）, playing sports（運動）, surfing（衝浪）, running a marathon（跑馬拉松）, travelling（旅遊）, cooking（烹飪）, collecting stamps（集郵）… |
| 個性 | outgoing（外向的）, introverted（內向的）, shy（害羞的）, friendly（友善的）, flexible（變通的）, considerate（體貼的）, timid（膽小的）, selfish（自私的）, passionate（熱情的）, broad-minded（心胸寬闊的）, sensitive（敏感的）, naïve（天真的）, humble（謙虛的）, self-centered（自我為中心的）, reliable（可靠的）, ordinary（平凡的）, rational（理性的）, nervous（易緊張的）, punctual（守時的）, talkative（多話的）, humorous（幽默的）… |

| 在學表現 | academic performance（學業表現）, passing grade（及格成績）, on the lower end of the curve（成績吊車尾）, flunked（被當）, get behind（成績落後）, mediocre（平凡的）… |
|---|---|
| 比賽 | story-tellig contest（說故事比賽）, basketball game（籃球比賽）, tennis match（網球比賽）, swimming contest（游泳比賽）, beauty contest（選美比賽）, singing contest（歌唱比賽）, debate contest（辯論比賽）, running race（跑步比賽）, Chinese calligraphy contest（書法比賽）, recital contest（朗讀比賽）, dancing competition（舞蹈比賽）… |
| 名次 | win 1$^{st}$, 2$^{nd}$, 3$^{rd}$ prize, etc; come in 1$^{st}$, 2$^{nd}$, 3$^{rd}$, etc; win 1$^{st}$, 2$^{nd}$, 3$^{rd}$ place, etc; finish 1$^{st}$, 2$^{nd}$, 3$^{rd}$, etc; rank 1$^{st}$, 2$^{nd}$, 3$^{rd}$, etc; win the consolation prize（安慰獎）; come out on top（冠軍） |
| 社團 | English conversation club（英語會話社）, recreation study club（康輔社）, mountain-climbing club（登山社）, photography club（攝影社）, debate club（辯論社）, guitar club（吉他社）, popular dance club（熱舞社）, magic club（魔術社）, drama club（話劇社）, sign language club（手語社）, scouts club（童軍社）, wind instrument club（管樂社）… |

2. 信件的結尾敬詞，信的開頭若是 Dear Sir/Madam（不知對方姓名時），結尾用 Yours faithfully; 若是開頭為 Dear Mr. Gary（有稱謂及姓氏時），結尾用 Yours sincerely。但建議花點時間將對方的姓名找出來，避免用 Dear Sir/Madam 或 To whom it may concern，這樣對方公司才覺得你有尊重他們並用心想得到這份工作。

3. 姓名拼法：可選擇漢語拼音等等，請參考教育部網站：http://crptransfer.moe.gov.tw/

※ 以上僅列出常見字詞，若讀者想查詢更多，請善用 google，至於查詢方法請至本書 "描寫文" 單元中所介紹之步驟。

**牛刀小試** 請依據所給的題目發展一篇文章，並請將文章上傳至本書前言中所列之作文評改網站

請就個人狀況寫一篇申請工作的自傳

_____

_____

_____

_____

_____

_____

_____

_____

_____

## 申請大學

| | | |
|---|---|---|
| 前言 | | 1. 言簡意賅（最好不要超過一張 A4）<br>2. 從實陳述、要有亮點、盡量強調自己與他人的不同點（不可誇大不實）<br>3. 仔細校稿 |
| 第一段 | 內容 | 1. 姓名、生長背景<br>2. 該學校科系、並讚美該科系可為本身培養未來職場能力。 |
| 第二段 | 內容 | 高中、職課內表現：<br>1. 個性、興趣（凸顯積極向上）<br>2. 學業表現<br>4. 專長（專業能力）<br>5. 特殊表現（得獎事蹟） |
| 第三段 | 內容 | 高中職課外表現：⇨ 連結該理想科系<br>1. 社團經驗與收穫和成長<br>2. 幹部經驗與收穫和成長<br>3. 打工經驗與收穫和成長 |
| 結論 | 內容 | 個人短期、長期的生涯期許及展望、並再次讚美該科系可為本身培養未來職場能力，並感謝對方。 |

**說明**

請依下面所提供的文字提示寫一篇英文作文，長度約 120 字（8 至 12 個句子）。作文可以是一個完整的段落，也可以分段。

提示：假設你 / 妳是高三生，考完大考，正準備申請心目中理想的大學，請就高中 / 高職這三年的課業表現及課外表現，請一篇大學申請書。

Dear Professor Edward:

I am writing to apply for the admission to your department.

My name is Huang Bailong. I am a senior at National Changhua Senior High School. I hope to study for a bachelor's degree in Department of Photonics and Optoelectronics at your university. I deeply believe that your program will enable me to sharpen my skills and assist me with both further study and my future career.

I have a wide variety of interests, especially in solar power, computer science and English. Participating in the contest of solar-power robots, I won the first place and represented my school for the national contest, surprisingly, winning second place. Moreover, to solve the battery problem of smartphones, I even cooperated with my classmates to design a cellphone case with the solar panel embedded. With this well-designed cellphone case, we were invited to a tech exposition to showcase our design. In addition, because of a strong interest in English, I came in second both in the English composition contest and speech contest. I also served as the leader of English drama club and ran the club for three years.

The Photonics-related courses offered by your department will help develop my solar power generation knowledge and techniques. If I have the honor to be admitted to your department, I will put all my efforts into how to increase the electricity generation rate of the current solar panels. Furthermore, I am considering pursuing a master's degree in your university, which certainly goes a long way in satisfying my learning desire.

To conclude, I believe your university will be very appropriate for my academic and career aims. If I have the honor and opportunity to enter your school, I will spare no efforts to pursue knowledge in this field. Thank you for your time and attention.

Yours sincerely,

Wei Li-an

---

參考單字：

| | |
|---|---|
| bachelor's degree 學士學位 (C) | embedded 內建式的 (adj) |
| Photonics and Optoelectronics 光電工程 | exposition 博覽會 (C) |
| sharpen 精煉（技術）(vt) | master's degree 碩士學位 (C) |
| solar power 太陽能 (U) | go a long way in 對……有很大幫助 |
| represent 代表 (vt) | pursue 追求 (vt) |

敬愛的 Edward 教授：

　　我此封信主要是要申請貴系的入學。

　　我的名字是韋里安。我是國立彰化高中的高三生。我希望可以進入貴大學的光電系。我深深相信貴系可以精煉我的技術並在我往後的學業及職業生涯有很大助益。

　　我有廣泛的興趣，特別是太陽能、電腦及英文。我曾參加太陽能機器人競賽，我贏得冠軍並且代表學校參加全國比賽，令我驚訝的是，我贏得第二名。此外，為了解決智慧型手機電池問題，我甚至和同學合作設計出一款內建太陽能板的手機殼。因為這設計精良的手機殼，我們受邀到科技博覽會去展示我們的作品。此外，因為對英文的濃濃興趣，我在英文演講和作文比賽中都拿過第二名。我也擔任英文話劇社的社長三年。

　　貴系所提供的光電相關課程將會培養我太陽能發電的知識和技術。如果我有榮幸可以進入到貴系，我將投入全部心力於如何增加目前太陽能板發電率。此外，我也考慮在貴大學攻讀碩士學位，這也會滿足我的求知慾。

　　總而言之，我相信貴大學將是我課業及職涯最佳選擇。如果我有榮幸和機會進入貴校，我將不餘遺力追求這領域的知識。謝謝您寶貴的時間和精神。

韋里安 敬上

## 文章分析

1.

| | | | |
|---|---|---|---|
| **第一段** | 姓名 | Wei Li-an | |
| | 畢業學校 | National Changhua Senior High School | |
| | 申請科系 | Department of Photonics and Optoelectronics | |
| | 未來能力 | sharpen my skills & assist me with both further study and my future career | |
| **第二段** | 興趣 | solar power, computer science & English | |
| | 競賽 | $1^{st}$ in the contest of solar-power robots & $2^{nd}$ in the national contest | |
| | | $2^{nd}$ in the English composition contest & speech contest | |
| | 課外表現 | smartphone solar-power case at a tech exposition | |
| | | the leader of English drama club | |
| **第三段** | 讚美對方 | develop my solar power generation knowledge and techniques | |
| | 展望 | master's degree in your university | |
| **結論段** | 讚美對方 | very appropriate for my academic and career aims | |
| | 強調求知慾 | spare no efforts to pursue knowledge in this field | |

2. 善用轉承詞：surprisingly, moreover, in addition, furthermore, to conclude

## 溫馨提醒

常用單字及片語（請參考 "申請工作" 篇）

 **牛刀小試** 請依據所給的題目發展一篇文章，並請將文章上傳至本書前
言中所列之作文評改網站

請就個人狀況寫一篇申請大學的自傳

## 9 Resume 履歷表

| 原則一 | 句型要一致（名詞對名詞、動詞片語對動詞片語） |
|---|---|
| 原則二 | 事蹟要由最新排到最舊（為使主考官印象深刻），除非之前事跡太驚人，才擺最前面。另外，活動及事績之後要附時間，且要有亮點。若是申請大學，不需提到國中階段的表現。 |
| 原則三 | 不要有過多的色彩或隔線。標題為了強調，可以用粗體字、底線、或斜體字。 |
| 原則四 | 確實檢查，絕對不可有文法、拼字錯誤。否則，主考官會認為你不專業。 |

### 申請大學

| 姓名<br>地址<br>電話　　　　　　　大頭照<br>電子信箱 |
|---|
| 目的 |
| To V |
| **教育背景** |
| • XXX（年） |
| **得獎事由** |
| • XXX（年）<br>• … |
| **學校活動** |
| • XXX（年）<br>• … |
| **專長 / 特殊技能 / 語言能力** |
| • XXX（年）<br>• … |
| **工作經驗** |
| • XXX（年）<br>• … |

【提示】請按照上表提示，將你／妳三年的高中／高職課內外表現寫入表格中。

# 申請大學

| |
|---|
| Qiyuan Huang<br>No.50, Xuefu Rd., Beidou Township,<br>Changhua County 521, Taiwan (R.O.C.)　　　picture<br>(04)1234567<br>jenie@gmail.com |
| **Purpose** |
| To be a candidate for college admission to National Taiwan University of Science and Technology |
| **Education** |
| A senior at National Beidou Senior Home Economic and Commercial Vocational High School (2016) |
| **Honors and Awards** |
| • First place in English speech contest (2016)<br>• First place in the school's table tennis competition (2015)<br>• First place in the English composition contest (2015)<br>• Second place in English speech contest (2015)<br>• Second place in the English singing contest (2014)<br>• Third place in the school's talent show (2014)<br>• First place in the school's tennis competition (2014) |
| **School Activities** |
| • Volunteer of Taiwan Fund for Children and Families (2014-2016)<br>• Table tennis club (2014-2016)<br>• English drama club (2014) |
| **Special Skills** |
| • Office systems: Word, Excel, Powerpoint<br>• Talent: table tennis, singing<br>• Languages: English (fluent), Chinese(native), Taiwanese (fluent), Japanese (basic) |
| **Work Experience** |
| • Part-time English teacher assistant at a cram school (2015)<br>• Part-time coach assistant at a table tennis club (2014) |

| 黃祺媛 |
| --- |
| 521 彰化縣北斗鎮學府路 50 號 |
| (04)1234567　　　　　　大頭照 |
| jenie@gmail.com |

**目的**

希望能錄取台灣科技大學

**教育背景**

國立北斗家商 (2016)

**得獎事由**

- 英文演講比賽第一名 (2016)
- 校內網球比賽第一名 (2015)
- 英文作文比賽第一名 (2015)
- 英文演講比賽第二名 (2015)
- 英文歌唱比賽第二名 (2014)
- 才藝秀第三名 (2014)
- 校內網球比賽第一名 (2014)

**學校活動**

- 台灣家扶基金會義工 (2014-2016)
- 網球社 (2014-2016)
- 英文話劇社 (2014)

**專長 / 特殊技能 / 語言能力**

- 微軟文書系統：Word, Excel, Powerpoint
- 才藝：網球、唱歌
- 語言：英文（流利）、中文（母語）、台語（流利）、日語（基本）

**工作經驗**

- 補習班兼職老師助理 (2015)
- 網球社兼職教練助理 (2014)

溫馨提醒

地址音譯可上郵局網頁查詢：

http://www.post.gov.tw/post/internet/SearchZone/index.jsp?ID=130112

 **牛刀小試** 請依據所給的題目發展一篇文章，並請將文章上傳至本書前言中所列之作文評改網站

請就個人狀況寫一篇申請大學的履歷

## 申請工作

| |
|---|
| 姓名<br>地址<br>電話　　　　　　　　大頭照<br>電子信箱 |
| 目的 |
| To V |
| **教育背景** |
| • XXX（年） |
| **興趣** |
| • XXX（年）<br>• … |
| **學校表現及榮譽** |
| • XXX（年）<br>• … |
| **語言能力（或其他）** |
| • XXX（年）<br>• … |
| **工作經驗** |
| • XXX（年）<br>• … |
| **義工經驗** |
| • XXX（年）<br>• … |

## 申請工作

| Junjie Lin<br>No.5, Aly. 2, Heping 1st Rd., Lingya Dist.,<br>Kaohsiung City 802, Taiwan (R.O.C.)<br>(07)8882000<br>JJlin@gmail.com | picture |
| --- | --- |

**Objective**

To seek a position of an accounting firm

**Education**

- Bachelor' Degree of Department of Accounting, National Taiwan University (2015)

**Interests**

Chess, football, swimming

**School Awards and Activities**

- Accounting 2nd-level certificate (2015)
- First place in the English debate contest (2014)
- Student of the Year (2014)
- Leader of the student union (2013)
- Leader of the chess club (2012)

**Languages**

- Mandarin (native), English (fluent)

**Work Experience**

- Part-time accountant assistant (2013-2014)
- Part-time English tutor (2012)

**Volunteer Experience**

- Volunteer of World Vision Taiwan (2014-2015)

| 林俊傑 |
|---|
| 802 高雄市苓雅區和平一路 2 巷 5 號 |
| (07)8882000　　　　　　大頭照 |
| JJlin@gmail.com |

**目的**

應徵外計事務所工作

**教育背景**

- 台大會計系 (2015)

**興趣**

西洋棋、足球、游泳

**學校表現及榮譽**

- 會計乙級證照 (2015)
- 英文辯論比賽第一名 (2014)
- 當選年度學生 (2014)
- 學生會會長 (2013)
- 西洋棋社長 (2012)

**語言能力**

- 中文（母語）、英文（流利）

**工作經驗**

- 兼職會計助理 (2013-2014)
- 兼職英文家教 (2012)

**義工經驗**

- 世界展望會義工 (2014-2015)

 **牛刀小試** 請依據所給的題目發展一篇文章,並請將文章上傳至本書前
言中所列之作文評改網站

請就個人狀況寫一篇申請工作的履歷,可自行增減項目:

| |
|---|
| |
| **Objective** |
| |
| **Education** |
| • |
| **Interests** |
| |
| **School Awards and Activities** |
| • |
| • |
| • |
| • |
| • |
| **Languages** |
| • |
| **Work Experience** |
| • |
| • |
| **Volunteer Experience** |
| • |
| • |

# Chapter 9

# Punctuations
## 標點符號

1. 句點（period）

   ⊙ 句子結束

   Monica used to drink a cup of hot milk before work.

   ⊙ 縮寫後

   P.S. We should be together too.

2. 逗號（comma）

   ⊙ 分隔所舉之例

   I have been to some countries, such as Japan, Germany, and England.

   ⊙ 同位語後

   Mr. Huang, an excellent mechanic, only fixes expensive sports cars.

   ⊙ 數個形容詞

   He is a hard-working, thin, tall guy.

   ⊙ 引述後

   My grandmother always says, "Honesty is the best policy."

   ⊙ 分隔副詞子句與主要子句

   After you are done with my computer, would you send it back to me?

⊙ 分隔對等連接詞（and, or, but），所連接的主要子句

William broke up with his girlfriend, and, even worse, his car was stolen.

⊙ 分隔分詞構句

Seeing a plate full of chicken bones, my dog kept jumping around and wagging its tail.

⊙ 非限定用法（關係代名詞）

Taipei 101, which is Taiwan's tallest building, attracts tourists around the world.

3. 分號（semicolon）

⊙ 分隔兩個主要句子

Tomic didn't show up at the contest; he got serious stage fright.

⊙ 分開一大串的舉例（因為已經太多逗點）

Many celebrities are invited tonight: Brad Pitt, an excellent actor; Ang Lee, an outstanding director; Jay Z, a popular rapper and producer; Lebron James, a famous NBA player.

4. 驚嘆號（exclamation mark）

⊙ 用於感嘆句後

What a gorgeous man!

How lovely the gift is!

⊙ 命令

Don't do it!

5. 連字號（hyphen）

⊙ 用於複合字

We sometimes have dinner at an all-you-can-eat buffet.

This is a woman-only party.

I work with my sister-in-law at a foreign trade corporation.

There is an anti-corruption march held next Sunday.

6. 引號（quotation marks）

   ⊙ 用於直接引述

   Leo said, "I proposed to my love yesterday."

   "Pay back my money," said Lillian, "or you'll be in a big trouble."

   The billboard reads, "Bicycle Renting. Free Parking."

7. 冒號（colon）

   ⊙ 列舉時

   My reasons that I oppose nuclear power plants are as follows: First, …
   Second, …Third, ….

8. 刪節號（ellipsis）

   ⊙ 用於省略（三點「…」，例句中的第 4 點為句點）

   Last month, I ran into my old flame, and ….

9. 破折號（dash）

   ⊙ 用於補充資訊

   The artist used disposable material in his works—disposable chopsticks,
   bowls, and cups.

   ⊙ 代替冒號

   She only loves one man—Mr. Andy Murray.

   ⊙ 思路或話語轉折

   He believed that Jennifer had some feelings for him—well, kind of.

10. 斜線（slash）

   ⊙ 用於分開兩個選項（功能類似 or）

   You can eat/drink anything on the table. Make yourself at home.

# Chapter 10

## Grammar:
## Some mistakes to avoid
## 文法（應避免的錯誤）

説明

以下皆為筆者於教學現場，所觀察學生在寫作時易犯的文法錯誤，希望讀者能從他人錯誤中學習，不要犯這些錯誤，在寫作過程中，能監控自己寫出的句子，更重要的是，在完成一篇作文後，能靠本身文法概念，找出錯誤。

**1** 不一致：包含主詞與動詞不一致、名詞單複數不一致、時態不一致等等。

(A) 主詞與動詞不一致：

(✕) Wearing uniforms are not a cool thing.

⇨ Wearing uniforms <u>is</u> not a cool thing.

**解析** 動名詞當主詞應為單數。

(✕) Mandy together with her siblings agree with the plan.

⇨ Mandy together with her siblings <u>agrees</u> with the plan.

**解析** together with 連接兩個主詞時，動詞單複數以第一個主詞決定。類似片語還有 as well as, along with。

(✗) How people purchase things have changed a lot since online shopping became popular.

⇨ How people purchase things <u>has</u> changed a lot since online shopping became popular.

**解析** 名詞子句當主詞時，要視為單數。

(✗) I did not went to your party because I did not finishing my job.

⇨ I did not <u>go</u> to your party because I did not <u>finish</u> my job.

**解析** 助動詞後的動詞應為原形動詞。

(✗) When you drunk, call a taxi or your friend to drive you home.

⇨ When you <u>are</u> drunk, call a taxi or your friend to drive you home.

**解析** drunk 為形容詞，需有動詞。句子基本定義：主詞 + 動詞。

(✗) Our company launches a series of new products which takes every consumer by storm.

⇨ Our company launches a series of new products which <u>take</u> every consumer by storm.

**解析** 主格關代後的動詞，需與先行詞單複數一致。

(B) 名詞單複數不一致

(✗) English is an universal language.

⇨ English is <u>a</u> universal language.

**解析** universal 寫成 KK 音標，應為 [ˌjunəˋvɝs!] 為子音開始。

(✗) We are such a good friend.

⇨ We are such good <u>friends</u>.

**解析** 主詞與補語應一致，改為複數。

(✗) All of the guests drank a few wine.

⇨ All of the guests drank <u>a little</u> wine.

**解析** a few 修飾複數名詞；a little 修飾不可數名詞。

(✕) Computer is to me as book is to my brother.

⇨ The computer to me as the book is to my brother.

Or

Computers are to me as books are to my brother.

**解析** 可數名詞都必須去「數它」，不限定的單數名詞加 a/an，限定的名詞加 the 或所有格，若為複數名詞，要記得加 s/es。

(✕) Our car broke down on the freeway and the credit card company sent other car to pick us up.

⇨ Our car broke down on the freeway and the credit card company sent another car to pick us up.

**解析** another 指「另一個」，並無限定是哪一個；other 意思為「其他的、剩下的」後面只能加複數名詞，但限定用法中 the other car/the other cars 是可行的。

(✕) In order to make a traffic smooth, people have to use the highway with at least three people in the car.

⇨ In order to make the traffic flow smoothly, people have to use the highway with at least three people in the car.

**解析** 不可數名詞前不可加 a，除非限定，那可以加定冠詞 the。

## (C) 時態不一致

(✕) We really have a blast on that day.

⇨ We really had a blast on that day.

**解析** on that day 為指「過去那一天」，所以該用過去式。溫馨提醒：動詞的時態變化，會隨時間片語而變化；倘若沒有明顯的時間片語，則可透過上下文來判斷。

(✕) This is the place where Josh meets her fiancee.

⇨ This is the place where Josh met her fiancee.

**解析** meet 這個動作就上下文推敲而言，應為已發生的動作，故用過去式。

(✕) Everyone congraduated him and give him a big hand.

⇨ Everyone congraduated him and <u>gave</u> him a big hand.

**解析** and 為對等連接詞，前面動詞 congraduated 為過去式，give 也應該為過去式。

(✕) Josh had fun camping with his college classmates. He is three hundred miles away from home. He does not have to hear his parents' nagging and can really enjoy himself.

⇨ Josh had fun camping with his college classmates. He <u>was</u> three hundred miles away from home. He <u>did</u> not have to hear his parents' nagging and <u>could</u> really enjoy himself.

（註：上下文語意判斷應該都是過去發生之事，故時態應統一。）

## 2 不對等

(✕) In my free time, I like to listen to music, read novels, and riding a bike in the countryside.

⇨ In my free time, I like to listen to music, read novels, and <u>ride</u> a bike in the countryside.

**解析** and 為對等連接詞，故連接的詞性要一致，在本句而言，三個不定詞片語。

(✕) I was uneasy and anxiety, waiting for the result of the singing contest.

⇨ I was uneasy and <u>anxious</u>, waiting for the result of the singing contest.

(✕) The little girl felt frightened and embarrassing.

⇨ The little girl felt frightened and <u>embarrassed</u>.

**解析** and 前後要詞性對等，v and v；adj and adj；adv and adv；N and N…

(✗) One cannot underestimate himself or herself because everyone is good for something.

⇨ One cannot underestimate oneself because everyone is good for something.

**解析** one 可指非限定的某人，所有格為 one's，受格為 one，反身代名詞為 oneself。

(✗) I learned a lesson that when I take a bath in winter, never close the window.

⇨ I learned a lesson that when I take a bath in winter, I should never close the window.

**解析** 原句 never close the window 為祈使句，與語意不符。

(✗) My father always says that it is better to prepare for the worst, and I should always be well-prepared for any promotion opportunities.

⇨ My father always says that it is better to prepare for the worst, and that I should always be well-prepared for any promotion opportunities.

**解析** and 對等兩個 that 子句，皆是當 say 的受詞。如果沒有加 that，會造成讀者誤會，因為有時會變成另一句意思。此句可能解讀為「不是都是我爸爸所講的事情」。

## 3 不完整的句子（少了主要子句或動詞）

(✗) When you go to school.

⇨ When you go to school, do not forget to bring the box lunch with you.

**解析** 副詞連接詞 when, before, after, if, although, though 等等，需要連接兩個句子。

(✗) Because no one can win the battle with natural disasters.

⇨ Because no one can win the battle with natural disasters, human beings should do whatever they can to protect the environment.

**解析** because 和 so 也須連接兩個獨立句子。

(✗) So it became the most embarrassing experience for me.

⇨ <u>Therefore</u>, it became the most embarrassing experience for me.

**解析** 以 so 開始的句子為口語用法，該用有因果關係的轉承詞來代替，如：therefore, as a result, thus, hence, consequently, accordingly 等等。

(✗) And fortunately every passenger miraculously survived the car accident.

⇨ Fortunately every passenger miraculously survived the car accident.

Or

⇨ <u>Besides</u>, fortunately every passenger miraculously survived the car accident.

**解析** 以 and 開始的句子亦為口語用法，應避免，可用表「此外」意思的轉承詞代替，如：besides, in addition, moreover, furthermore, what is more 等等。

(✗) But by reading magazines, we can keep abreast with the latest news.

⇨ <u>However</u>, by reading magazines, we can keep abreast with the latest news.

**解析** 以 but 開始的句子亦為口語用法，可用表「轉折」意思的轉承詞代替，如：however, nevertheless, nonetheless, yet 等等。

(✗) The reason why I was crying.

⇨ The reason that I was crying <u>was that I got lost.</u>

**解析** 原句 the reason why I was crying 中 why I was crying 是用來修飾 reason，所以整個充其量只能視為一個名詞片語，如此，並無動詞。切記：句子基本定義：S+V。

**4** 詞性誤用

(✗) What with lazy and what with rudeness, Dickson was fired by his angry boss.

⇨ What with <u>laziness</u> and what with rudeness, Dickson was fired by his angry boss.

**解析** 介系詞後可接名詞、動名詞，但不可接形容詞或副詞。

(✗) Drunk-driving causes over 30,000 people dead each year.

⇨ Drunk-driving causes over 30,000 <u>deaths</u> each year.

**解析** 原句太中式英文，應將 dead 改為名詞。

(✗) To be safety, people should watch both sides when crossing the road.

⇨ To be <u>safe</u>, people should watch both sides when crossing the road.

**解析** 原句 safety 應改為形容詞 safe，因為是 people are safe 而不是 people are safety。

(✗) We very appreciated your concern.

⇨ We appreciated your concern <u>very much.</u>

**解析** very 不可修飾動詞，應該用 very much 或 a lot 代替。very 基本上修飾形容詞或副詞，如：very excited, very quickly。另外，名詞前若加 very，有強調功能，如：He was the very man that sent you flowers.

(✗) People who take exercise regular are health.

⇨ People who take exercise <u>regularly</u> are <u>healthy</u>.

**解析** 副詞修飾形容詞與動詞。

(✗) We all unlike the noise from modified cars and motorcycles.

⇨ We all <u>dislike</u> the noise from modified cars and motorcycles.

**解析** unlike 可當形容詞或介系詞，意思為「不像……」；dislike 為動詞，意思為「不喜歡……」。

**5** 不間斷句子（兩個主要子句中間無連接詞或適當標點符號）

(✗) There exist many problems between us we need to deal with them.

⇨ There exist many problems between us<u>, and</u> we need to deal with them.

Or

There exist many problems between us<u>;</u> we need to deal with them.

Or

There exist many problems between us<u>.</u> We need to deal with them.

**解析** 獨立句子與獨立句子間，可用適當連接詞、句點、分號來串連。

(✗) I took an injured stray cat home, then took good care of it.

⇨ I took an injured stray cat home, <u>and then</u> took good care of it.（then 為副詞）

**解析** 副詞無法當連接詞功能來連接兩個獨立句子，或詞性相同的字或片語。

(✗) Please do not lie to me even it is merely a white lie.

⇨ Please do not lie to me <u>even if</u> it is merely a white lie.（even 為副詞）

**解析** 副詞無法當連接詞功能來連接兩個獨立句子，或詞性相同的字或片語。

**6** 格格不入的單字（用字深度要一致，不要突然出現很難的字；或是非正式用法的字，如：俚語、舊式、口語用字等等，皆不宜出現正式寫作中）

(✗) It is time for us to hit the sack.

⇨ It is time for us to <u>go to bed</u>.

**解析** hit the sack 為舊式英文，現代英文會用 go to bed/go to sleep 來表達「上床睡覺」的意思。

(✗) When I was on the stage ready to speak, <u>you know</u>, I was frightened to death.

⇨ When I was on the stage ready to speak, I was frightened to death.

**解析** 插入語 you know 為口語用法，不宜出現在正式文章。另外，也不要用 well, so,but, and 來開始句子。

(✗) Mr. Wang <u>bought the farm</u> at the age of 95.

⇨ Mr. Wang <u>died</u> at the age of 95.

**解析** buy the farm 為俚語用法，應避免。

(✗) I came from an impoverished family. My father does not have a job, nor does my mother.

⇨ I came from a <u>poor</u> family. My father does not have a job, nor does my mother.

**解析** impoverished 這個字在文章中，略顯突兀，因為難度與其他字差距太大，應該使用 poor 來代替。

**7** 不縮寫（英文縮寫適用於非正式場合、非正式用語（口語、俚語），我們在寫英文作文時應極力避免出現縮寫字）

(×) He didn't listen to my warning and slipped on the banana peel.

⇨ He <u>did not</u> listen to my warning and slipped on the banana peel.

**解析** 英文縮寫適用於非正式文體。

(×) Richard's gone to Hawaii and he won't be back until next Saturday.

⇨ Richard <u>has</u> gone to Hawaii and he <u>will not</u> be back until next Saturday.

**解析** 英文縮寫適用於非正式文體。

**8** 雙動詞（動詞與動詞之間，無連接詞或 to，或 be 動詞與一般動詞擺在一起）

(×) We should remind people don't jaywalk because it is dangerous.

⇨ We should remind people <u>not to</u> jaywalk because it is dangerous.

**解析** 英文句子忌諱出現兩個動詞以上，但卻不合文法。解決方式為：使用連接詞、to、改為分詞等等。

(×) Whenever we encounter difficulty feel frustrated, we can ask our teachers for advice.

⇨ Whenever we encounter difficulty <u>or</u> feel frustrated, we can ask our teachers for advice.

**解析** 此句使用連接詞來連接兩個動詞片語。

(×) He is sometimes contact his old classmates and catch up on some gossips.

⇨ He sometimes <u>contacts</u> his old classmates and <u>catches</u> up on some gossips.

**解析** 由於國小到國中，動詞先學 Be 動詞，導致有些學習者會誤把 Be 動詞與一般動詞會同時使用，但這是相當大的錯誤。Be 動詞與一般動詞只有在進行式中，才會一起使用，如：He is hailing a taxi.

(×) Don't drive after you drink alcohol is very important.

⇨ <u>Not to drive</u> after you drink alcohol is very important.

**解析** 此句亦犯了兩個動詞錯誤，請記得：直述句的主詞詞性必須是名詞功能，如：一般名詞、代名詞、動名詞、不定詞、名詞子句、名詞片語、虛主詞 it 等等。

**9** 主詞虛懸（主要是發生在分詞構句的時候，沒有注意到其實主詞前後兩句要一致，而在省略掉主詞之後所用的動詞又不是原本的主詞，這時候就造成主詞是指誰不清楚的虛懸狀況。另外，用 To+V, S+V 的句子也是容易出現這種問題。）

(✗) After robbing the bank, the police strived to hunt them down.

⇨ After several criminals robbed the bank, the police strived to hunt them down.

**解析** 此句不可能是警察去搶銀行又去抓嫌犯，改法為：將另一句主詞寫出，讀者才有辦法理解。

(✗) Badly hurt, an ambulance rushed the injured to the hospital.

⇨ Badly hurt, the injured was rushed to the hospital by an ambulance.

**解析** 此句不可能是救護車受重傷，而應該是傷者嚴重受傷，所以主要子句主詞應為傷者這樣才合理。

(✗) When the waiter served water, accidentally spilling it onto a customer.

⇨ When serving water, the waiter accidentally spilled it onto a customer.

**解析** 分詞構句應在副詞連接詞當句，而不是在主要子句。

(✗) To get a better grade, my computer will not be turned on until the test is over.

⇨ To get a better grade, I will not turn on the computer until the test is over.

**解析** 此句不可能電腦為了要得到好成績，應該是 I 才對。

**10** 用字不精準

(?) Ronald ate a big bowl of ramen and hiccuped.

⇨ Ronald gulped down a big bowl of ramen and burped loudly.

**解析** ate 用字雖然文法上沒問題，在不夠精準呈現，gulp down 為「狼吞虎嚥」的意思，搭配後面大聲打嗝，此外，burp 才是「打飽嗝」。

(?) My favorite dish is cooked fish.

⇨ My favorite dish is <u>smoked</u> fish.

> **解析** cooked fish 文法上亦無誤，但 smoked salmon 為煙燻鮭魚，訊息比較豐富。

(?) Anna walked into her sister's room, trying to scare her.

⇨ Anna <u>tiptoed</u> into her sister's room, trying to scare her.

> **解析** walk in 不足以表達上下文的精確含意，tiptoe 意思為「躡手躡腳地走」，搭配後面要嚇她妹妹，比較切合。

## 11 太浮誇的修辭

(✕) The truck ran into a tree on the roadside as the airplane crashed into the World Trade Center.

⇨ The truck ran into a tree on the roadside at high speeds and <u>was broken to pieces</u>.

> **解析** 筆者在大學時有一次英文作文將小客車衝撞路邊的大樹比喻成美國 911 的飛機撞大樓，光這一句就被教授評為 pompous，意思是說我比喻的太誇張。此後，便知道在寫英文作文時，比喻要恰到好處，過與不及皆不好。

## 12 洋涇邦英文（多使用 idiomatic English，所謂的涇邦英文就是將中文直接翻譯成英文的中式英文，也不考慮中英文的句子結構是有些差異）

(✕) People mountain people sea on the square.（人山人海？）

⇨ This square is crowded with of people.

> **解析** 原句就是直接從中文翻譯為英文。

(✕) My friend said me to drive him to go home.

⇨ My friend asked me to drive him home.

> **解析** 原句中式英文。

**13** 避免寫出陳腔濫調（好的作文是要充滿原創性不應該拾人牙慧。以下列舉一些的 cliché 的例子，應要避免）

| | |
|---|---|
| between a rock and a hard place | 兩難 |
| last but not least | 最後但並非最不重要 |
| raining cats and dogs | 傾盆大雨 |
| as dry as a bone | 十分乾燥 |
| skeletons in the closet | 不可告人的家醜或秘密 |
| to add salt to the wound | 傷口撒鹽 |
| so on and so forth | 如此等等 |

**14** 避免偏見文字（除非明確知道所指稱對象的性別，否則應該用右邊欄）

| 避免 | 該用 |
|---|---|
| anchorman | anchor（主播） |
| mailman | mail carrier（郵差） |
| chairman | chairperson（主席） |
| policeman | police officer（警官） |
| businessman | businessperson（商人） |
| salesman | salesperson（銷售員） |
| waiter/waitress | server（服務生） |
| forefathers | ancestors（祖先） |
| stewardess | flight attendant（空服員） |

**15** 句型誤用

(✗) Hardly are we know what accident will happen.

⇨ Hardly can we know what accident will happen.

**解析** 否定詞擺句首，其後的主詞、動詞需倒裝，若是 Be 動詞，直接主詞與 Be 動詞互換；若為一般動詞，則需借用適當的助動詞，來進行倒裝。

(✗) No one here understood what was the speaker talking about.

⇨ No one here understood what the speaker was talking about.

**解析** 名詞子句公式應為 5W1H＋S＋V，而不是 5W1H＋V＋S。

(✗) How fashion!

⇨ How fashionable!

**解析** 感嘆句中，若是以 how 引導出來，則要加形容詞或副詞；what 引導的感嘆句才是加名詞。

(✗) The man whose fly was down.

⇨ The man whose fly was down embarrassed all the ladies in the meeting.
Or
No one knew the man whose fly was down.

**解析** 原句利用所有格關代寫出，充其量只不過是個名詞片語，修改辦法：(1) 將此名詞片語當主詞用，再補一動詞；或 (2) 將此一名詞片語當受詞用，前面補一個主詞和動詞。

(✗) The plane which lost power and crashed into the forest killing everyone on board.

⇨ The plane which lost power and crashed into the forest killing everyone on board was expected to land at Osaka Airport.
Or
Some witnesses saw the plane which lost power and crashed into the forest killing everyone on board.

**解析** 原句由主格關代所寫出，但先行詞 plane 與關代這句，也只是名詞片語，無法形成句子，修改辦法：(1) 將此名詞片語當主詞用，再補一動詞；或 (2) 將此一名詞片語當受詞用，前面補一個主詞和動詞。

(✗) Here comes exciting news which the rock band, Mayday, is coming to Taichung.

⇨ Here comes exciting news that the rock band, Mayday, is coming to Taichung.

**解析** 原句應利用名詞與名詞子句 that＋S＋V 為同位語，而不是 which＋S＋V。

**16** 搭配詞錯誤及用字錯誤（指在特定的句子中如何適當地選用詞語的問題。用字的精準與否會影響到一句話的解讀，光是一個字的誤用就很有可能造成無法理解，更有可能會貽笑大方。改善辦法，多看別人文章，多查字典）

(✕) The chicken lies a gold egg every day.

⇨ The chicken <u>lays</u> a gold egg every day.

**解析** 躺：lie-lay-lain；下蛋 / 放置：lay-laid-laid；說謊：lie-lied-lied。

(✕) I cost 2,000 dollars to buy the NIKE shoes.

⇨ I <u>spent</u> 2,000 dollars buying the NIKE shoes.

**解析** cost 與 spend 兩字都可當「花費（金錢）」，但 cost 的主詞為物，spend 主詞為人。另外，take 亦是指花費，但是「花費時間」，主詞亦為物。

(✕) Professor Li was glad to participate the international conference.

⇨ Professor Li was glad to <u>participate in</u> the international conference.

**解析** 參加可用 join(vt), participate in, take part in。

(✕) Take a example to my friend, her sister was died of a car accident.

⇨ <u>Take my friend for example</u>. Her sister died from a car accident.

**解析** 舉......為例的片語為：take...... for example, take...... for instance, 或 take......，溫馨提醒：這三種用法皆為句子，類似祈使句，所以需要以句點結尾。

(✕) Thank you for being so considerable to us.

⇨ Thank you for being so <u>considerate</u> to us.

**解析** considerable 是指「大量的」；considerate 則是「體貼的」= thoughtful。

(✕) Kim rose his hand and cried for help.

⇨ Kim <u>raised</u> his hand and cried for help.

**解析** 上升：rise-rose-risen (vi)；舉起...... / 扶養：raise-raised-raised (vt)。

**17** 修飾語錯位（英語與中文不同，同一個修飾語置於句子不同的位置，句子的含義可能引起變化，也有不同的解讀，最經典的詞莫過於 only，看以下的例子。）

Only I kissed my wife at home at night.（註：只有我晚上在家親我老婆。）

I only kissed my wife at home at night.（註：晚上在家我只有親我老婆。）

I kissed only my wife at home at night.（註：晚上在家我只親我老婆。）

I kissed my wife only at home at night.（註：晚上我只有在家才親我老婆。）

I kissed my wife at home only at night.（註：我只有在晚上在家才親我老婆。）

**18** 標點符號誤用

A. 千萬不可將逗點移到下一行的句首。另外，拼字分兩行書寫時，不可未加連號 hyphen，或未按音節把字作適當的劃分。例如 commencement 誤 分 為 comm-ence-ment，school 誤 分 為 sch-ool，happened 誤 分 為 happen-ed。

B. (✗) Taipei 101 which is located in Xinyi District is the tallest building in Taiwan.

   ⇨ Taipei 101, which is located in Xinyi District, is the tallest building in Taiwan.

   **解析** 若先行詞為獨一無二、專有名詞、人名、地名時，為非限定用法，其中關代前須有逗點。

**19** 人稱變來變去

英文作文忌諱人稱反覆無常，因為會讓讀者丈二金剛，一般說來，記敘文通篇用第一人稱或第三人稱；論說類文體，通篇盡量用第三人稱，這樣比較客觀，但絕對不會一段裡面人稱變來變去，雜亂無章。

People who have been to Taroko Gorge must be impressed by its marvelous scenery…. I am considering moving to Haulien after I retire. In my opinion, you should do the same thing. Even my father who seldom leaves his hometown has been searching for some information about it…. Mr. Lin told me….

**20** 以數字開始一個句子（儘管以數字開始一個句子文法上沒有錯，但容易使讀者感到不整齊與凌亂，所以盡量以英文字來代替或者改寫整個句子。）

(×) 75% of the rivers in this country have been polluted by industrial waste.

⇨ Seventy-five of the rivers in this country have been polluted by industrial waste.

 假設以下句子皆出現在作文中，請將錯誤或不適當的部分改正

1. How to travel on a tight budget trouble me very much.

2. People can't dream about success without putting any effort into it.

3. After transferring the money, the products customers order online will be shipped to them within 24 hours.

4. I am very thank you for what you have done for me.

5. Thompson cooked the beef for two hours for his family.

6. It is important for me to focus on my studies, I have a midterm test tomorrow.

7. But evacuating all the villagers near the volcano is our top priority.

8. We visited many historic palaces and, you know, several ancient temples.

9. He is enjoying his carefree life since retirement.

10. Our government provides every citizen for a sound welfare system.

1. trouble ⇨ troubles

**解析** 名詞片語 How to travel on a tight budget 當主詞時，要視為單數。

2. can't ⇨ cannot; can not

**解析** 作文句子不縮寫。

3. After transferring ⇨ After they transfer

　**解析** 因為兩邊的句子主詞不同，故要將另一主詞寫出，不然會犯了主詞虛懸問題。

4. am ⇨ X; 或 thank for ⇨ grateful

　**解析** am 若加進去會造成雙動詞錯誤；或者保留 am，將動詞 thank for 換成形容詞 grateful for。

5. cooked ⇨ stewed

　**解析** stew 意思為「燉…」，會比 cook 意思來的精準。

6. ⇨ It is important for me to focus on my studies because I have a midterm test tomorrow.

　OR

　It is important for me to focus on my studies; I have a midterm test tomorrow.

　**解析** 原本的兩個句子，並無連接詞，造成"不間斷句子"的錯誤。

7. However, evacuating all the villagers near the volcano is our top priority.

　**解析** but 在寫作上為連接詞，不宜放在句首來開始一個句子，應換成副詞的 however。

8. We visited many historic palaces and several ancient temples.

　**解析** 刪除口語的 you know。

9. He has been enjoying/has enjoyed his carefree life since retirement.

　**解析** since 句型中，主要子句應用完成式來寫。

10. for ⇨ with

　**解析** provide 意思為「提供」，用法為：provide sb with sth；provide sth for sb。

# 淺談中譯英

## 1. 評分標準

中翻英這一大題,是中級複試寫作的第一大題,而且都是一段文章的翻譯,文章主題包羅萬象,例如:生活、環保、科技、人文、健康等等,總分為 40 分。評分標準,依據大考中心公告如下:

| 級分 | 分數 | 說明 |
|---|---|---|
| 5 | 40 | **翻譯能力佳**<br>內容能充分表達題意;文段組織、連貫性甚佳,能充分掌握句型結構;用字遣詞、文法、拼字、標點及大小寫幾乎無誤。 |
| 4 | 32 | **翻譯能力可**<br>內容適切表達題意;文段組織、連貫性及句型結構大致良好;用字遣詞、文法、拼字、標點及大小寫偶有錯誤,但不妨礙題意之表達。 |
| 3 | 24 | **翻譯能力有限**<br>內容未能完全表達題意;文段組織鬆散,連貫性不足,未能完全掌握句型結構;用字遣詞及文法時有錯誤,妨礙題意之表達,拼字、標點及大小寫也有錯誤。 |

| 級分 | 分數 | 說明 |
|---|---|---|
| 2 | 16 | **稍具翻譯能力**<br>僅能局部表達原文題意；文段組織不良並缺乏連貫性，句型結構掌握欠佳，大多難以理解；用字遣詞、文法、拼字、標點及大小寫錯誤嚴重。 |
| 1 | 8 | **無翻譯能力**<br>內容無法表達題意；句型結構掌握差，無法理解；用字遣詞、文法、拼字、標點及大小寫之錯誤多且嚴重。 |
| 0 | 0 | **未答 / 等同未答** |

## 2. 翻譯技巧

1. 分析中文

    (1) 在分析過後：將每句的的主詞、動詞、連接詞、句型等，畫底線，並做標記：S; V; N; adj; adv; 何種句型…等等，如此的分解句子，除了可以增加翻譯的正確性，亦可避免遺漏一些字沒翻譯到。

    (2) 抓出主詞與主要動詞：找出主詞與動詞，特別注意：主詞的詞性（功能）必須是名詞，例如：一般名詞、代名詞、動名詞（Ving）、不定詞（to+V）、名詞子句（5W1H+S+V）等等；而句子的主要動詞，則有以下兩個特性：第一，會因為主詞的單複數而變化；第二，會因為時態而做變化。

    (3) 找出相對應的英文片語：要找得出片語，必須要勤背狄克生片語，以及單字的用法或搭配詞，例如：refrain...from...（克制不去…）、be interested in...（對…感到興趣）等等。

    (4) 找出連接詞：基本上，連接詞需要連接前後兩句，如果看不出明顯的連接詞，則須適時加入合乎文法的連接詞。表時間（如：while, when, before, after, since, as, etc）、表轉折（如：while, but, whereas, etc）、表讓步（如：although, though, etc）、表假設（如：if, providing that, provided that, given that, etc）等等。

    (5) 加入轉承詞。評分項目中，有一項是文章的連貫性這個標準，所以適當的加入轉承詞是必須的，請參考本書中的相關章節。

(6) 找出特殊句型：要找出特殊句型，前提就是要將本書所列的句型公式及用法都牢記。

## 2. 判斷時態

判斷句子時態而言，可藉由句子所提及的時間片語來決定，如果沒有明確的時間片語，則必須藉由邏輯，或一些關鍵字來決斷動詞到底是何種時態，因為中翻英這一大題，都是一段文章，所以請注意，句子與句子的時態關係，通常不會整篇段落上下兩句的時態變來變去。

以下是最常見的時態：

⊙ 現在簡單式：凡是提到習慣、個性、常理、常態、格言的事。最常用！

⊙ 現在進行式：現在此刻正在發生或進行的事。

⊙ 未來式：未來時間點會發生的事。

⊙ 過去簡單式：過去一個時間做了某事、過去習慣、過去狀態。最常用！

⊙ 現在完成式：動作從以前持續到現在；或動作持續多久；或表一個經驗（ever, once, three times）。常用！

⊙ 過去完成式：過去的一個動作在某一個時間點前早就完成；或兩個過去的動作，先發生用過去完成式，後發生用過去式。

## 3. 下筆書寫

一般直述句通常會以：主詞＋動詞＋副詞＋地點＋時間的順序來書寫，副詞有時可以放在動詞前面來做為強調；若要強調地點或時間，也可以將其置於句首。若為疑問句，則須判斷是否為 yes-no 問句或 Wh- 問句，並借適當的 Be 動詞或助動詞；另外，如果為倒裝句，則需將主詞與動詞顛倒放，更多用法，請翻至本書之句型章節。

## 4. 檢查

(1) 主詞與動詞的一致性：單數主詞配單數動詞，複數主詞則搭配複數動詞；

(2) 主動或被動：簡單來說，主詞可以"主動"執行"動詞"這個動作，用主動語氣；相反地，如果不行，則用被動語氣，公式為：be + p.p.+ (by…)

(3) 名詞：是否有注意到該名詞的單複數，並加上適當的冠詞（非限定：a/an; 限定時：the/ 所有格）或在字尾加 s/es 來形成複數；

(4) 動詞：是否合乎該句的時態，另外，該動詞是否為及物動詞（後面需加一個名詞作為受詞）或不及物動詞（先加介系詞，才可以加名詞作為受詞）。另外，也需注意是否為特殊動詞（如：imagine，後面應加動名詞或名詞；hate，後面可加動名詞或不定詞）；

(5) 介系詞：介系詞後面是否記得動詞改為動名詞；

(6) 特殊句型的用法是否正確等等。

### 範例

（以下範例為英檢中心所公告 5 級分的譯文。）

説明：請將下列的一段中文翻譯成通順、達意且前後連貫的英文。

去年暑假我在一家便利商店打工，那是我第一次打工。工作很辛苦，但是很有趣。我不但從工作中學到很多，還結交不少好朋友。雖然離開工作已經一年，但我們還是經常聚會。

### 譯文

Last summer vacation, I had a part-time job in a convenience store, and that was my first time working part-time. The work was really tough, but was very interesting. Not merely did I learn much from work, but also made a few good friends. Although I <u>had left</u> the work for a year, we still often <u>met</u> together.

### 評語

整體而言，能流暢而清楚表達題意。用字遣詞、句夠完整、時態掌握大致良好，雖然最後一句應使用現在完成式與現在式，而非過去完成式（had left）及過去式（met），但仍已達 5 級分的標準。

去年暑假　我　在一家便利商店　打工，那　是　我第一次打工。

分析：　時間　　S　　　地點　　　　V　　S　V　　　N

時態：過去式。因為時間為去年暑假

下筆：直述句，並補連接詞。因為中文沒有明顯的連接詞


工作　很辛苦，但是　　很有趣。

分析：　S　　adj　　連接詞　　adj

時態：過去式。因為整件事為去年暑假所發生

下筆：直述句。並使用對等連接詞 and


我　不但　從工作中　　學到　很多，還　結交　不少好朋友。

分析：S　　　　介系詞片語　　V　N　　V　　　　N

時態：過去式。因為整件事為去年暑假所發生

下筆：直述句。並使用套用句型 not only...but also...（不但…還…），譯文中採用
　　　倒裝句寫法。


雖然　　離開工作　已經一年，　　但　　我們　還是　經常　聚會。

分析：　連接詞　　　V　　　時間片語　　連接詞　S　　adv　　adv　　V

時態：現在式。因為整件事為主角的現況

下筆：直述句。第一句補主詞 I


## 3. 勤加練習

筆者建議大家可以至訪間的書局，買英檢中級難度的雜誌，試著將雜誌後的中文
譯文，翻譯成英文，再與英文原文相互比對，檢視自己的遣詞用字、結構、文
法，及連貫性是否還有加強空間，並學習英文原文的諸多優點，相信勤加練習
後，必會帶來長足進步！

# 戰勝 GEPT 全民英檢中級的 16 堂課--用心智圖搞懂英文作文與句型

作　　者：黃百隆
企劃編輯：溫珮妤
文字編輯：江雅鈴
設計裝幀：張寶莉
發 行 人：廖文良

發 行 所：碁峰資訊股份有限公司
地　　址：台北市南港區三重路 66 號 7 樓之 6
電　　話：(02)2788-2408
傳　　真：(02)8192-4433
網　　站：www.gotop.com.tw
書　　號：ARE000800
版　　次：2017 年 04 月初版
建議售價：NT$300

國家圖書館出版品預行編目資料

戰勝 GEPT 全民英檢中級的 16 堂課：用心智圖搞懂英文作文與
　句型 / 黃百隆著. -- 初版. -- 臺北市：碁峰資訊, 2017.04
　　面；　公分
　ISBN 978-986-476-333-7(平裝)
　1.英語　2.作文　3.句法
805.1892　　　　　　　　　　　　　　　　　106001618

## 讀者服務

● 感謝您購買碁峰圖書，如果您對本書的內容或表達上有不清楚的地方或其他建議，請至碁峰網站：「聯絡我們」\「圖書問題」留下您所購買之書籍及問題。(請註明購買書籍之書號及書名，以及問題頁數，以便能儘快為您處理)
http://www.gotop.com.tw

● 售後服務僅限書籍本身內容，若是軟、硬體問題，請您直接與軟體廠商聯絡。

● 若於購買書籍後發現有破損、缺頁、裝訂錯誤之問題，請直接將書寄回更換，並註明您的姓名、連絡電話及地址，將有專人與您連絡補寄商品。

● 歡迎至碁峰購物網
http://shopping.gotop.com.tw
選購所需產品。